DENIS VOIGN

MARY CHELTENHAM

dv-éditions

Translated from French by Cecily A. Norris

dv-editions

29 A rue de Dalis
67100 Strasbourg France

9782914644525
9782914644518 (ebook)

acknowledgements

Thank you to Cecily Norris for her formidable translation work, a process of almost five months, executed with accuracy and conscientiousness for a high-quality result. Thanks also to Catherine and Viv, my two proof-readers.

Special thanks to my wife Muriel for her sound advice and invaluable assistance.

About the author

Denis Voignier is a French educator an novelist. He specializes in crime fiction and children's literature. He has travelled extensively throughout England, Scotland and Wales and is fascinated by the United Kingdom, its landscapes, its people and the language of Shakespeare. The United Kingdom is the setting for one of his first crime novels, "Après la Pluie", which was and stil continues to be a remarkable success.

Now comes "Mary Cheltenham", which he has had translated into English, in hope enhancing the satisfaction of readers on the other side of the Channel.

1

Gloucestershire, September 1882

It was an autumn morning, one typical of our region. Milky mist covered the countryside, and through the dew-covered carriage door, I could barely see the roadside. The clip-clop of hooves on the ground, hardened by the cold weather, filled the air, and my uncle, sitting in front of me, had not yet uttered a word since our departure.

Now and then, the coachman, in a loud and raucous voice, emitted a shout to the horses. The whip, sometimes, cracked hard and made me jump.

Finally, the pace slowed, the road followed a long curve and as the layers of mist thinned and frayed in places, I made out the massive shape of a building, grey and sombre in the blinding landscape.

The rolling of wheels on the ground was replaced by the crunching of gravel on a walkway and the carriage came to a halt.

"We are here, Jeremy. Get out."

As my uncle had the right to the services of the coachman, who having reached the door, invited him to get out, I came out by myself on the other side, jumping out of the vehicle. The air was cool and I turned up my coat collar.

The sun finally broke through, the mist quickly thinned out and

I could see the residence looming in front of me like a gigantic ship.

It was a yellow stone structure, with a roof of bluish slates. Three tall chimneys rose to the sky, like sentinels on watch. The two levels each had a long line of high mullioned windows. At the centre, a staircase with a few steps gave access to a wide landing. The entire picture was very symmetrical, rather cold, and indeed austere.

While I was losing myself in this reverie, my uncle grabbed me by the arm.

"Stop dreaming, will you. They're waiting for us."

His voice was a monotone, almost without expression. In my memory, I had never, over the last ten years, seen him smile, at least with me. Emotions seemed to slide over his face and he often looked expressionless. He handed me a canvas bag that the coachman had taken from the trunk of the vehicle. It was my meagre luggage.

The whip cracked again, the team made a half-turn and came to a halt. The coachman had instructions to wait. As we moved forward, my uncle looked frequently at the heavy silver watch that he pulled from his coat pocket.

We were still a few yards from the stairs when the door overlooking the landing opened. A man in a yellow and gold uniform with black trousers appeared. He walked stiffly like an automaton, came down the few steps and stood in front of us. That was both to welcome us, as well as to warn us not to go any further.

"Sir Jenkins, I believe?"

The major-domo — or simply valet — had a strong, funny accent which I had never heard before. His dark eyes were rather suspicious and he stared at us in turn as though we were some strange beasts.

"Osmond Alexander Matthew Jenkins, indeed. And this is my

nephew Jeremy. Jeremy Page."

My uncle had spoken in a dry voice, leaving no room for comment.

"Very well. Follow me."

The servant led us up the stairs, pulled open the heavy, solid wooden door and let us into a white marble vestibule. Antique statues decorated the place, and the majestic busts seemed to be staring at us. The man directed us to a small sitting-room at the side of this entrance hall. There were three garnet-red velvet chairs, along with a polished table. The room smelled of beeswax.

"Have a seat. I will let Lady Cheltenham know you are here."

My uncle did not seem to like these ponderous formalities. As a businessman and formidable shopkeeper, he could not bear having to wait. He liked situations that were quickly settled or negotiated. But, this time, he had little choice and had to be patient.

Luckily for his temper, the wait was not long.

Rhythmic footsteps sounded and approached rapidly. Finally, Lady Cheltenham appeared in the doorframe.

My uncle got up, taking off his top hat. A rough tap on my shoulder made me understand that I, too, should stand up.

She was a beautiful woman, about thirty years old. She was fairly tall, slender, and rather svelte in her overall appearance. Two big bright eyes shone in her pleasant smiling face. Her fine blonde hair was drawn into a sort of bun at the back of her head.

"Sir Jenkins."

"My Lady."

And my uncle bowed somewhat reverently.

"Did you have a good trip from Gloucester?"

"Yes, My Lady. An excellent trip."

"Very well. This is the young man you spoke to me about in your correspondence..."

"Yes, My Lady. Jeremy Page, the only son of my deceased sister, Joan. If our agreement still holds…."

"Of course. We need staff and to me, this young man already has a very robust appearance for his age."

"That is so, you can be sure of it, My Lady. He does not shirk his duties."

"Well, in that case we will put him to the test very soon. There is no shortage of work here, such a large building…"

"I am really grateful to you, My Lady. It is also reassuring to know that he will be in good hands and safe from want. You know with my never ending business, I can't manage to…"

"I understand, Sir Jenkins. I understand perfectly."

What my uncle was not saying openly was that his business was somewhat limping along. This arrangement with Lady Cheltenham would allow him, temporarily, to boost back up his finances. However, the young lady called her major-domo.

"Wickney! Wickney!"

"My Lady?" responded a voice quite close by.

"Bring me what's necessary, please."

Wickney — I could now put a name to this character — reappeared, with a little brown leather satchel in his hand.

"Here it is, My Lady."

The bag passed from Wickney's hands to those of the young woman and finally into my uncle's. I believed I could discern this time the semblance of a smile and his eyes gleamed, for a fleeting moment, with a little spark of joy. The business was settled; my uncle, as usual, had no reason to linger.

"Thank you, My Lady. I do not wish to inconvenience you any longer. Moreover, my business…"

"Of course, Sir Jenkins. Of course. Wickney will see you out."

My uncle turned towards me and, for a brief moment, rested his large hand on my shoulder. He stared at me with that look, which had become expressionless again.

"Goodbye, my boy. Behave yourself."

"Goodbye, uncle."

He turned on his heels, after having bowed respectfully to the mistress of the house. Wickney preceded him and they both disappeared from my view.

I remained alone with the beautiful lady.

"Very well, young man. Welcome to Cheltenham. As soon as Wickney returns, he will show you around, take you to your lodgings and let you know what duties will be yours from tomorrow."

"Very well, Madam."

She wore a little smile. Was it a smile of tenderness, of benevolence, or that smile used by people in high places? At that moment I could not tell.

Some footsteps sounded, but they certainly were not Wickney's. These were a lot lighter, dancing and youthful. One could say carefreeness pervading the house.

"Mary, what are you doing there?"

This time the voice was stern, harsh, cutting like a Toledo blade.

"Mother…"

"Mary, how many times do I have to tell you not to turn up like that, in front of strangers, especially when they are servants?"

"Yes, mother."

I leaned forward a bit, as the doorframe was blocking the view. And I saw her… She was my age, without a doubt, about sixteen or seventeen years old. Her oval shaped face, pale like a November moon, was all smiles. Her eyes, bright like her mother's, shone with life and mischievousness. Her blond hair hung in curls around her alabaster cheeks.

"Go back upstairs at once. You will come out when I say so."

And the young girl, throwing me a brief glance, disappeared rather quickly, without waiting for anything more. I kept in my memory her fleeting, but enchanting image.

Wickney reappeared during this time.

"My Lady?"

"Take this young man to the outbuildings. Let him look around and give him his instructions. I'm depending on you."

"Of course, My Lady."

And I followed in the footsteps of this sinister character, who, all the same, was giving me the shivers.

2

I followed the major-domo, who was moving straight ahead with a determined gait. On my right, I saw a wide staircase, leading upstairs. It was probably from there Mary had come.

The corridor was endless, and after making a turn to our right, Wickney pushed a wide door with the back of his hand. The decor changed quickly. This was certainly the servants' quarters. Several rooms followed. They were obviously dedicated to storage, maintenance, housekeeping, stores or the kitchen. Moreover, I glimpsed several persons, men and women, busy at various tasks.

As I had slowed down, Wickney announced:

"Useless to linger here. You will be working in the stables, perhaps, and in the upkeep of the grounds."

Horses. I had always loved horses. In Gloucester, I often used to go and visit my uncle's neighbour, Sir Ladington. He had three fine animals that he rode on Sundays to go on trips in the surrounding countryside. I had easy access to the stalls and used to observe the animals for long periods of time. Sir Ladington, a very likeable gentleman, had allowed me several times to mount one of the horses, Cesarus, and I then taught myself to ride. According to Sir Ladington, I managed it rather well. But these escapades did not last long, as my uncle did not like to see me having fun. He thought that it was wasted time and systematically put me back to work.

A little door gave access to outside, probably an entrance for staff who did not have at their disposal use of the main door located above the landing. This time, I was at the back of the building and I came across the outbuildings that I was unable to see when I had arrived. A long wooden building very likely housed the horses, at least about ten, from my estimation. Nearby were other huts, which perhaps were the lodgings Lady Cheltenham had mentioned. Located there, also, were sheds for feed, carts, tools for gardening and upkeep of the huge grounds now before my eyes.

Wickney stopped for a moment and turned to me. His unemotional expression was hardly reassuring. But perhaps it was a mere demeanour that the man adopted. If he was the major-domo and consequently the head of all these servants, he had to, permanently, seek respect.

"From here, you have a rather precise view of the Cheltenham estate. These large grounds, the main building and its outbuildings. The grounds are no less than 25,000 acres, so there is much to keep one busy, between the lawns, the paths, the ornamental trees, the lake and the riding stables. Milady owns also several miles of forest north of the town, but that does not concern us. I am now going to show you your lodgings, which you will share with Cadell."

"Cadell?"

He did not respond, but led me to a hut, at a considerable distance from the main building. This shack, of moderate size, was wooden. The walls were made of squared logs and the roof of long, flat, greyish stones. There was one door at the front and at that moment I could see only one window.

"This is it. You see it's rather rustic, but you will only be there to sleep and for your meals, if you wish. To get water, there is a pump by the wall, behind the stables."

Wickney went to the window pane, removed a spider web with his hand and looked inside.

"Cadell is not there. He must be still at the far end of the grounds. He had some trimming to do over there. I advise you not to go in if he isn't there. Sit on the steps and wait for him here; I have things to do. Oh, I forgot, midday meal with the others. You will find it."

And Wickney, briskly turning on his heels, took the path to the manor.

I put down my canvas bag and sat on the steps leading to the entrance of the shack. In fact, it was raised, placed on several solid logs. This, surely, was for protection from rodents and the prevalent dampness.

While observing the grounds, I wondered what this Cadell, with whom, if I had understood it correctly, I was going to share the lodgings, looked like. Perhaps a boy, also taken on here, and with whom I could make friends. That reassured me; so I was not alone in this world, which for me was totally new.

I did not wait long. At the end of the path which led to the lake, a figure appeared. The man, tall, with broad shoulders, approached at a brisk pace. His boots crunched the gravel. When he was just a few feet away, I could finally make out his features.

He was a man of about forty years old, with an emaciated face. His features were drawn, his sparkling black eyes were circled with purple lines. His hair, curly and unkempt, fell over his wide forehead. A thin beard covered his hollow cheeks. At first sight, his general appearance was one of distrust and fear. He put down the long, curved saw that he was carrying on his shoulder and wiped his hands on his thick overalls.

"What are you doing here?" he grunted in a hoarse voice.

"I am Jeremy, the new worker…"

"Hmm… the new worker. I heard about that, in fact. Well, here you are."

"Yes, I…"

"You didn't go in?"

"No, I was waiting for you."

"You did well. This is my home. You must not disturb me. You will have to be discreet. But don't stand there like a scarecrow."

He went up the three steps and opened the door. He turned his head and beckoned me to follow him.

Inside, it was rather dark. Another window overlooked the back, but it was hidden by a thick brown-coloured curtain. From the threshold I made out a table and three poorly built chairs, two basic beds, one of which was immediately at the left of the door. The other one was at the back, under the second window. On the right were some shelves which supported quite a collection of curios, but now, I would not be able to say what they were.

A musty odour hit my throat. On the table were two bottles of cheap alcohol.

"Please come in. No need to be difficult."

"Yes, sir, of course."

"Sir… Oh! Oh!"

And Cadell gave a loud laugh which chilled my bones.

"Get yourself settled and don't worry about me. We are just here to work hard."

"Yes, sir"

"The slave-driver told you about getting a bite?"

In light of my dumbfounded expression, he thought it best to rephrase.

"Wickney explained how you get your meals?"

"Er…yes…no…"

"On the stroke of midday and seven o'clock in the evening. If you don't have a watch, you will hear the bell."

"Understood."

"And in the morning, six thirty on the dot. You will get your food at the manor house with the servants. Try to be early, if not you will get nothing at all. Regarding work, Wickney will give you the plan. If you want to go to the toilet, the hut is at the back. That's okay with you?"

"Yes, sir."

"Very well, now leave me; it's time for my break."

Cadell placed his tool along the wall, grabbed a bottle from the shelf and gulped a long mouthful. He clicked his tongue as a sign of deep satisfaction. He took off his overalls and threw them over the back of one of the chairs. Then, reaching the bed on the left, he stretched out, turning his back to me.

I understood that I should not disturb him. It was better to be in his good graces. On tiptoe, I reached the back of the shack. The bed seemed comfortable enough and a large woollen blanket covered it. A sort of rack allowed me to put away my bag. I had to be satisfied with this very rough furniture, nonetheless. Cadell began to snore noisily. Work must have worn him out greatly for him to fall asleep so quickly.

The alcohol, which he seemed to be accustomed to imbibing, without a doubt also had something to do with it. Having nothing particular to do at the moment — my work did not officially begin until the next day — I decided to go and take a walk around the stables.

3

As I made my way to the stables, my mind wandered. Really, everything had happened so quickly. I think that I had not yet realized that I was going to have to stand on my own feet. My uncle, who had kept me under his thumb for years, had detached himself from me. His business was not doing very well and getting rid of one mouth to feed was rather convenient for him.

On the death of my parents, ten years earlier, he had taken me in, clearly because he could not do otherwise. It was the housekeeper, Juliet, who had raised me. My uncle, occupied with his business, very often on the road, could not bother with me, but I had quickly realized that to him I was a load with which he wanted to be burdened as little as possible.

I learnt to read, to write, I studied history and geography, I took an interest in science, and I was fascinated with books, although there were few at my uncle's home. In his big house on Armory Street, the bookcase in the drawing room did not have many. Juliet, who had had a grandmother of French origin, taught me some basics of that language and I managed quite well. It was at school that I found my reading matter and I was able to take these books home to devour them in the evenings, in my humble room, by the light of a smoky paraffin lamp. The 1870 Education Act established compulsory education only up to the age of ten years.

So, as soon as I was ten years old, my uncle took me out of school to put me to work. I was deeply disappointed. I had to quit school at the height of the academic year, in the middle of spring. My schoolmaster viewed my departure with regret. He thought I was a brilliant student and that I should have been able to continue my studies at secondary level, but my uncle would have none of it. My classmates were rather few and I quickly forgot them.

From then on, I had to work in my uncle's firm. He managed a small textile factory and, using raw material imported from the West Indian colonies, he created fabrics which he exported to the four corners of the realm. It was a firm that my uncle had bought for next to nothing from a desperate manufacturer. If the business had been doing well in its early days, the competition manifested by rival concerns in Bristol rapidly began to be felt. The neighbouring town, with a better location, endowed with a fully developed port, equipped with a new railway, had much better advantages. But my uncle could not relocate. To sell his firm at a loss, to try to acquire a new one, extremely expensive, was impossible.

From the age of ten, I was therefore assigned, with some boys of my age, to packaging cloth. The difference with these other employees was that I was not paid. My uncle thought that room and board constituted a kind of salary. At most, he gave me a modest amount of pocket money, with which I could buy little.

However, my uncle's business continued to be in jeopardy. Sales dwindled, competition was stronger than ever. He laid off some of his employees and even dismissed my dear Juliet. That was for me — and evidently for her also — a very difficult moment.

Then, to boost up his business, my uncle entrusted me, as you just learnt, to the care of Lady Cheltenham. He was economizing on one mouth to feed and I understood that a part of my —

meagre — salary would be sent to him.

I had got near to the stables. The atmosphere was filled with those odours so peculiar to stalls. The hay, the horses, all of it intoxicated me. A wild desire to ride seized me. Pushing a small wooden gate, I skirted the stalls, glancing inside. Of the ten locations, five were occupied. Some magnificent animals, thoroughbreds, with gleaming coats and slender legs, occupied these stalls. Their heads projected from the stalls and each one in turn rapidly recoiled as I passed by. That was understandable. I drew near to a mare with a light brown coat. She had a tuft of beige hair, which hung over her eyes, giving her a comical appearance. After a motion of retreat, she allowed me to get close. I gently caressed her head.

"Hello, my pretty one," I whispered. "So, what's your name?"

"Grace… her name is Grace."

I turned around. This little, high-pitched voice belonged to Mary, whom I had glimpsed a while before in the manor. She was looking at me with a cheerful expression, obviously happy to have surprised me.

I moved away from the horse. I had, at that moment, the impression of being caught in the act. But of what? Perhaps because I found myself in the presence of the daughter of the mistress of the house. I was a mere worker. Mary must have noticed my uneasiness.

"Have no fear. I won't tell."

"What do you mean by that, Miss?"

"Here is Brackett's private domain. No one enters without his authorization or else on the specific order of my mother or Wickney."

"Oh."

"That will remain our secret. You like horses?"

"Yes, Miss. I love them."

"My mother has preserved this passion of my late father. A

riding accident, nonetheless. She hardly rides, but keeps these animals, feeds them, takes care of them. I myself go riding from time to time, but it's Brackett who regularly takes them out to keep them fit and in good health."

"I see."

"Are you always so talkative?"

"The fact is, Miss, I only know…"

How would I be able to admit that her sudden appearance had thrown me into a state of uneasiness and confusion? And then, it is true, I was not a great talker.

At school, I was more often absorbed in my books rather than playing with my friends, and at my uncle's firm, days often passed without my saying a single word, while packaging the fabrics for export. As for interactions with my uncle, they were limited to what was strictly necessary.

I could clearly see that Mary was trying to lighten up the atmosphere.

"And do you like it here?"

"I don't know, Miss, I just got here."

"That lout Cadell hasn't upset you too much?"

"No, Miss, that's alright."

"He's a bit sullen, though, but he's not a bad chap. He is a good worker who gets through the work of at least two men in his day's work."

"Indeed."

"We must leave now. Brackett should be here soon. He left a while ago with Azurea. It would be better if he does not find you here, for the moment, at least."

"Very well, Miss."

I left to explore the surroundings of the building. I heard the young girl shout:

"You can call me Mary!"

"Very well... Mary."

And she took off with a joyful laugh, which made a flock of starlings take flight.

I saw her sky-blue dress disappear round the corner of the manor, just as I heard the trotting of a horse.

4

The horseman quickly drew near. Azurea's nostrils released clouds of steam with each of the loud exhalations of the animal. Without a word or a look, the individual passed near me, directed the mare towards the first stall, dismounted and immediately covered the back of his mount with a thick woollen blanket.

When he had completed these preliminary tasks, essential, it is true, to prevent the animal catching a cold, he turned his head towards me. Under a broad-brimmed hat, his hair fell in long, stiff strands, framing an elongated face. His eyes, small and somewhat mocking, deep black, ardently scrutinized me. His upper lip was slightly deformed by a purple scar and revealed yellowed or almost black teeth. He could have been a little over twenty years old. Lanky, rather thin, he gave the impression of being irritable, touchy, and anti-social.

"What are you doing here?" he yelled at me in a cantankerous tone of voice.

"I'm the new worker, Jeremy. I just got here."

"Oh yes? You are lodging with Cadell?"

"Yes, that's right, with Cadell."

"Oh! Oh! Good luck!"

I did not respond to that remark. At the time, I did not have any particular opinion about Cadell to express.

"In any case, you must not hang around the stables; bear that in mind. You must not go near the horses; they don't like strangers. You understand? If I see you in the stalls, I will give you a thrashing."

"Oh, I have no business with the horses. I think I'm going to work on the grounds, with Cadell."

"Good, good. And now leave me alone, go away!"

I did not wait for any more. This Brackett was unpleasant and aggressive. I decided not to bother with him. He definitely was not worth the trouble.

I still had a little time before the midday meal. I decided to push on as far as the lake. I understood that it was at the end of the path which ran directly north.

The trees bordering it were magnificent. Golden beeches, flaming oaks, weeping willows. The lawns were well kept and here and there, autumn leaves had been gathered in heaps. That showed that the maintenance was very regular, as leaves fell daily in this season. They would be destined to be burnt, some of them, because I knew that they could also be used as manure in preparing the land for future cultivation.

The path followed a slight bend, then meandered between areas with clusters of plants, whose flowers had now disappeared. Around one of these bends, the lake appeared. Relatively circular, about one hundred and eighty feet in diameter, its smooth surface was covered in some places by large, flowerless water lilies. Rushes fringed the opposite shore and I saw three ash-coloured herons, on the bank, foraging for food. I stayed there for a moment, breathing deeply, and enjoying the quiet of the surroundings. If the work was not too hard I figured I should be happy here. I no longer had to put up with my uncle's bad temper and work hard for his firm. It was therefore with a light heart and boosted morale that I retraced my steps. This time, I was in a hurry to get to know the staff working at the manor. When I passed back in front of the shack, Cadell, who had finished his siesta, was sitting on the steps. He was chomping heartily on a greasy piece of meat and had placed, next to him, one of his bottles of alcohol. He gave me a little nod, which I would have sworn, was almost friendly.

The bell rang twelve times. Lunchtime. Being anxious not to be late, I quickened my step and reached the door I had used with Wickney. In the corridor, a slight hubbub, as well as a pleasant smell of food immediately showed me the way.

Hesitant, I stood in the doorway. One of the servants, who was about fifty years old, turned towards me.

"Come in, young man, come on in. You must eat while it's still warm."

Saying this, she pointed at a chair.

"Don't be afraid, we won't eat you," yelled another woman, a bit younger.

"My name is Cathy," the one who had invited me to sit down began again. "And this is Lauren and this is Joanna."

"What's your name and where are you from?" asked the one named Lauren.

"My name is Jeremy, I'm from Gloucester and my uncle…"

"Eat up," Cathy continued, "and pay no mind to Lauren; she always asks a lot of questions, always wants to know everything."

Lauren began to laugh and sat down in front of me. Her blond curls hung over the sides of her head-scarf. Her big blue eyes focused their attention on me.

The meal consisted of boiled meat and good-sized potatoes. There was also green cabbage. It was a considerable amount.

I looked around. Two large wood stoves, which generated a mild heat, took up an entire wall in the room. The stoves hummed and the food simmered in casseroles and stewpots. Shelves held white dishes and a large cupboard contained the necessities for setting tables. I also glimpsed a low sideboard. The third worker was on her feet and bustling about in front of the stoves. In response to my questioning look, Cathy explained:

"Today, it's Joanna who is on duty. She will serve the meal for Milady and her daughter. She will eat later."

"And Wickney?" I dared to ask.

"He also will eat later. He often has things to do at this time. But he will probably pass by to give you your instructions. As for Brackett, he rarely comes, just like Cadell, also. They prefer to fend for themselves and eat alone. They are uncouth fellows."

"Oh."

"You like it here?"

"I don't know, Madam, I just got here." I gave the same reply that I had given to Mary.

"Madam! You hear, girls. Jeremy, you are in the same boat as us. Employed by an extremely rich Lady who is going to decide everything for you. Let's not be fussy, you can call us by our first names."

"Understood… Cathy."

The three workers rather looked alike with their light blue aprons and their head-scarves. Only age differentiated them.

In any case, they seemed nice to me and I told myself that I would be able to find here, at meal times, a friendly and comforting place.

Lauren handed me a piece of apple pie.

"Here, Jeremy, build up your strength. I made it myself. With apples from the orchard. Tell me what you think."

The pie was scrumptious. It reminded me of those my dear Juliet used to make.

She also served me a cup of rather strong coffee which was kept hot on a corner of the stove. It was delicious.

"Well, Jeremy, you seem to enjoy it."

"It was excellent. All the more because I ate very early this morning, because of the journey."

As the women began to clear the table, footsteps sounded in the corridor.

"Wickney," Lauren whispered to me.

Indeed, the major-domo appeared in the doorway. He looked around.

"Jeremy has finished eating, Wickney; so have we," stated Cathy.

"Very well, I need to talk to him about his work."

"Yes, sir," I replied.

"You can remain in your seat."

Wickney sat down opposite me, while Lauren placed in front of him a large plate filled with meat and vegetables.

"Well, you are going to begin tomorrow morning. As you may know, breakfast at six thirty in order to get work going. In the middle of winter, you will begin later; it is not light enough at that time. As I don't yet know what you are capable of, you will start off with Cadell. You will help him with trimming the trees at the far end of the grounds and with gathering the leaves. That should not be too complicated. For the time being, that will be for two weeks. The instructions are therefore valid for the duration. Then we will see how the work is progressing. On Sundays, rest, of course and gathering at the chapel for the ten o'clock mass. Then, after the service, you will pass and see me for your week's pay."

"Understood, sir."

"You have understood everything clearly?"

"I think so."

"Well, you can go now."

After a moment of hesitation, Cathy intervened.

"Joanna has to go to Prestbury to run some errands; you can go with her if you like."

"With pleasure."

I was happy with this prospect. I was very much interested in discovering the surroundings.

"Then be in the yard about two o'clock. I will be there with the cart," explained Joanna.

"Understood. See you soon."

And I took off, elated at the prospect of this escapade.

5

Prestbury was only three and a half miles away. Joanna handled the cart skilfully, the horse moving at a good pace. It was one of the animals I had seen when I visited the stables.

As soon as we left the estate, we had travelled through a majestic forest with delightful colours. Russet, yellow, brown, all these hues which under the rays of a generous sun enchanted me. The air smelled of damp earth, humus and mushrooms.

At the edge of this wood, the road sloped gently and traversed a small valley, in the hollow of which nestled the village of Prestbury. A stream meandered through the hollow of the valley, a bluish ribbon with gentle curves, bordered by tall poplars which danced in the breeze.

Although the Cheltenham estate rather belonged to the town with the same name, the workers were in the habit of shopping in Prestbury. The village was, actually, closer than the town, and they were supplied by farmers or merchants who offered articles and food of a high quality.

"We are going to drop in on Prescott first," declared Joanna. "He has autumn potatoes that resemble those of spring. He has a technique, he says, of cultivating them, which enables that. Something borrowed from the peasants of the Loire Valley, in France."

I consented. In fact, I was happy to just go along. Joanna could take me wherever she wished; I was really delighted with this excursion. Moreover, the young woman was kind, spoke in a soft voice and I felt rather comfortable next to her. During the short journey, she had spoken a bit about her family. About her father who beat her mother every day; about the latter who finally succumbed to the beatings. Joanna was only ten years old then. Her father, a hardened drinker, had died shortly after, his liver eroded by alcohol.

She had been placed here, at Cheltenham, thanks to the kind courtesies of Cathy, who had known her mother for a long time.

She had therefore had a hard life, but said she was happy at the manor. She was well treated there; Lady Cheltenham was a fair person; in spite of his cold demeanour, Wickney was not a wicked man. I should not bother with Brackett, who simply wanted to be left in peace and although Cadell was rather grumpy, he was not a bad person.

Joanna stopped the cart in front of a wretched looking building. A hovel rather than a house, with stone walls in a terrible state. The roof also seemed damaged.

"This is it?" I asked.

Seeing my surprise, Joanna began to laugh.

"This is it, but don't be fooled by appearances. Just follow me."

At the side of this miserable building was a metal gate which was not even closed. We went in and I encountered a yard filled with cases, boxes and casks. Beyond, a kind of shed, which seemed new, with roughcast walls and roofing in perfect condition. Another moderately sized house adjoined this building. This one was spruce.

"You see, Jeremy, how ugliness can hide unsuspected beauty?"

"Indeed, what a contrast."

"That is because Mr Prescott does excellent business. He sends his vegetables, and especially potatoes, throughout the entire region. So he had this shed and this house built. The dwelling by the road is a family house which he did not want to live in."

At that moment, no doubt after having heard us talking, a young boy, about ten years old, came up. He was wearing a big, brown linen jacket and had a cap stuck on his head.

"This is Tom, his son," Joanna whispered to me.

Then, addressing the boy:

"Good morning, Tom. Is your father in?"

"Good morning, Miss Joanna. Yes, he is in the shed preparing a big order. I won't ask why you are here."

"Indeed, Tom, as usual. I'm taking the opportunity to introduce Jeremy, who will be working at the manor from now on. Perhaps you will see him from time to time."

The boy gave me a nod and I immediately gave him one in return.

"I'm going to look for my father, Miss Joanna."

And the boy disappeared running into the shed. We heard him call his father several times.

A plump little man appeared then. He did not look like much. Nothing about him denoted a rich producer whose business was doing wonderfully well. Very plainly dressed, dishevelled hair, crooked moustache, he sported a big smile on his rather jovial face.

"Miss Joanna, I am happy to see you. You are always so radiant."

Joanna turned crimson for a brief moment before regaining her composure.

"Thank you, Mr Prescott, thank you."

"And this young fellow?"

"This is Jeremy. He is working with us. He just got here."

"Very well. I think he will be happy at the manor. What would you like today?"

"I would say two hundred pounds. Dutch, as usual. We consume a lot of them."

"That's not a problem. You're taking them now?"

"I would like to. And bring me your bill; Wickney will come by to settle it."

"Agreed. Tom," shouted the producer, "did you hear? Hurry up."

Tom, who was keeping his distance, went back unto the shed to prepare the order.

"It won't be long. Perhaps Lady Cheltenham might want something else. I have some excellent cabbages now, autumn lettuce, and some nice carrots, with just the right sweetness."

"Put in some for me as well, enough for a week; you know what we need."

"Ever since, as you can imagine."

And Mr Prescott also went off to the shed to prepare this additional order.

The matter was quickly settled in fact. The potatoes were divided into five cloth sacks and the vegetables in perforated crates. Mr Prescott himself undertook to put everything in our cart.

"Next time, Joanna, remember to bring back the sacks; they are very useful to me," he said, handing her the bill for Lady Cheltenham.

"I will bear that in mind, Mr Prescott, I promise. See you soon."

And we resumed our journey, while Tom kept his eyes on us.

Joanna headed for the centre of the market-town. The village was very quiet. The men were working in the fields or in the orchards; the women must have been busy with household chores. The children were probably at school. She pulled up at a lovely square, in the centre of which was a hundred-year-old plane-tree and a grey stone fountain from which ran crystal clear water.

"We are going to the General Store, Mrs Appleton's place, on that side," she said. "Wickney wants some wire, some twelve-penny nails, and a new scythe blade. There are always things to be done at the manor, as you will understand very soon."

At the General Store, Mrs Appleton held sway behind a mahogany counter like a queen in her palace. She was wearing a pair of metal-rimmed glasses and her pulled back grey hair gave her a rather stern appearance. But her soft eyes and her permanent smile immediately put me at ease.

"Good morning, Joanna, what lucky chance brings you here?"

"Always tools and work materials."

"And who is this charming young man?"

And Joanna repeated her explanation. Mrs Appleton was looking at me in a kindly manner.

"You won't be idle up there, my lad. You won't be bored. Good luck!"

I gave Joanna a questioning look. She indicated that I should not be worried.

Mrs Appleton prepared what was needed and, she too, handed over a bill of expenses for the attention of Lady Cheltenham. Before leaving the premises, the shopkeeper slipped a barley sugar, shaped like a lollipop, into my hand.

"For the road."

"Thank you, Mrs Appleton."

"Don't mention it, young man. Have a safe return."

And we continued on our way. Joanna made another detour to the apothecary's dispensary. Lady Cheltenham wanted wild rose syrup for her daughter Mary, who had a sore throat. I almost replied that I had met Mary that very morning and that she seemed quite healthy, but I refrained. Bringing up that encounter was perhaps not a good thing.

"I believe that this time, we are finished, Jeremy. Now that you have seen the place, you can come back, during your breaks. There is a tavern at the end of this street where the lemonade is excellent."

"I'll remember that, Miss Joanna."

And we got back on the road to the manor. The trip seemed to me as delightful as the outward journey. We saw two yearling roe deer, who were leaping about over the slopes. The sun played hide-and-seek with the trunks of the beech trees and a light breeze set the last golden leaves dancing.

At the end of the road the chapel bell sounded. Five o'clock already!

6

The evening meal took place in that congenial atmosphere that I had already experienced at midday.

Cathy had made bread. She seemed to be an expert on the matter and, twice a week, she prepared several pounds of soft, sweet-smelling bread. The loaves were wrapped in dish-cloths and put away in the larder, located in the basement. The temperature and the humidity level there being constant, the bread did not get hard and kept all its savour throughout the week. She had also prepared a soup with numerous vegetables. In it I detected potato, leek, carrots, parsley and chervil. These two aromatic herbs were excellent for one's health, she said, which made her put them very often in the food.

She had prepared cold chicken, drumsticks which I gnawed on heartily. We finished off with goat's cheese and the remainder of the apple pie.

"Well, this outing to Prestbury has opened up your appetite," she said to me.

"It's the fresh air here," added Lauren. "That must be a change from Gloucester for you."

In Gloucester, with my uncle and Juliet, we lived in the middle of town. From October to April, the chimneys of the houses, it is true, discharged their yellowish or grey smoke, according to the fuel used. Fine dust infiltrated the houses and naturally the air was contaminated. Doctors recorded several lung diseases due to this pollution. Here, at Cheltenham, I breathed to my heart's content. The air was pure, fresh, invigorating and stimulating.

Wickney did not turn up for the meal. No doubt he had been detained by an urgent task. Brackett and Cadell were also conspicuous by their absence. Joanna waited at table for Lady Cheltenham and when she reappeared, we had finished eating.

"So, it's the big day tomorrow," said Cathy.

"Yes, I will start working. With Cadell."

"Well, he will take you into the grounds for trimming and for collecting leaves. These grounds are huge, it will take a while. But you look strong."

It is true that the work at my uncle's place had developed my muscle structure. The packing cases and boxes to be lifted constantly had developed the muscles in my arms, my shoulders and my thighs. So, in spite of my youth, I had a certain amount of physical strength.

Looking through the window, I observed that the daylight was fading. I decided to disappear.

"I'm going to turn in. Thank you for this fine meal. It was truly delicious."

"Don't mention, Jeremy," Lauren responded. "And tomorrow, don't forget, half past six."

"I will be there. Good evening."

They wished me goodnight in a chorus, but I did not wish to go to bed immediately. I was tempted to take a walk in the grounds and I decided to follow the gravel path.

There was still a little light, and I was able to proceed without difficulty. So I again went in the direction of the lake at a rapid pace. The place was quiet. The water was still; only a few ripples appeared here and there, caused by ducks and swans which I had not seen in the morning. The herons had disappeared. I stayed there a while, listening to the silence and breathing the fresh air.

I was alerted by some rustling on my left. Someone was coming for sure. Some noises could be heard in the leafy part of the estate, which rose in a gentle slope towards the road to Prestbury. Nut trees and other more or less decorative shrubs grew in this section of the grounds. So someone could be rather easily concealed there. But then who would hide away like that in the grounds at this hour?

I decided to get out of sight. I espied a thicket which made a perfect hiding-place for me. Through the branches, I could still make out the undergrowth. It was close to nightfall, this time, but an almost full moon emitted sufficient light to see.

Two shadows emerged from the undergrowth. Two persons fairly tall in stature, at any rate taller than me. They seemed to be clutching each other like two men quarrelling or fighting. I thought I heard some muffled shouts and it seemed very much to me that one of the protagonists had let fly several punches in the face of his adversary. The one who was hit shouted angrily, raised his arms and quickly disappeared. I was very surprised by this scene. So what was happening? The figure I could still see came down the hill, making his way towards the path, in my direction. I was scared to death and had to curl up, praying not to be discovered.

The man passed about twelve feet from my hiding place. In the light from the moon, I recognized him immediately. It was Brackett heading back to the stables, with an angry expression. He was muttering, swearing and seemed very agitated. I waited until he had disappeared before heading for my shack. After all, Brackett's troubles with friends of his kind did not concern me. So I decided to forget about this matter.

I cautiously entered the hut, avoiding making the floor creak. But Cadell was not sleeping. Sitting on a chair, by the light of a paraffin lamp, he was sculpting, with a penknife, an animal in a piece of wood. He raised his eyes as I came in.

"Oh, there you are."

"Yes, sir."

"Go to sleep; tomorrow there will be no idling. You need to be fit."

"Yes, sir. Good night."

"Hmm…"

While Cadell was extinguishing the lamp, I slipped under the blanket. The day's images came one after another before my eyes. My uncle, Lady Cheltenham, Wickney, Brackett, the trip to Prestbury, the nice servants Cathy, Lauren and Joanna… But one image kept coming back incessantly, and lay over the others. It was the image of a pale blue dress, an oval face with perfect features and blond curls dancing in the wind. Mary. Mary Cheltenham…

7

During the night, Mary's image had become blurred and was replaced by the more disturbing one of Brackett. I saw his face, distorted by anger, his broken-toothed mouth emitting a stinking breath on me. He was threatening me; I don't know why, but the situation was very unpleasant. He hoisted a long cutlass in my direction and I gave a frightful yell.

Cadell was bending over me.

"What's happening to you?" he grunted.

His voice was harsh.

"A nightmare, sir, nothing serious."

"Try not to wake up the whole household like that every night."

I smiled in the dark, as it was just the two of us.

And he went back to his bed grumbling.

The chapel bell rang five times. I could still go back to sleep. It was a bit cold and I pulled up the blanket.

At six o'clock, I was up. Cadell stirred, turned over several times and opened one eye. Without a word, he stood up and slipped on his overalls. He dashed outside and I heard the toilet door.

I decided to have a quick wash and I remembered that the pump was outside. It was a hand device, fixed against the wall behind the stables. My uncle had one like it in the yard at his business place. I was able to prime it with the help of a half-filled bucket that I found there and very cool water began to run. Sprinkling my torso and my face brought me fully awake. However, I wondered what I would do in the middle of winter, when the weather was very cold or turned freezing?

I heard footsteps near the stables. Brackett appeared. He gave me a look of disgust which signified that this water pump was the boundary beyond which I should not go. He did not say a word to me and disappeared immediately.

I was hungry and did not waste any time joining the kitchen staff again.

"Oh, there's Jeremy!"

Cathy was already in top form. The kitchen smelled of coffee and fresh bread.

"I advise you to eat well, Jeremy," she went on. "It will be a long time until midday and the work is sometimes hard. Build up your strength."

Joanna and Lauren had not yet arrived. Footsteps sounded in the corridor.

"That's Cadell. He always comes in the morning; he doesn't say it, but he loves my coffee," Cathy whispered.

My roommate appeared.

"Good morning, Cadell," the servant cheerfully called out.

"Hmm…"

Without further comment, he took a seat, while Cathy served us each a large bowl of steaming coffee. I cut a big slice of bread which I spread generously with rhubarb jam, also home-made. Cadell wolfed down two poached eggs and a rather thick slice of bacon. I mimicked him with the eggs; as for the bacon I decided to try that another time. There was also porridge, which succeeded in filling our stomachs. I took some more coffee, as it was really excellent.

"Are you ready, young man?" Cadell then asked.

"Yes, sir, I think so."

"Oh! Oh! You hear that Cathy? Since yesterday this boy has been calling me sir. Here, everybody calls me Cadell."

"Understood, Cadell. I will do that."

"Good. Meet me at the shack in five minutes. I will tell you about the tools and the work."

"Yes, s… Cadell."

Although Cadell had already left Cathy whispered to me:

"I think he likes you. He hardly speaks so much in such a short time. It's a rather good sign. Because with the one who was here before you…"

But she did not want to say any more about it to me. I realized that it was useless to ask her about this matter.

"Off you go! And good luck!"

Cadell and I had reached the back of the grounds, almost quarter of a mile from the manor. As we were leaving we had seen Brackett, who seemed to be busy near the fences around the training-area. So the wire and twelve-penny nails that had been bought the day before at Mrs Appleton's were for him.

The back of the grounds, bordered by a rather high drystone wall, was overrun, that's the word, by numerous shrubs. Lilacs, hazels, others unknown to me, and which were growing in a disorganized fashion, according to Lady Cheltenham. A number of creepers clung to the enclosure wall and were succeeding in loosening the stones. Cadell explained to me, in a rather curt manner, that the priority was at that spot. Cutting, pulling out these kinds of creeping lianas growing by the hundreds and burning them. We thus had, in my estimation, twelve to eighteen hundred feet in length to clear, which would keep us busy for a good fortnight.

For the whole morning, we pulled out the awful fibrous stems which were not letting go so easily. The stems, thumb-sized, had multiple branches and insinuated themselves between the stones, thus managing to dislodge them. We each had a sort of metal hook which allowed us, as far as possible, to pull the plants out of the crevices. In two hours, we had not progressed beyond sixty feet. However, Cadell seemed satisfied with my work.

Perhaps to allow me to catch my breath a bit, he suggested burning what we had already pulled out.

"You will find what's needed in the bag there."

In fact, I found a box of safety matches as well as some newspaper. So it was not very difficult to light a fire, on a blackened site that Cadell must have used before. The paper caught quickly, the print becoming distorted from the combustion. However, I had time to make out a headline in bold type: '*Drama at Cheltenham manor.*' I was extremely intrigued by that. I rummaged in the bag to dig out other sheets of this newspaper. It was dated May of the previous year. So what had happened there for the newspaper to print such an article? Had Cadell read this newspaper?

I lit the fire and began to burn the plants. Thick, acrid smoke rose from it. Cadell put on some pieces of wood to feed the fire and for it to remain alight. I was thus able to resume my clearing work and regularly throw lianas into the flames.

The morning went on like that, quickly, and Cadell did not seem discontented. Not that he would have expressed it, as he had not uttered ten words, but I could see by his expression that my work satisfied him.

"The midday bell will ring soon," he told me. "You can go on; I will finish up this remaining bit."

"Thank you, sir…"

"Cadell! My name is Cadell"

But I had already dashed towards the lake and the gravel path. I was racked by hunger pangs. I was in a hurry to get back to the warmth of the kitchen.

This time, it was Lauren who was on duty. She was preparing and serving the meal for Lady Cheltenham and her daughter

Mary. I would have liked to go with her to meet up with Mary again, but very much doubted whether that was a good idea. Why did I then have this desire to see the girl again? This was something that had never happened to me before. I must say that at school I had only kept close to boys and at the business place moreover, girls of my age were conspicuous by their absence. Cathy must have noticed my frowning.

"Is something bothering you, Jeremy? Was it Cadell?"

"No, no Cathy. Everything went well. Cadell isn't unpleasant. Not talkative, but not unpleasant."

"That's good, that's good. But I told you so; he has a soft spot for you."

After the meal, I was again able to take a walk in the grounds. This time I visited the part at the front, where I had arrived. I saw again the majestic façade, its lovely slate roof and numerous windows. Behind one of them, on the first level of the building, I thought I saw movement. I blinked my eyes. Yes, a little blonde head had passed behind the windowpane and it very much seemed that Mary, since it could only be her, was waving to me. My heart leapt in my chest. To me, who was in despair about seeing her again, this fleeting apparition gave new impetus to my desire to meet her again, to speak to her, about nothing, the manor, horses…

The chapel bell called me to order. Soon I would have to resume work. Time to get back to the shack where Cadell must be waiting. It was better not to be late.

The afternoon passed without mishap. We had made good progress along the wall. Cadell, who was a little more talkative, estimated that it would take us about one more week. But I realized that other tasks awaited us later and that when we had finished at one end of the grounds, we could begin again at the other end.

The evening meal was enjoyable, and I was able to talk about my day.

"You seem to be happy," Lauren commented.

"I quite like this outdoor work. It's rather pleasant."

"But I guess that you have no intention of making a career here," said Cathy.

"No, it's a temporary position. Perhaps my uncle's business will be straightened out and then, when I come of age, I would be able to decide. Only one thing is missing…"

"Yes?"

"Books. I would really like to be able to continue to read. I don't know how to do that."

Joanna and Cathy exchanged looks.

"Perhaps there is a solution," announced the young woman. "Lady Cheltenham owns, from her late husband, a fairly complete, excellent library. Perhaps you could…?"

"Oh yes, that's an idea. But when and how?"

"Sunday, after mass, that would be the opportunity."

"Sunday… that's the day after tomorrow. I don't know if I will be bold enough."

"I will come with you," Joanna reassured me. "I will speak to Milady."

"Thank you, Joanna, thank you. I can't wait for Sunday."

In fact, I knew that waiting would be difficult.

8

The chapel was half full. It was an unpretentious place, soberly decorated. The architecture, in the purest Roman style, was magnificent.

I settled myself in the back row and I was able to see the whole congregation. The pastor, Peter Van Meylen, who was of Dutch origin, Lady Cheltenham in the front row, with her daughter Mary, Wickney, the major-domo, Cathy, Joanna and Lauren, Cadell and even Brackett. The latter was seated in the same row with me, right at the end of the bench, undoubtedly in order to remain undisturbed.

I had never much frequented Protestant churches, no more than other churches for that matter. Also the pastor's words and his references to biblical texts hardly inspired me. His monotonous style, his dispassionate and staid voice, and his rather slow delivery were putting the congregation to sleep. Only Mary, right in front, did not stop fidgeting. I saw her moving about and I feverishly awaited the moment when she would look back, but that, to my great despair, did not happen.

When the pastor had ended his sermon and had recited his words of advice on how to behave in society, the congregation prepared to leave the premises. Joanna quickly got up, came back up the aisle and came to look for me.

"Let's go," she whispered. "We will await Milady outside. She usually comes to see each one of us to hear what is happening. That will be the opportunity."

I was anxious to see Lady Cheltenham again to ask permission to access the library. Perhaps I would also get close to Mary?

The congregation was leaving the church.

Lady Cheltenham led the way and she sported a big smile when she saw us. Joanna gave her a little hand signal.

"Good morning, Joanna"

"My Lady."

"And good morning to you, Jeremy."

"Good morning, Madam."

I made an attempt at a sort of bow, which made her laugh.

"How are you? These first days? All is going well?"

"Yes, Madam. I like the work and we are making good progress."

"I will go and see that, Jeremy. I will go and see. And you, Joanna, you wanted to speak to me?"

"I have a request, My Lady."

"Yes, Joanna, go ahead."

"Our young Jeremy would like to have access to your library."

"Well then. It's the first time anyone has made such a request to me. That is rare. Can you read?"

"Yes, Madam. I went to school and I was a rather good pupil. I have a real passion for books, especially those dealing with explorers or the history of ancient civilizations."

"That's a difficult topic. So you must be very interested. You are lucky, my late husband collected this type of work."

Joanna had a big smile and Mary, who meanwhile had come up, gave me a wink. This time she was wearing a garnet-red velvet dress, which went wonderfully well with her pale complexion.

Lady Cheltenham pondered for a moment and looked at me benevolently.

44

"I think that can be done. You can take out one book per week, for example. Does that suit you?"

"Oh yes, Madam."

"In that case, you will arrange that with Wickney. He can attend to that on Mondays, during his break, after the midday meal."

The major-domo, who was standing behind and certainly had not missed a bit of the conversation, nodded in a sign of approval.

"So Wickney will pass by to see you tomorrow," added Lady Cheltenham.

"Thank you, Madam."

"Thank you, My Lady," Joanna concluded.

Sunday being a day of rest, I decided, after the meal, to go and stroll around. I would like to have gone back by the horses, but Brackett's presence dissuaded me. After the mass, he had returned to the stables and shut himself in the little shack which was his place of abode. According to Cathy, he very often spent his Sundays drinking and sleeping. But he could also disappear until the evening, leaving the estate for an unknown destination.

By chance on my walk, when I had left the property and taken a short cut, I saw two riders appear, riding side by side.

As they approached, I recognized, on one of the mounts, Mary's slender figure. The man who was with her was about forty years old. His stern appearance, thin, pinched mouth, his menacing look, nothing about him was very attractive.

"Whoa!" Mary shouted to stop her horse.

"Miss," then said the horseman, turning aside. "Remember not to pull so hard on the reins. That's not necessary."

"Yes, Mr Crowd. I will be careful."

Then Mary smiled, while the man persistently stared at me.

"Young man?"

"Jeremy. Jeremy Page…"

"This boy is a friend," Mary interrupted. "Leave us a while, please, Mr Crowd."

The man hesitated, but no doubt he had to comply with the wishes of his pupil and moved forward his horse about twenty paces. He seemed to be annoyed.

"Jeremy, what are you doing here?"

"Friend? Did you say friend?"

"Yes, exactly. That was the only way to get away from this bird of ill omen. My mother makes me take lessons twice a week and this Mr Crowd is as cheerful as a jail door."

I understood this strategy, but I was wondering all the same if the term 'friend' was not going beyond a mere tactic here.

"I'm making use of my rest day. This quiet retreat is superb; I really like it here. And then, the work is not too difficult and Cadell is not giving me a rough time."

"Cadell is not a bad fellow. Brackett is more disturbing. Stay far from him, if you want my opinion."

"I had noticed it too and I avoid crossing his path."

"I will have to go. Mr Crowd is getting impatient. We will see each other tomorrow."

"Tomorrow?" I asked, astonished.

"Yes, in the library. I will come with Wickney."

"Oh! Good."

And she galloped off to meet up with her riding teacher. I don't know why, but the continuation of my walk was very different. The persistent image of Mary was superimposed on the magnificent landscapes that I was discovering. Her face, her blond curls, her dignified gait on the magnificent horse.

It was like that up to the evening and right up to when I fell asleep. I had an additional reason to go to that library.

That evening, Cadell returned a little later than usual. He seemed uneasy, troubled and at one moment I thought he was going to tell me something in confidence. He changed his mind and as usual he tossed off a big gulp of his cheap whisky before going to bed.

The next day, we resumed our work. I truly had the impression that this clearing was endless. The morning seemed to me all the longer because I was impatiently awaiting the midday meal. Cathy was surprised to see me eating faster than usual.

"Well, take time to breathe, Jeremy. You have a rendezvous?"

She could not have said it better.

"It's true, you seem to be in a hurry," added Lauren, who was struggling with one of the stoves.

"I'm waiting for Wickney."

"Wickney?"

"Yes, he has to escort me to the library."

"The library?"

In a few words, I told Cathy and Lauren about the arrangement with Lady Cheltenham.

"So it's the books that have you in this state," Lauren commented.

"Yes, yes, the books. I really have trouble doing without them."

I dared not admit, that from then on, the fact that I would meet Mary again motivated me as much, if not more, than finding the works of the late Lord Cheltenham.

I had just finished lunch when Wickney made his appearance. Dressed in black, stiff in his somewhat tight suit, with an imperturbable expression, he stopped on the threshold.

"Jeremy, if you are ready, we can proceed."

"I'm coming right now, sir."

And I followed the major-domo who led me to the staircase that I had seen on my arrival. It was a fine piece of work with white marble steps streaked with carmine red. The banister, on the right, comprised some elaborate columns. On the walls, three paintings of hunting scenes followed one after the other. At the stairhead, Wickney turned left and pushed a painted wooden door.

Over his shoulder, he glanced at my shoes. Obviously satisfied with the inspection, he gave me the signal to enter.

The room, with a high ceiling, was brightened by two large windows. In spite of the fairly grey sky, there was nevertheless enough light.

Very quickly, my eyes were attracted to the varnished wooden shelves which took up two wall-surfaces. These shelves had a phenomenal number of works. The books, mostly bound with light brown, dark brown or also black leather, displayed on their spines prestigious names of authors of the period, Burney, Radcliffe, Austen, Byron, Shelley, Scott and so many others, and also more ancient ones of Greek or Roman antiquity. It was ecstasy. I had never seen so many books at one time. The collection of all these authors in this room had a profound impression on me.

"Well, Jeremy, satisfied?"

I turned around. In my reverie, I had not noticed that Mary had arrived.

"And Wickney?"

"He's waiting at the stairhead."

I was overcome. Mary seemed to rule the roost in this house. But after all, wasn't she the daughter of the mistress of the house?

I was so happy with Mary's presence that I almost forgot about the books. It was she who brought me out of my torpor.

"There's a stool, there, if you wish."

"Er...yes."

I had spotted on a shelf at the top some works in a larger format. They clearly appeared to deal with travel and exploration. I would deal with Ivanhoe later.

I grabbed the stool so I could get a closer look.

There were several books there that were likely to interest me. One of them, in particular, held my attention. I turned to Mary, who continued to observe me.

"May I?"

"Of course, that's what you are here for, isn't it?"

I grasped the book and turned over the leaves carefully. This one was adorned with magnificent lithographs. A true marvel. My choice was therefore settled.

"I'm borrowing this one."

"You just need to let Wickney know. You know him now. He will make a note of what you take away."

I understood that perfectly. I also suspected that I had to return this book in an impeccable state. I again glanced at several other titles and got down off the stool.

"Agreed."

Before I reached the door, Mary held me by the arm. This contact, the very first in fact, had a strange effect on me, like a kind of wave that came and overwhelmed my nervous system. An electric current which would have circulated in me, of which the origin or the trigger, was none other than Mary.

"Tell me, Jeremy, it was my understanding that you liked horses."

"Yes, that's correct," I stammered.

"Would you like to go riding?"

"Yes, I think so, but…"

"But? You are only a worker, that's it? And you believe that it's not possible?"

"Yes, it's pretty much that. And then, Cadell and Brackett?"

"Cadell doesn't care about the horses. As for Brackett, rest assured, he often has the opportunity. That is a part of his duties."

"And your mother?"

Mary gave a little mischievous smile.

"Don't worry about my mother. I will no doubt be able to convince her."

9

This work by Edward Augustus Inglefield about his exploration of Canada kept me awake rather late. I had brought a paraffin lamp close to my bed and I was able to immerse myself in the narration of these extraordinary adventures. I envied these characters who set off for the unknown, ready to face all the dangers for the mere pleasure of discovering new territory. One detail intrigued me: the author, and explorer, was born in Cheltenham. Retired, he presently lived in Kensington.

Cadell, who had at first grumbled a little because of the light, fell asleep rather quickly. His regular breathing and his sudden and irregular snores proved he was sleeping the sleep of the just. Cadell was a strange character. Sullen, bad-tempered, a little brutish sometimes in attitude, but kind, when all is said and done. He was a hard, conscientious worker, who liked to give his best. He had taken me under his wing and I did not have any complaints about him. He had not spoken to me about his past life and I felt that there was something there that he did not want to recall. Perhaps he had gone through some painful and difficult moments, which could explain his unsociable behaviour.

I was dragged from my reading by some unusual noises. Outside, someone seemed to be running. The noise on the gravel indicated it. I pricked up my ears. There were several persons there.

I hurriedly got up and slipping on my leather slippers, I half-opened the door.

About sixty feet away, three persons were fighting. I recognized the figure of Brackett, who was struggling with two other men. Insults were flying, punches were exchanged on all sides. Brackett was swift, supple, elusive, and for a moment he had the upper hand over his two adversaries.

Then, suddenly, a blade glinted in the moonlight and Brackett uttered a cry of pain, falling to his knees while clutching his belly.

Behind me, Cadell sprang up. He pushed me aside with his powerful arm.

"Bastards," he shouted. "Clear off."

I saw a rifle gleaming in his hands. He shouldered his rifle and fired twice. The loud noise of the detonations echoed throughout the grounds, while the strangers, surprised, fled without waiting for anything else.

Meanwhile, Wickney had arrived, running towards Brackett to try and give him some help.

The young man was now stretched out, on the side of the path. He seemed to be in great pain and he was losing a lot of blood. I realized, from Wickney's expression that nothing much could be done.

"Brackett, Brackett, what happened?" asked the major-domo.

"Young man… young man…" responded Brackett, pointing at me, "take care … of the horses. You…"

His sentence ended with a death-rattle, while blood poured from the corner of his lips.

"Burglars?" Wickney conjectured.

"I don't think so," Cadell replied.

The major-domo turned around. He seemed to understand this remark. Brackett was known for engaging in shady and

51

unsavoury activities. This attack looked very much like a settling of scores.

No matter that I had not much approved of Brackett, this situation pained me. Even if Brackett was rather often disagreeable, he had never caused me harm and I had no particular reason to wish any on him.

The young man uttered a final moan and did not move any more. His eyes had become lifeless and seemed to stare at the stars. We were dismayed.

"The attackers?" asked Wickney.

"The bastards ran away," Cadell replied in a loud voice.

"I will go to Cheltenham first thing tomorrow morning to inform the Police."

"Bah!"

Cadell did not seem to believe in the effectiveness of the Police in this situation.

"Meanwhile, don't touch anything. I am going to cover the body and we will await the policemen."

This matter was astonishing. However, I recalled that evening when I had seen Brackett returning from the back of the grounds. Did that perhaps have a direct connection with this evening's altercation?

Cathy came and covered the body of the unfortunate man with a large, thick cotton sheet. She seemed shocked and did not understand what had just happened.

"I'm going to make tea for everyone, if you wish."

We were no longer really sleepy, so we again made our way to the kitchen.

The tea was still steaming in the cups when Lady Cheltenham came to join us. She was uneasy and disturbed. I had never seen her like that.

She sat near to us while Cathy served her a beverage.

"So, what happened?"

"Brackett ran into a brick wall," remarked Cadell, who for once had come along with us.

"What's that, Cadell? Explain yourself," demanded the young woman.

"I think, My Lady, that Brackett was involved in dealings with alcohol. I had spotted him several times before with some shady individuals, on the grounds."

"You are very sure of that?"

"Yes, My Lady."

"Very well, Wickney will be in charge of searching his shack."

After that, we drank our tea in silence. This incident had really crushed us. It had been so unexpected and so violent.

"Were you able to hit them?" Lady Cheltenham went on.

"I don't think so, My Lady; it was dark, you know."

"Of course, of course."

Then, as she got up to leave:

"I suggest that everybody take a rest. Tomorrow morning, don't go far; it's highly possible the Police would wish to question you. And you, Jeremy, come and see me before lunch. I have to speak to you."

"Yes, Madam."

That morning, Cadell and I therefore stayed close to the manor. There was no shortage of dead leaves, and we made huge piles of them in order to burn them. Wickney, who had gone to town, returned, accompanied by two police sergeants.

Cartridge and Holden, the two investigators with really surly expressions, then asked us several routine questions.

Cadell was rather evasive and for my part, I did not know Brackett enough to provide any information of interest. According to the policemen, the young man had a past of petty delinquency, and they were not surprised by his tragic end. The two men informed us that it would be difficult, if not impossible, to find the culprits. We ourselves did not have enough information to provide. The policemen inspected the grounds, but did not pick up any trace of blood. So Cadell had not hit the aggressors. The visit to Brackett's shack offered nothing; it must be said that Wickney had passed there before. Perhaps he had got rid of any clues. In fact, Lady Cheltenham perhaps did not want this matter made known and become a significantly negative rumour circulating in the surrounding countryside.

As we were finishing piling up a fair quantity of beech leaves, Wickney turned up.

"Jeremy, follow me; Milady is waiting for you."

"Go, go," Cadell added. "I will finish it."

I followed the major-domo, vaguely disquieted by this sort of summons. What could the mistress of the house want with me? Did it have any connection with Brackett's death?

Wickney led me into the little sitting-room where I had been received with my uncle.

"Oh, there you are, Jeremy. I sent for you as a result of last night's events. We now have a problem to fix."

"Yes, Madam."

"I no longer have anyone to look after the horses."

"I understand, Madam; that is very upsetting."

"It is a daily job. I must find a solution today."

I guessed what was to follow, not really believing it.

"Would you like that, Jeremy?"

"I think so, Madam."

"I know that you aren't afraid at work and that you like horses."

"Yes Madam, I love horses."

"Then listen, Jeremy. It is very simple; from this afternoon you will attend to the stables. It is a heavy responsibility, but I think you are capable of taking it on. We are going to arrange your day so that you can still help Cadell, while we wait to find someone else to lend him a hand. You will also need to change your lodgings."

"Do I have to, Madam?"

Lady Cheltenham seemed surprised by this question.

"It's because I am now familiar, with Cadell…"

"That's not a problem. You can keep your lodgings. So let us do it like that. Wickney will pass by and give you some information after the meal."

"Thank you, Madam"

"You can go now, Jeremy. See you very soon."

"Goodbye, Madam."

She questioned me as I was leaving the room:

"And the library, did you find everything you wanted there?"

"Yes, My Lady. I believe so."

Were we, she and I, speaking about the same thing?

I left again, almost gleeful, in a hurry to announce the news to Cathy. I was also a little worried about Cadell, but all the same, I would be able to continue to help him. Taking care of horses! A dream that I was cherishing for a long time.

10

So I assumed my duties, but with fairly relative enthusiasm. I was well aware that the opportunity offered to me that day was the consequence of a tragedy. I was not to forget that.

Attending to these horses took time. Feeding them, brushing them, cleaning their loose boxes, changing the stable litter and taking them out, one after the other, to restore the circulation in their legs in the training-area, on the grounds and sometimes outside the estate on the surrounding forest paths. It was thus that I made serious progress in horsemanship.

My life now seemed quite settled here, at Cheltenham, and I had no cause for complaint. The work was pleasant and I always found time to assist Cadell, usually at the end of the morning when I had completed the cleaning of the stables. The man bore me no grudge for my new position and always greeted me in an agreeable manner. One would have said that he missed my company. Lady Cheltenham had not yet been able to hire anyone to assist him and when all was said and done, I liked it like that.

The investigation carried out by the Police produced nothing. Really and truly, alcohol trafficking existed in the town of Cheltenham — as in other places as well — and one could suppose that Brackett had been involved in it in one way or another. Perhaps he had wanted to go it alone and his accomplices had not appreciated such a move. This murder would surely remain unpunished.

Young Brackett was buried in the modest cemetery in Prestbury. He had no known family and only Lady Cheltenham and the staff of the manor attended the ceremony. It was an opportunity moreover, a little peculiar it is true, to meet Mary. But I was unable to approach her that day.

The day after that sad day, Mary came and joined me at training-area. She rode Azurea.

"Oh Jeremy! You have made progress," she said to me.

"As you can see. I try to train regularly."

"Do you want to take a turn in the grounds?"

"You think that's possible?"

"Seeing that you have to take out the horses and let them run, what does it matter?"

This argument, rather correct in the final analysis, persuaded me instantly. A ride in the grounds in the company of Mary, what bliss!

On the gravel path, we rode the horses at a trot. I was riding Calix, a fine black mare with a shiny coat. She was frisky, supple, and precise in her gait. All the same I remained cautious as I certainly did not have Mary's expertise. Her hair floated in the wind and she followed the rhythm of the movements of her horse. She really seemed very much at ease, and I was very impressed. She was laughing out loud and her crystalline voice filled my heart with astonishing happiness.

As we moved along, I spoke to her about my childhood, about my uncle and his decision to place me there. As for Mary, she recalled the riding accident that had cost her father his life. A commonplace fall on a path in the grounds, which had turned into tragedy. Her father, although an accomplished rider, had landed badly and had broken his neck on a stump. I did not seek to question her any further on this sensitive topic.

We had passed the lake. Mary stepped up the pace. Nothing seemed likely to stop her.

The recent rainfall had made the ground very resilient, even soft in places, in spite of the gravel. Azurea shied and Mary, taken off course, slipped sideways. Her right shoulder crashed into the trunk of an oak at the edge of the path. The collision threw her off balance and she was hurled to the ground, luckily on a grassy patch.

I immediately brought my mount to a halt.

"Mary! Mary!" I shouted, as I dismounted.

"Jeremy... Jeremy..."

Her voice was weak; she was lying there, like a broken puppet, very much paler than usual.

"Does anywhere hurt?"

"My shoulder, my shoulder..."

I gently touched the shoulder; she responded with a wince of pain.

"Can you move your legs?"

"Yes, I think so."

And she moved her legs to show me that all seemed well in that area.

"Listen, I am going to take you back to the manor."

I tied the horses to a young birch tree. I would retrieve them later. I gently lifted Mary and carried her in my arms. She felt like a featherweight to me and I thought I would be able to take her home without difficulty.

During the whole journey, which really, I would have liked to prolong, Mary kept her eyes on me. I felt her hands clutching my clothes perhaps a little more tightly than necessary.

Before approaching the stretch leading to the building, I dared to do the unthinkable. I placed a delicate kiss on the young woman's forehead. I was expecting the worst, but she responded with an enchanting smile.

"Jeremy…"

From that moment, I did not know why, but I thought I realized that our fates were linked by something intense, something that I had not yet managed to define precisely.

Dr Frazer arrived in the afternoon. I was in the kitchen and I was waiting to get some news about Mary. When we returned to the manor, her mother, at first incensed by this riding escapade, had then thanked me for having brought Mary home. She promised to keep me informed.

It was Wickney, the unavoidable major-domo, who came to inform us.

"Miss Mary has no serious injury. A slight dislocation of the shoulder from which she will quickly recover, according to Dr Frazer. She has to stay in bed for a day or two."

"Good," Cathy remarked. "Is your mind at ease, Jeremy?"

"Yes, Cathy; all the same that upsets me."

"I understand, but don't worry, she will soon be up and about."

If I had dared, I would have asked to see her, but I suspected that there were certain limits that a mere worker could not be allowed to breach. So I decided to grin and bear it. I had high hopes that we would find a way to see each other again, as soon as Mary was back on her feet.

11

Mary recovered quite quickly. She resumed her riding lessons and Mr Crowd took advantage of this incident to be even more attentive than before, that is to say even more annoying. We met regularly in the training area only because Lady Cheltenham had officially forbidden escapades in the grounds without the presence of the teacher. Since the accident, Mary looked at me differently, at least that is the impression that I had. Her eyes became very soft, her look seemed to envelop me in a sort of protective cocoon. Sometimes our hands happened to touch and a strange wave passed from one to the other. Then we looked at each other and together roared with laughter. But deep within us, something was being born, something new, strong, brilliant, and uncontrollable.

Life went on. The stables, work with Cadell. I had succeeded in dissuading Lady Cheltenham from hiring anyone. I was really determined to participate in the upkeep of the grounds in the company of this strange character with whom I felt secure. Little by little, his tongue loosened and in his own way, in a rather rustic manner perhaps, he passed on to me his knowledge of plants, of the art of pruning them, looking after them and maintaining them.

Autumn ended without being really noticed and winter quickly asserted its rights. The trees were bare, the sky grey most of the time, and the light dull. The prevalent humidity was rather strong and snow made its appearance, fashioning the scenery as it liked, according to whether the wind, light or stronger, blew from the north or from the east. I took out the horses a little less often; I had made the loose boxes draught-proof with thick bundles of straw and I had put warm, thick blankets on the animals' backs.

Cadell and I were busy with firewood, spending a lot of time cutting, sawing and stacking. As it was out of the question to cut the trees on the grounds, we went into some surrounding woods where Lady Cheltenham owned some parcels of land. It is there that we got trunks of beeches, which, when dried by the wind, would supply the manor's fireplaces and stoves.

This work took us a great part of the winter. Outside activity being then less important, we proceeded with inside maintenance jobs which Wickney indicated to us. Doors which were jamming in their frames, floors to be repaired, walls on which the plaster needed a fresh coat, and tiles to be stuck back. In a word, there was no shortage of work.

At the very beginning of March, Lady Cheltenham made a big announcement. She was having a party at the manor.

She had invited Sir Garmond, an eminent man from Gloucester who had, besides a considerable fortune, a transportation company, properties and lands. It was rumoured that he would no doubt soon be the new husband of the mistress of the house. This man, very aristocratic in appearance, recently widowed, his forty years or so borne with ease, impeccably dressed and always carrying an ivory cane, had two sons, John and Perdy, two young rascals about fifteen years old, who did as they liked. It must be said that the father, despite his stern and intransigent appearance, let them get away with almost anything.

The party took place on a Sunday afternoon. Fortunately, the sun, generous on that day, already casting pleasant rays, allowed

Cathy, Lauren and Joanna to set up long tables in the yard of the estate. Cadell and I had put up a wooden frame and stretched some canvas to protect the guests from a light easterly breeze. From the beginning of the afternoon, there was a procession of carriages. The guests, who came from Gloucester mostly, or even from Brockworth, Great Witcombe and Tewkesbury, competed for prestige. They had dressed, especially the ladies, in their finest clothes, with brilliant colours and in the latest fashion. Wide-brimmed bonnets with ribbons were side by side with picture hats; long cloaks with puffed sleeves revealed velvet wrist-bands. Mary, who had put on a canary yellow dress with sky-blue ribbons, whirled around among all these people, transported, happy, light-hearted. I looked at her walking, running, dancing, and my heart also shared in her joy and her radiance.

Among about twenty guests, Sir Garmond seemed to attract the attention. In a loud and confident voice, he boasted about the sound health of his various transportation enterprises and stuck out his chest like a rooster strutting in the hen-house. Lady Cheltenham, who was never very far from him, was smiling, looking at him with admiration and very often acquiesced to his remarks. This couple seemed ill-matched to me, but it is one of those matches that the best logic cannot explain.

About two o'clock, when everybody was present, they served tea. When I say "they," I mean Cathy and her friends from the kitchen. The servant had made sumptuous fruit-cakes with apples, as well as raisin biscuits, for which she had the secret recipe. The guests seemed to appreciate these cakes.

Cadell and I found ourselves being offered coffee and a slice of fruit cake. Lady Cheltenham introduced us, unstinting in praises of us. Cadell even seemed moved by it. Milady related the episode when I had brought Mary back to the manor after her fall from the horse. I felt myself blushing right up to my hair when all the guests stared at me and applauded.

Mary disappeared afterwards along with a group of children, including the two boys, John and Perdy. They had gone off running into the grounds and that succeeded, who knows why, in annoying me. Cadell and I went back to our lodgings as we were no longer needed, for the moment.

Cadell sat on the steps of the shack. From time to time, he drank a large gulp of his whisky and smacked his lips.

"You want a taste, young fellow?" he said, holding out the bottle to me.

"Oh no, Cadell. I'm not used to it."

"Soon to be seventeen years old, you can well have a drink. As for me, at your age…"

He did not finish his sentence. A veil fell over his eyes. Not wanting to offend him, I took hold of the bottle and swallowed a gulp of his drink. I thought, at that moment, that the flames of hell were devouring my throat and gullet. A ball of fire irradiated my stomach, then a gentle warmth invaded my body. I coughed several times.

"Well then, lad? It's going down well, isn't it?"

"That stuff of yours is very strong."

"True, that's true, no bourgeois crap. That one cleans your guts."

I did not doubt it. How could Cadell drink this brew all the time?

"I'm going to have a nap," he said to me. "Don't make any noise."

"Don't worry, Cadell, I'm going to the lake. I think the frogs have spawned."

"Go on, lad."

As I got up, I heard him murmuring.

"I had a son, once… You look like him…"

I paid no attention to this remark. Had Cadell wanted me to hear him? Perhaps another time he would speak to me about this son whom he had just mentioned.

I reached the lake, interested in finding the frogs' eggs and perhaps tadpoles.

I heard, to the left of the path, the shouts of the children who had left the buffet. These shouts seemed strange to me. They were not shouts of joy, of children playing. There was a cry for help there, a call for assistance.

I branched off and rushed through the undergrowth, under the cover of the trees. I drew near and, rounding a clump of trees, I saw the whole scene.

Mary, lying on her back, on the still wet grass, pressed flat on the ground by John, to me it seemed to be him, while his brother, Perdy, astride her, and having raised up her dress, was devoting his attention to what I dared not imagine. Mary was struggling and yelling over and over again. My heart missed a beat. I grabbed Perdy by the collar of his tweed coat and violently dragging him backwards, I flung him several feet away. He was a lightweight. John, alerted, more thickset, reacted very quickly by rushing towards me. But I had already evaded the collision and my fist, let loose with force, smashed into his jaw. I followed up my momentum and, sitting on him in order to restrain him, I continued to land more punches on him. John's nose was nothing but a piece of bloodied flesh. He looked at me, rolling his eyes wildly.

A grip stopped my action. Cadell was behind me.

"Stop, lad, stop. You can't do that. It's his word against yours and there, you will be the loser."

Then turning towards the two rascals:

"Clear off!"

Sobbing, Mary threw herself into my arms.

12

This episode did not reach Lady Cheltenham's ears. The two boys, out of fear of receiving a severe reprimand, preferred to remain silent. As for their condition, they used a quarrel as a pretext, which did not at all surprise their father, undoubtedly accustomed to his sons quarrelling like that. John and Perdy did not try to make me take any blame. Cadell's menacing shadow dictated that they should instead keep a low profile. As for Mary, she did not breathe a word of this matter, perhaps in order not to upset her mother or quite simply because she thought that she was a little guilty.

We discussed it later and I reassured Mary. The boys would surely not have gone as far as rape. They had acted to frighten her, amuse themselves, in a strange way indeed, but some doubt remained. What really would have happened if I had not intervened? After some time, we forgot this event and joy once again lit up my friend's face.

In mid-April, Mary told me that her mother was preparing to enrol her in a private school. Up to that time, she attended classes at home, two tutors coming regularly, during the week, to give her lessons in language, mathematics, sciences, as well as singing and instrument playing. Mary played the piano. It was time, her mother insisted, that Mary gained entry into a secondary school, in order to get a more complete education there in all subjects. She said that in her family, heads had always been well filled and it would be the same for Mary. Mary was not opposed to this plan, but she was surely going to miss life at the manor where she had, when all is said and done, a lot more freedom to organize her timetable.

The choice made was Cheltenham Ladies' College, which had opened its doors about thirty years before. The establishment, a top-class one in England, headed by Dorothea Beale, called into question old principles and old methods of teaching. Even though young girls continued to receive a very moralizing education, the subjects taught were opened up to the world. Finished with embroidery and singing, they learnt from then on, besides literature and mathematics, geography, history, a foreign language — French — and they practised open-air sports. Religious education was also less prevalent. Mary was not displeased with this programme; on the contrary really.

However, when we discussed this plan, very often when we met on the grounds, a veil of sadness passed over the usually bright eyes of the young girl.

"You are lucky," I said to Mary, as we sat on the new grass on the lawn.

"Would you have liked to continue your studies?"

"Oh yes. All the more because I was a rather good pupil. But my uncle had decided otherwise."

"I have an idea," she replied, with this mischievous expression that I knew too well.

"You have my attention, Mary…"

"I will return to the manor each weekend. I will be able to pass on my lessons to you. Literature, mathematics, history and geography, you will only have the difficulty of choice. I will certainly have homework and doing it together can only be to your advantage."

"But Mary, where will I find the time?"

"We will find it, we will find it."

The veil of sadness had vanished. In conclusion, this separation had a very advantageous compensation. I would be able to gain from the education Mary got. She was right. We would find the time.

That day in May was splendid. The trees were competing in beauty, the colours were bursting out, and scents filled the air. The lawn had this colour that it only possesses once a year, when the new shoots sprout up tight and thick. The flowers, scattered in the grass or bunched in clusters were simply an explosion of colours.

Mary had changed. Her doll-like face was now that of a young lady. Her cheekbones were slightly prominent; it looked like her almond-shaped eyes had lengthened. Her body, which I was imagining under this light dress in a lovely beige, allowed me to imagine new curves that unsettled me. The afternoon was coming to an end; golden rays of sunlight danced in her hair. We were in perfect harmony; nothing else seemed to exist.

Mary rested her head on my shoulder. I slipped one arm around her waist to draw her closer to me. Her body responded to my demand and she turned her face to me.

In an instant, our lips met in a wild kiss which seemed to go on forever. Time had stopped.

13

The plunge was taken. This result was inevitable, for, since the first day on which we had seen each other, we knew that had to happen. We were not complaining about it, very much on the contrary; but we were well aware that this relationship had to remain secret. The servant, stable-man, orphan, penniless one with the young lady of the Cheltenham family! That was not possible, that was inconceivable, and worse, that was not permitted. That existed only in stories, in tales of chivalry or only if the person of humble circumstances was the young girl and not the man. That is why we were hopeless. Happy, but hopeless. Our budding love, so strong, no doubt indestructible, had no future.

Moreover, the deadline for Mary's departure was drawing near. Her mother had prepared her belongings and the trunks were almost packed. Her entry into college was the day after the next.

"You are going to leave," I said, sick at heart.

"I won't be so far, as you well know. The college is only two miles from here. And think about all that I will bring back for you, all those things that will allow you to study, like me."

Mary was right. This separation had a positive side. Perhaps this education would allow me to elevate myself, to leave these humble circumstances of a servant and to hope… No, I was not of aristocratic birth; consequently, that world was out of reach and I could not aspire to anything.

"Would you be able to come and get me on weekends?"

"Do you think that's possible?"

"My mother will not object. She has a lot of confidence in you; she appreciates your work and your seriousness. So I am not worried about that."

"That would be wonderful."

Thus, things, at least those that were part of the immediate future, took a more acceptable turn. I would wait the whole week long, absorbed in my work and the weekend would therefore only be all the more delightful.

So I was living on a sort of cloud, a smile on my face, tranquil mood. Cathy considered me weird.

"Well, Jeremy, what is happening to you? You have a strange expression. A happy expression, but unusual."

"It's the spring, Cathy. This season is splendid and it delights my heart. These flowers, these colours, this renewal…"

"You are right Jeremy, nature presents us its greatest beauty at this time. Let's make the most of it. You know, for a moment, I thought you had met a girl on your outings to Prestbury."

"Oh no, Cathy!"

As for Cadell, when he met me, he had a strange smile — which was rather rare. He must have suspected something. Moreover, Cadell was always informed about everything and was always there when needed. He had proved it several times. But I could count on his discretion, so I was not worried about that.

The fateful day, the terrible day, was fast approaching. Already two days before I was having a lot of trouble sleeping, endlessly tossing in my bed.

The day before, I had cleaned the stables more quickly than usual. I knew, we had agreed on it, that Mary was to pass by to see me.

I was therefore impatient, nervous and continued to keep an eye on the walkway leading to the building.

At four o'clock — the chapel bell had just rung — she appeared. At her rapid pace, skipping, as light as a water-sprite, she moved forward, bathed in sunlight.

"Jeremy…"

"Mary. I just finished."

"Ah, good. Azurea is doing well today?"

"Yes, much better; she has got back her appetite."

"You will take good care of her in my absence, won't you?"

"Of course. You will be able to ride her when you come back."

For a few days, the mare had seemed exhausted, in poor shape. She was hardly eating and Lady Cheltenham had arranged for Mr Pickenbrock, the vet, to come.

"Is everything ready?" I asked.

"Yes, the trunks are packed. Wickney will take me very early tomorrow morning."

"Two weeks; so it's two weeks."

"Yes, during registration, students are not allowed to go off on the first weekend."

"So I will have to work twice as hard, to avoid thinking too much…"

"It's Cadell who is going to be happy, then."

Mary grasped my hand and carried me off to the barn. This building was an extension of the stables and housed the stores of food for the horses, as well as a considerable supply of straw. Several cats roamed around the place and so protected the grain against the ravages of mice and rats.

I allowed myself to be led, without resistance. We reached the back of the building, a place where the straw, widely spread out, made a sort of comfortable bed.

In a few minutes, our two naked bodies became one. The suppleness of hers responded to my demands and a sublime wave overwhelmed us at the same time. Her body arched, eyes skyward, Mary was experiencing this shared bliss and squeezed me even more tightly, in a final, almost violent embrace. We took a moment, in silence, to catch our breath. We were stretched out, side by side, happy, soaked in sweat in spite of the chilliness. Nothing else mattered at present but this magic moment that we were enjoying, without saying a word. Mary turned to me.

"Jeremy…"

"Mary, so why are you leaving?"

"I may be leaving, but we won't be apart; that's what matters. Now, we are bound together for ever."

"Yes, forever."

The next day, early, Wickney brought the carriage around to the front of the manor. He had installed a stiff awning to protect the passengers, as the east wind was a bit chilly.

Having bolted down my breakfast, I dashed into the yard to witness the departure. All the workers were present. That relieved me, as in that case, my presence seemed quite normal. The team began to move off. Lady Cheltenham and her daughter gave us a little wave and I saw Mary's misty eyes staring at me for a second.

Cadell put his huge hand on my shoulder.

"It will be all right, lad, it will be all right."

Work resumed. By drowning myself in work, I expected to forget Mary. Forgetting her, that is to say not to be permanently thinking about her, so that I would not sink into a state of extreme sadness. But that did not work. Her image was there, constantly, before my eyes, wherever I was, whatever I was doing. I had to accept the inevitable. Two weeks; that was not so long. Mary would bring me a great deal of things to study and we would be able to spend time again in the grounds and… in the barn.

But events, very often unforeseen, were going to determine otherwise.

On Tuesday morning, while I was bustling about in the stables, checking the horses for which shoes had to be changed, Wickney came looking for me. Lady Cheltenham wished to see me, and the matter seemed to be urgent.

Wickney led me into the little sitting-room.

"Jeremy, I have bad news for you," she said with a sad expression.

Immediately, I thought of Mary. Did some misfortune befall her? Had there been an unexpected accident? Was she ill?

"Yes, Madam," I replied in a toneless voice.

"Your uncle Osmond passed away the day before yesterday, Sunday. I got the news this morning."

"Oh!"

This news did not really sadden me, I had to admit, but it affected me somehow all the same.

"I also have to tell you that he killed himself."

"What?"

"He ended his own life. According to the people who were still working with him, his company was in great difficulty. He was up to his ears in debt, which undoubtedly is what drove him to this unfortunate action."

I did not know how to respond. Lady Cheltenham further explained to me:

"The solicitor, Sir Radcliff, wrote me a long letter which I will hand over to you. He wishes to meet with you as quickly as possible in order to settle the inheritance from your uncle."

"Inheritance?"

"Yes, that is to say the handing over of the property he owned. You are his only relative, so that is normal. The trouble is that your uncle no longer owned anything. Even his business was mortgaged. The only thing he has left you are his debts."

I thought lightning had struck me on my head. I did not know much, practically nothing, about this matter of inheritance. But I figured that in this particular case there were difficulties lying in wait for me.

"So what should I do, Madam?"

"Meet with this solicitor and probably settle all this business."

"But then, I…"

"Yes, Jeremy, you are going to have to leave us. That is very painful for me, as you are a good, hard-working and pleasant young man. Everybody here will miss you a lot."

Lady Cheltenham could not have said it better.

"But perhaps I won't be gone for a very long time?"

"I don't know, Jeremy. I can wait a few days, at most. You know well that for the horses, I need to get someone very quickly. I will try Cadell, but he already has a lot of work, all the more because you will no longer be there to help him."

"I understand, Madam."

In fact, I understood nothing that was happening to me. Everything was still so amazing.

The next morning, I packed my meagre bags. Wickney was responsible for taking me to Gloucester, to the house of my late uncle. I said my goodbyes to Cathy, Joanna and Lauren. This parting was very difficult. Cadell hugged me tightly.

"It will be all right, lad, it will be all right."

"Here, Cadell, that's for Mary."

Cadell discreetly grasped the letter that I was handing him.

"You can count on me, lad. I will give it to her."

At ten o'clock, the team moved off. I turned my head and contemplated Cheltenham manor for the last time, no doubt.

DESCENT INTO HELL

14

The house of my uncle Osmond Jenkins was situated not far from the town centre, on Armory Street. It was a beautiful looking structure, entirely of white stone, with red brick chimneys. Both levels had a row of lovely sash-windows and three skylights could be seen under the roof. A little garden, in the front, separated it from the street. The latter had hardly ever been maintained and weeds had invaded the spot for a long time. The place that I had known when I was younger seemed different. It was as if I was seeing it for the first time.

Wickney let me off in front of the little wrought-iron gate.

"Good luck, Jeremy."

"Thank you, Mr Wickney. I think I'm going to need it, indeed."

The man did not comment. True to himself, as I had known him during the nine months spent at the manor, he turned on his heels and set off again immediately. For a moment I kept watching the crown of his top-hat which jiggled to the rhythm of the horses.

Lady Cheltenham had handed over the house key to me. Sir Radcliff had sent it to her with the letter, thus allowing me to save time and especially, to have a place to stay, temporarily. All the more because the solicitor was away that day and I did not have an appointment with him until the next day.

On closer examination it was evident that the house was not in very good condition. The plaster of the façade was falling off in places and the lower part of the building was corroded by greenish mould. My uncle certainly had neither the time nor the money to undertake regular maintenance.

The key turned with a grating sound in an obviously worn-out lock. The passage smelled of that mould which was climbing along the substructure. The wall at the entrance was covered with stringy fungus. The lack of heat could also have been responsible for this damage.

I went into the drawing-room. Dark, depressing, occupied by furniture with dull colours, the place smelled stuffy and dusty. A little table, in the centre of the room, placed on a filthy rug, was crowded with bottles. My uncle must have sunk into alcoholism and so into disgrace. But this trap nevertheless had not solved his problem and had driven him to a fatal act. I found myself pitying him, feeling a sort of compassion for this man who, however, had not made life easy for me. When he had taken me in, I was almost six years old. He quickly handed me over to Juliet's care. This good, devoted individual, without thinking about the task, alone and childless, had raised me like her son. With her, I had learnt about life; she had taught me humility and modesty, as well as courage. I learnt the basics of reading with her, for the stories she told me each evening had given me the desire to learn to read. During this rather happy period, my uncle more or less did not concern himself about me. Besides, I rarely saw him, as he was very preoccupied with his business. Then came school, where I could perfect my knowledge, for I was eager and curious. But, as you know, that did not last, since my uncle then made me work in his firm, thereby getting cheap labour.

In spite of everything, I was astonished. Without being luxurious, the house that I had known was clean and warm. But no doubt Juliet had a lot to do with it. Since my departure, and hers, my uncle had allowed the place to decline. I climbed the staircase leading to the first floor. The little bedroom that I had occupied was relatively preserved. It was in order, somewhat spared by the dust. So I decided to settle in there for the moment. My first concern was to light a fire in the fireplace in order to combat the prevailing dampness which was pervading my bones. The wood pile was at the back of the small kitchen and I quickly got the fire going. Luckily, the beech, very dry, had no difficulty catching.

I did a little tidying in the kitchen, which was extremely overcrowded. Bottles were lying on the floor, in the sandstone sink or on the sideboard tray as well. The water pump in the garden was working and I was able to do a little cleaning up of the place, which did not seem very healthy to me. Then, exhausted, I ended up sitting in front of the little table in the drawing-room, looking at the golden flames dancing in the hearth.

"Mary, Mary, where are you at this moment? So what are you doing? When am I going to see you again? If you knew…"

How could she have known? She would hear the news in close to two weeks when she returned to the manor. I dared not consider the grief that was going to overwhelm her then.

I had a disturbed night. Noises of rodents making a racket in the attic woke me several times. Other noises, coming from the ground floor also kept me on the alert. That was more astounding. Perhaps the wood, with which I had rekindled the fire was crackling ominously from the effect of the heat? But it seemed very much to me that these noises were coming from the kitchen. I went downstairs to check the door which gave access to the backyard and the small garden. The bolt was completely drawn. So I did not have to worry and moreover, who would come prowling around here and for what reason? I ended up going to sleep towards morning, worn out. It was a cock — the neighbours had poultry — that woke me.

Cathy, thinking ahead, had slipped something for me to eat into my bag, which would last several days. Eggs, dried meat, apples, homemade biscuits, a jar of orange marmalade and squares of dark chocolate wrapped in a flowered cloth were all there.

The kitchen stove gave no trouble to get going. Very quickly, it gave off good heat, the cast-iron top even beginning to glow. I was able to cook the eggs, drink some hot tea and taste the delicious biscuits. Now, I had to get to Sir Radcliff's. He had his practice in the centre of the town, but I knew Gloucester well enough to get there easily.

So I went down towards the town centre. The magnificent cathedral, on my right, pointed its double spire to the sky. The historic building, of white stone, shone, as if polished, in the morning sun. I observed, on my left, the loops of the Severn and the fork of the canal which led to the estuary, to the south. The docks were quite close by. It was there that numerous boats set sail from or came alongside, bringing in or carrying away various kinds of merchandise. My uncle had recourse to this means of transport when his products were being shipped in other vessels, further south, to neighbouring countries like France or The Netherlands.

I found Sir Radcliff's practice on St John's Lane. The establishment, plush, painted white, very well maintained, supplied with a garden full of flowers, could not go unnoticed. Obviously, the position of solicitor provided a good living for its master.

At the first ring of the doorbell, a servant in a yellow and gold uniform appeared on the threshold. His slicked back hair, protuberant chin and aquiline nose gave him the appearance of a crow. He drew near, with a suspicious look and pursed lips.

"Young man?"

"I have an appointment with Sir Radcliff. I am Jeremy Page."

"Ah yes, very well. Master Radcliff told me. Come in, please."

He pulled the open-work metal gate to him and signalled me to follow. I was ushered into a dark hall, with entirely tiled walls. Three leather armchairs were conspicuous along one of the walls.

"Please have a seat. I will inform Master Radcliff."

This ritual, a bit pompous, made me uncomfortable. Even Wickney was not so formal. But I was discovering a new environment and its different rules.

Master Radcliff himself came to meet me. He was a rather small man, corpulent, with a round, pink face. That confirmed that the profession of solicitor did not leave one in poverty.

"Ah, dear young man. Come on, I was expecting you. Did you have a good trip? Oh! What a matter! Your uncle, such a nice man, so charming, how is that possible? I won't bring it up again. Look, last week…"

I was only listening to him with one ear. This chattering was making me giddy. I had come to get answers to precise and essential questions.

"Sit down. Make yourself comfortable. A cigar?"

"No thank you, I don't smoke."

"You're wrong, these are excellent."

And with a tinder lighter, the solicitor lit a huge cigar, and the almost purple smoke from it filled the office.

"Let us come to our business," he finally said, digging with his sausage-shaped fingers into a pile of hardback files stacked on a corner of his desk.

"So, where the hell is it? Ah, here it is. Jenkins, that's it. What a story!"

He began to read over, silently, a document that he had extracted from the file.

"Yes, this is it indeed. Young man, you are the only family member of Osmond Jenkins."

"Yes, sir. I am his nephew, Jeremy Page. My mother…"

"Yes, I know that. According to the law and according to the last will and testament of your uncle, you are the sole beneficiary of his estate, both personal and financial possessions."

"That's what Lady Cheltenham explained to me."

"Oh, that dear Lady Cheltenham. An extraordinary woman, extremely pretty, and ..."

He did not finish his sentence. His sparkling eyes betrayed what he was thinking.

Sir Radcliff seemed to come to his senses and returned to the text that he had just read.

"So, to be precise, your uncle bequeaths to you the house, the business, the machinery and supplies belonging to it."

"So all of this is my property, is that right?"

"That's just the point, young man, but there is a problem that we have to take into account."

I was well aware of what the solicitor was driving at. The critical moment was approaching.

"Your uncle, by his actions, with which you were well acquainted, having been his employee for a while..."

"Yes."

The solicitor blew out a thick cloud of smoke, in order to continue.

"Your uncle has, how should I put it, incurred considerable debts. He invested a lot in new machines, ordered phenomenal quantities of raw material, but his sales fell at a mad speed. He had also proceeded with some Stock Exchange investments, but these proved to be catastrophic, and he lost large sums of money. Briefly, the situation is not good. The creditors are jostling to collect their money; the company is mortgaged. Only the house remains, which unfortunately would not suffice to fill the pit your uncle has dug..."

"And how much is that?"

"Close to fifty thousand pounds."

The amount seemed immense to me of course, but never having

owned more than a few shillings, I had trouble estimating the real value. The solicitor must have noticed it.

"It's a lot of money, you know. The company, the supplies and machinery, the sale of the house, all that would not be enough. Far from it."

15

I had two weeks before me to find a solution. The solicitor, having estimated the possible financial returns — sale of all that it was possible to sell — it would still be more than fifteen thousand pounds short, a sum which I did not have, of course. I could try to find a job, but I would have to cut my salary by three quarters and thus pay almost all my life. My uncle had not done things by halves. He had given me a poisoned gift which I could have done without.

I was devastated. I did not see any solution to escape this situation. The only one was to throw myself from the top of a bridge into the Severn or to flee to France or even to Ireland. But that was impossible; I could not leave Mary; our lives were connected; we had become inseparable; no event, however serious it may be, could separate us from each other. For a moment, I was tempted to set off for Cheltenham and to seek financial help from Milady. But I abandoned that very quickly; I was only a humble worker and no doubt I would never have been able to repay her.

Sir Radcliff had warned me. Fifteen days from then, the creditors were going to claim their due. In case of impossibility on my part to repay the sums demanded, the courts of justice would take over. I would be condemned to hard labour, perhaps deported to the colonies.

I nibbled some of Cathy's biscuits. The few shillings earned at Cheltenham jingled in my pocket. A modest sum which would not keep me for long. I had rarely, if ever, found myself in such a dilemma. I recalled Juliet's advice; she used to tell me often never to lose hope and that each problem had its solution. I was going to have to, now, here, find a way out alone. Juliet had gone back to her native Wales and I did not know the most recent employees of the business well enough to be able to seek their assistance.

So I decided to go in search of a job, from the very next day. There had to be recruitment at the docks as traffic through the canal was booming. Carrying bales of cloth to be loaded on to the boats did not frighten me. I could try my luck; at least I would not be totally reduced to begging and I would have enough to be able to eat properly.

By the light of a candle, I wrote a long letter to Cadell, to inform him about the recent events. He would pass it on to Mary, so she would be fully aware of the situation. Perhaps she might have an idea, perhaps she would find a solution? With two of us, even at a distance, it would always be less difficult, and knowing that she was in search of a positive outcome would console me.

So, early, I made my way to the port. Already, dockers, sailors and porters were at work. This activity seemed endless. I observed the various gangs, trying to figure out which ones I should speak to.

Two men, in ill-fitting, long, thick black coats, like Black Friars, emerged from a nearby warehouse. They were coming towards me. Was this a sign? They should certainly be able to give me some information.

"Hey! Boy! You're looking for work?"

I couldn't believe what I was hearing. I was making progress.

"Er, yes, that's right."

"You're just in time!"

Saying this, the two men had come up. They each grabbed me by an arm and slipping their hands under each of my arm-pits, lifted me off the ground to drag me towards another building.

"But, what are you doing?"

"Shut up, will you!"

The tone of voice was threatening, cutting. The fellow did not seem to be joking.

I struggled in vain; nothing helped and soon we entered the warehouse, which at the time was deserted. They dragged me towards the back of the building, where there was a sort of office. They put me down there and closed the heavy door again.

"We have some work for you, seriously."

"But why this way?"

"You will get an explanation, but first we are going to confirm that we have the right fellow."

I did not understand any of that.

"Are you really the nephew of the scumbag who tried to swindle us?"

"Who? What?"

"Jenkins, the big man Jenkins, your uncle."

"Yes, I am really his nephew."

"Then that's good. We'll be able to settle our accounts."

I began to wonder what shady business my uncle could have had a hand in.

"Your uncle flogged some goods for us, you see; he was short of money."

It was always the same one who spoke, quite a tall fellow, rather thin, with a face like a knife blade. His figure was not unfamiliar to me.

"Your uncle worked for us, but he wanted to double-cross us; that was a very bad idea. So, bye-bye."

"Suicide! It was not a suicide!"

"You catch on quickly, boy. Your uncle kept the goods and the money; that was unacceptable, right."

His accomplice, a smaller chap, brown, his face swallowed up by a thick beard, confirmed:

"Right."

I noticed that the latter had a bandage on his left arm, as if he had been the victim of a recent injury.

"So there, you are going to work hard for us, to pay back the money your uncle stole from us. When your debt is repaid, you will choose to continue or not. We understand that you have big money troubles."

I preferred not to respond. These two had to be touchy and I surely did not need to irritate them too much. I was rather robust for my age, but these two fellows were scaring me and they were probably armed with knives.

"You understand what I'm telling you?"

"Yes, sir, yes."

"Good, we are both going to understand each other. Moreover, it's better."

I stared in astonishment. That was really and truly a threat.

"If you try to be clever, we will turn our attention to little Mary. Little Mary's pretty, isn't she? You at least banged her?"

How did these fellows know about all that? But this threat unleashed a violent reaction in me. My fist swung forward towards the face of this monster, but it only hit empty space. On the other hand, the response was not long in coming. The man let fly an uppercut at me, which took my breath away. A series of kicks followed and finally a terrible blow on my skull which knocked me out for good.

"Don't ever do that again, you filthy little brat."

I heard the office door close again before sinking into darkness.

16

I felt like I had been hit on the head by an anvil. My blood was beating against my temples and my ears whistled loudly. I opened my eyes and light that was coming through the only window in the office increased the pain. That fellow had really struck hard. His words came back to me little by little and I was trying to sort out these pieces of information. Clearly, my uncle, financially strapped, had got himself involved with these two traffickers to get a new injection of funds, but had wanted to go it alone. This thing was falling back on top of me, since these two crooks were demanding that I work for them in order to pay back the loss of profits. I was cornered on all fronts, in a sort of double impasse. I could not see how to get out of it.

I got to my feet painfully, my legs trembling. Through the window I made out the warehouse. Cases, boxes, bales, goods that were waiting to be loaded. In front of the entrance, the figures of my two assailants. I could have been mistaken, but the tall threadlike fellow, who had spoken to me and hit me, reminded me of the chap in the grounds, the one who had the violent quarrel with Brackett and who had stabbed him with a knife.

I gently turned the door handle, but it was locked. I was caught in a trap. So I tapped hard on the window pane. The two men turned up immediately.

"You've finished your siesta?" the one who after all had to be the ringleader started up again. "You thought about it?"

"Yes, sir, I've thought about it."

"All the better. It would have been very annoying to us if we had to hurt little Mary, right?"

I clenched my fists. If only I could, soon, make him eat his bloody words!

"I am going to explain it to you. An intelligent boy like you should easily understand. You turn up here, certain nights; we will let you know on which days. The goods come in by boat. You unload them and reload them into a cart. You take the lot to an address which will be clearly indicated to you. If you do the job well, your share is deducted from what your uncle owes us. Until you have paid us back, in the first instance. Easy."

The other character repeated:

"Easy."

"Oh, one more thing. Go and take a walk around your uncle's business. If he kept any of the goods, try to find them; that will give you a head start."

"Yes, sir."

And the man let fly a punch on my shoulder.

"Now, run along. Under normal circumstances, you begin tonight. We will let you know. And don't forget, if you try to be clever... Mary... that's it..."

Before I left the premises, the man let loose on me again:

"And of course, we don't know each other, we have never met. If you get caught by the coppers, forget us; that would be best; you don't want to end up like your uncle? Oh! Oh!"

I had very well understood the threat. But for the moment it was in my interest to go along with them. At any rate, I was not up to it and Mary's life was more important than everything else.

The two men let me leave. They had nothing to fear; they knew I would not talk.

87

I spent the day moping about in my uncle's house. I examined the problem from every angle in vain. I could not see any solution, except to kill these two devils; but that was something of which I felt totally incapable.

In the afternoon, I heard two light knocks on the window overlooking the street. Then, someone slipped a sheet of paper under the door.

I unfolded the document.

"Eight o'clock, dock 3. Frank"

The appointment was fixed. I rolled this message into a ball and threw it into the fire. I had a little time left; I decided to have a snack.

A little before eight o'clock, I approached the docks. I had put on a thick coat, as the wind was blowing. With my wool cap on my head and the darkness, I had little chance of being recognized, just in case...

On dock 3, two boats of average tonnage were moored. The *Cornwall King* and the *Brave*. I decided to go and try to get some information. Porters were coming and going, putting down bales of cloth on the platforms of the carts that were waiting there. At the lower side of the *Cornwall King*, one of the sailors turned towards me. He approached with a determined step.

"You are the brat?"

"I beg your pardon," I said in a voice meant to be confident.

"The new fellow, for the job?"

"You're Frank?"

"That's right. Go to the end of the wharf. You will find a cart with the wheels painted red. Get in and take off. That's all you have to do. Take this," he ended, slipping a piece of paper folded in his hand to me.

I did not ask anything more. In fact, a little further on, I saw a cart, a bit to one side. It matched the description. The platform was covered with a thick tarpaulin of dark-coloured material. I climbed on to the seat and consulted the piece of paper. It showed an address, Frogfurlong Lane, Innsworth. I knew this northern suburb a little and could get there without any problem. I whipped the two horses and the team moved off. I had not seen my two 'employers'. I supposed they carefully avoided being found on the premises at the time of the deliveries. A police raid was always to be feared. Perhaps they were going to recover the goods at the place where I was to take them.

The rest of this very specific mission unfolded without any problem. I reached Innsworth and the house, a dilapidated building, where I was to make the delivery. Two chaps wearing hoods came and unloaded the platform without uttering a single word. They were not my assailants; their appearances did not match. I saw only the forearm of one of the two men, which was tattooed with an eagle with its wings spread. When they had finished transferring the casks into a cluster of poorly joined boards, one of them came to meet me.

"Go back to where you came from and put back the cart at the starting-point."

I did not argue; the fewer questions I asked, the better off I would be. I made the return journey, deposited the cart and went back to Armory Street. I had trouble going to sleep. I did not like this situation at all. How long was it going to last? Months, years? If I got caught, alone, I would really be in trouble and the scoundrels would continue with their crookery. Moreover, I was not at all happy working with these crooks and murderers. I did not particularly like Brackett, but a desire for vengeance was rising in me. I had to think about a desirable outcome without risks.

The solicitor, Sir Radcliff, had succeeded in obtaining a delay. I had three months to reimburse the creditors. That was because I had, officially, found a respectable job. In the day, I worked at the docks as a porter and at night, at least two or three nights per week, I carried out this dirty job for my bosses. They, at least the more talkative one, demanded that I call them that.

One morning, I received a letter from Mary. Cadell must have given my letters to her and my pretty Mary was quick in responding to me.

Jeremy, my love for ever,

Cadell has delivered your letters to me. I am distraught, sad and I would be crying every day if I did not have to put on a brave face in front of my mother, so that she does not suspect anything. Strangely, Cadell, to whom I did not often speak, has become my indispensable confidant.

So I have learnt about your misfortunes and the obligations that you have to cope with. We are going to find a solution. I am going, I believe, very soon, to speak to my mother and inform her about the entire matter. She will not refuse to get you out of this scrape. I know her well and I know that she likes you a lot. Keep the faith.

Let me know how you are doing.

I'm sending you a kiss.

Your Mary who thinks about you only...

This letter broke my heart. We could have had a life of perfect bliss and instead of that...

But Mary also brought me hope. I knew her fighting spirit and I did not doubt that she would find the words to speak to her mother. I would surely very soon be out of danger and I would be able to flee from this wretched place.

It was therefore necessary for me to bear my misfortune patiently. These various initiatives could take time, but the delay granted by the creditors gave me some hope. While waiting, I had to continue to play my role of zealous servant.

My nocturnal missions were uneventful, until one night at the end of July. My bosses were present, lurking in the shadow of a warehouse. That night, the delivery was more important than usual, and they had insisted on keeping an eye on it. When I was guiding my team out of the docks, some whistles sounded.

"The coppers! The coppers!" I heard someone shout.

I jumped down from the vehicle and dashed between the buildings. Noises of cavalcades resounded almost everywhere on the docks. I heard several shots and the smell of gunpowder filled the place.

I dashed at full gallop, zigzagging between the warehouses, doing my best to get away as quickly as possible. To the east was waste ground, uncultivated, where clumps of trees grew here and there. I was able to reach it and hide for a while, taking the opportunity to catch my breath. On the other side, several hundred feet away, there was a great commotion. The Police must have been cursing and swearing, for if they had seized the alcohol, they had not been able to catch the perpetrators. I smiled in the dark. My patrons were going to have to review their plans.

"So what, little brat? You wanted to double-cross us?"

A heavy hand had landed on my shoulder.

"How so?"

"It's you who informed the Police, you bastard! Ron, deal with him and do what you need to do."

"I didn't inform anyone, I swear."

"Hogwash. You tried to get us caught; you will pay dearly for that, believe me. Ron, what are you waiting for?"

The one called Ron, who hardly spoke except to repeat the words of his mate, pulled me by the hair, dragging me to the ground. Grabbing my arms, he tied my wrists. I twisted and turned in vain; I could not defend myself. Moreover, he delivered a swift kick to my ribs which stopped me dead in my tracks.

"Little brat," the man repeated. "When we are finished with you, we will pay little Mary a visit. We will have a little fun with her first, rest assured."

"You dirty bastards!" I yelled.

It was the first time that I was really rebelling.

"I will kill you, I will kill you, both of you."

"Ron, hurry up, we aren't going to spend the whole night here."

The one called Ron slipped a great big canvas sack over my head and swallowed me up entirely with it. He tied up the end and carried me on his shoulder as if I was nothing but a piece of straw.

"Excellent. Now throw him in the water. Goodbye brat."

And I was dealt another final blow on the skull.

17

I had been knocked out, but I felt when I was being placed on the platform of a cart. The Police must have left the premises and the two crooks were able to operate without risk. The team moved off and I was tossed about at the will of the road, which was in a bad state. With my hands bound and the sack tied up, I could not try anything; I was cornered and I was well aware that in a short space of time I would be floating in the canal or in the estuary. My thoughts — the final ones? — were about Mary. Her sweet face brought me a little comfort and I hoped with all my heart that she would find happiness in the end.

The horses came to a stop. Ron lifted me up and I felt we were moving forward.

"Release me! Let me out! I won't say anything…"

Ron did not respond. This stupid, half-brained man was satisfied with carrying out the orders. I knew that he would not deviate from his mission. We stopped and the sensation that followed was very strange. In a few seconds I had left the massive shoulder of my bearer and I fell rapidly. Contact with the water was rather violent. Very quickly the sack filled up and I began to sink. The end was near. In spite of my efforts not to swallow the water, I was beginning to be dangerously short of air.

"Goodbye Mary… Goodbye…"

My descent continued and I had not noticed it. If I had paid a little more attention, I would have understood that I was not in the canal, but in the estuary, which was deeper.

The sack, in the fall, hooked on a pointed object. Perhaps a sort of pike or a piece of wood left by some ship or other. The latter, piercing the canvas, tore it a good length, ripping my thigh at the same time. But this wound faded into the background as I had before me the opening which was going to allow me to escape a fatal destiny. With a few moves I came out of my cloth prison; some leg movements allowed me to get back to the surface where I inhaled a big gulp of fresh air.

I could not get over it. Luck was with me, extraordinary luck, and I had to take advantage of the opportunity.

At the surface of the water, which was freezing, I could not see much. It was pitch-dark and I barely distinguished, at a good distance, the lights of a few ships cruising in the estuary. A rather strong current was pulling me towards the open sea.

That was not good news, all the more because with my hands bound, swimming and struggling was not an easy matter. Inexorably, I was being swept away; it seemed impossible to get back to dry land. At any rate, was I going to fail now?

I suddenly heard the splashing of a hull cutting through the water, which I had not seen coming. The stem grazed me, but the keel directly collided with me. The impact on my head was quite severe and this time I really sank like a stone.

"He's waking up," came a voice which seemed distant to me.

"So it would seem. He had a narrow escape."

Two faces leaned over me. When the mist covering my eyes faded, I could see my rescuers. Two bearded men, their heads covered by woollen caps. Their strong accents reminded me of Welshmen.

"So, young man, you swallowed water?"

I raised myself on one elbow, seized by a sudden fit of coughing. My left leg was hurting me and I grimaced.

"Don't worry about your leg. Larry has taken care of it; his mother used to do embroidery, oh! Oh!"

The other man, Larry no doubt, acquiesced with a nod.

"Where am I?"

"On the *Terrific,* my lad, an indestructible boat that criss-crosses the seas continuously. You have the devil's luck for the ship's cook to have spotted you. Just at the moment when he was throwing potato-peelings overboard."

"The cook? Potato-peelings? Oh, yes, the boat…"

"But explain how you found yourself in that situation. With your hands bound?"

"It's a long story; I don't really want to speak about it."

"I understand, young man, I understand. Meanwhile, you can go next door and get a bite to eat; there's some bacon left."

"Thank you, gentlemen, without you…"

"Without us, poof! Lost, vanished… But we have to believe that your time had not come. We're leaving you; go and get something to eat and meet us again on the deck."

The bacon was very tempting. This unexpected outcome had restored my hope and appetite. The crooks thought I had drowned; a plan began to take shape in my mind. But one always thinks better with a full stomach, so I headed for the kitchen.

The cook was bustling about in front of the stove. He turned his head. He was thin fellow, with a bony face and high cheek-bones. His black hair, stiff like rope, was plastered obliquely across his forehead.

"Ah, there you are! Glad to see you're alive and well."

"Thank you, Mr Cook, so it's you who…"

"You had the devil's luck, as I usually empty the rubbish earlier. But that time I had been delayed. Strange, isn't it?"

"Indeed. My name is Jeremy."

"Ling Thieng, from Singapore. I have been on this boat for more than ten years."

We shook hands. I owed a debt of gratitude to Ling, but how could I thank him?

"Sit down and have a bite. You need to recover your strength."

"Thank you, Ling."

I settled down and heartily devoured the bacon, which was still warm.

"The *Terrific* is a fine boat. Captain Lockwood is a good captain. A good sailor and a good captain. And then, we eat well. You want to stay? We are looking for a sailor."

"The fact is… I have some things to settle."

Ling frowned.

"In connection with your bound hands?"

"Yes."

"You want to settle the score, right?"

"That's about it."

"That will serve no purpose, apart from causing fresh trouble for yourself."

"I have no choice."

"That's what people always believe. Look, it's fate that sent us in your direction. See that as a sign. Forget your troubles, forget those who have done you harm, and change your life."

"I can't… they are going to harm someone else."

Ling nodded his head.

"I understand. In that case. It's up to you. You will be very welcome here."

"I thank you, Ling, but that will not be possible. Where is the *Terrific* going to?"

"Next stop Abertowe[1], beg your pardon Swansea, then Waterford in Ireland."

---

1   Abertowe is the Celtic name for Swansea.

"Good, I will get off in Swansea."

My decision was made. I was going to deal with my abductors. I had no choice.

The sea was not rough. However, the captain had to sail close, as the wind was coming from the north-west sector. He was rather proud of his boat, which had an engine with over two hundred and fifty horsepower. Besides, he was using the very latest model of propeller for improved performance.

So we were able to put into Swansea in less than two days. The wound on my leg was not a cause for concern; it was only the surface layer of the skin that had been torn. That would heal very quickly.

"There is Abertowe," the captain said to me, as he stood at the starboard rail. "We are going to fill up with coal and take it to Ireland. It's a business that is in full swing."

The development of steam engines, the manufacture of steel, a booming construction industry, all that made great demands on coal, and Wales, in the space of a few years, had become the leading European producer. Some cities, like Swansea or Cardiff, had seen their populations triple.

"We stop for two days, time to fill the bunkers. You can take part in the loading if you want to make a little money."

"I won't say no to that, as I'm penniless."

"Agreed. I'm going to take care of it."

The future seemed a little brighter to me. I was going to make a little money to get back to Gloucester. The crooks had to keep quiet for the moment; I had a little time ahead of me. It was Monday, Mary was at school, therefore relatively safe. I sent off a letter to Cadell, asking him to keep an eye on her on weekends. I explained to him that she was in danger and that he should not hesitate to use his rifle if necessary. I could trust him.

18

The few shillings earned at the port had allowed me to have enough to eat, to find a place to live and to recover my strength. I had had unbelievable luck. Was a lucky star watching over me? And over Mary at the same time? I had forgotten, partially it's true, the money troubles caused by the disappearance of my uncle. Moreover, the issue would no longer arise, as I was thinking of taking Mary very far away, to France, very probably. When the *Terrific* put out to sea again, I left the city of Swansea.

Seventy-five miles separated me from Gloucester. Making the journey on foot could take four days, provided that I walked from morning to evening, at a brisk pace. That was not impossible, but I risked arriving too late, as it was already Wednesday.

Luckily, a pedlar was travelling in that direction. He was making his way to Glynneath, then to Abergavenny to sell, or try to sell, his bric-a-brac, and he agreed to take me up to that point in exchange for a few pennies. For me, it was half the journey in a single day and therefore good news.

The pedlar, one Tynderwearth, was a born and bred Welshman. He spent the greater part of his time humming Welsh songs and swore by his country only. He did not display any hostility towards the English, but he was clearly proclaiming his origins. He was not a bad chap. He was a single man, since he had lost his wife Margreth and his two daughters, Claire and Dorothy, in a fire at his house. He criss-crossed the roads of the country, selling quite a collection of curios, buying to resell, and so lived according to the spirit of the times, good fortune and the uncertain benevolence of people. On the road to Glynneath, the horse began to hobble. It was dragging its left leg, but continued to move on, as these courageous animals that never complain would do.

"Now we're in trouble," Tynderwearth remarked, after having halted his horse. "We will need to look for a farrier, perhaps a vet."

"Don't distress yourself, sir, I will sort it out."

"How would you be able to do that?"

"That's my occupation somewhat. I know horses well and know how to take care of them, if necessary."

I examined the horse's leg. Its horseshoe was askew. A sharp stone had jammed one of the nails, had twisted its head and the shoe was no longer in its right place.

"It's nothing; it will be quickly fixed. Do you happen to have any pliers?"

"Pliers? Of course, I have a bit of everything in my cart. Look, here is a rather fine one."

With the help of the tool, I was able to take out the nail. It was then rather easy to straighten it with a heavy hammer, which the cart also had, and I fixed everything on the spot. The horseshoe, properly level now, no longer upset the horse.

"Your farrier did not do a good job, Mr Tynderwearth. The nails are not driven in sufficiently and the heads are beginning to get twisted."

"Oh! That scoundrel Terry John! The one who always asks for a little extra, while assuring me that he is doing the best job! And you, what are you asking for?"

"Nothing at all, Mr Tynderwearth. I am already so happy that you are helping me make my way. If only you knew."

"What are you going to do over there, in Gloucester?"

"Settle some business. It is very important."

"Listen, young man, you are a good lad. I know a lot of people in the area, rest assured. I am going to hook you up with some pals of mine. They would be able to carry you for the continuation of your journey. Trust me."

"Thank you, Mr Tynderwearth."

And the journey resumed, the pedlar humming his songs, which I was beginning to know by heart and which I hummed along with him.

The stop at Glynneath was not long. At the market-place of the little town, there were not a lot of people. I must say that a persistent drizzle failed to encourage anyone to set foot outside. All the same, Tynderwearth sold three well-made copper saucepans, an oil lamp with frosted glass and nicely engraved, a milking stool and a set of butcher knives. He said that when he managed to sell a saucepan in a day, that allowed him to fill his own.

We got on our way again, the horse having taken on a quicker pace, doubtless in a hurry to reach the next stage and its ration of oats.

The journey seemed strangely rather long to me, but no doubt it was because I was in a hurry to achieve my goal.

The woods came after the vales, the meadows after the fields, the farms after the shepherds' huts; we reached the town of Abergavenny in the middle of the afternoon. The first thing that Tynderwearth did was to go in search of potential colleagues. He found one of them at the Red Fox, a tavern which overlooked the village square.

"This is Woodblock, a friend," he said to me, introducing a red-haired giant whose arms were like trunks of young fir-trees.

Woodblock crushed my knuckles.

"Can you do me a favour, Woodblock?"

"That depends on the favour; tell me anyhow."

"This young fellow is going to Gloucester. That's your route?"

"Yes, I'm leaving soon. I expect to travel part of the night."

"So we're in luck. Can you take him with you?"

"I can, if we can come to an arrangement."

I was looking at and listening to the two men settle their business.

"Rudford? That's it?"

"That's it indeed. You let me have the space for the next market and it's done."

The two men slapped each other's palm.

"That will do, Woodblock. Thanks on behalf of the young man. I think that will help him out a lot."

I confirmed it.

"Yes, sir. That will suit me fine. Thank you."

"Hmm... Let's have a drink then!"

And the publican brought three glasses of beer filled to the brim.

So Woodblock took me with him. He had a cart similar to his pal's, and we set off a little before nightfall. Woodblock did not hum; he spoke very little and was rather uncommunicative. He controlled his horse skilfully, avoided ruts or holes in the ground, and from time to time glanced sideways towards the grasslands or woods we were travelling through.

Night had fallen and with it, chilliness. Woodblock, impassive, threw me a blanket to cover myself. I even ended up falling asleep on the wooden seat, in spite of the inevitable jolts.

"Wake up, young fellow. Wake up."

It was Woodblock, with his deep voice, who woke me, from my enchanting dreams in which Mary's face was smiling at me. The giant put an end to the spell.

"Yes? Oh, yes..."

While I was recovering my wits, Woodblock handed me a cup

of coffee. The cart had stopped at the side of the road. A saucepan was on a paraffin stove in the back. The sun was coming up, shyly, greenish-blue reflections filled the horizon and the nearby forest was soon covered with glittering gold.

"We're here. Gloucester is over there, a quarter of a mile away, at most."

"Well, I'm going to leave you, Mr Woodblock. I think you are heading north."

"That's right. First to the north. Gloucester afterwards."

"Thank you for the journey. That has really helped me, I must say."

"That's good, young fellow, that's good. If that helps you out."

I jumped down from the cart, retrieving my bag, which contained some belongings and provisions. I waved my hand and the team began to move, Woodblock very quickly branching off towards a path that went off on the left. He responded to my wave and I saw, little by little, his figure merging into the depths of the forest. There were some good people on this earth. But also some crooks, characters of the worst sort, prepared to do anything for money. The proximity of Gloucester brought me back, inevitably, to more sombre thoughts. I was going to have to face up to reality, now. Was I ready?

As I walked, I nibbled a few biscuits and crunched a very sour apple. I had, in a leather flask, some cool water, pumped when we had stopped in Abergavenny. That succeeded in waking me up and put me in rather good shape. I approached the city with determination. From this side, the south-west, I first had to cross the Severn, then turn due south to reach the docks. I had to be very cautious and very discreet. The effect of surprise is a definite advantage; it very often guarantees victory in dangerous operations. So I reached the harbour rather quickly and slipped behind the bales of merchandise waiting to be loaded. I only had to wait. But wait for what? I realized, then, that I had not decided on any plan, and that in any case, I certainly was unequal to the task. Only my thoughts about Mary could dictate this irrational, if not suicidal, behaviour.

19

I had finally decided to abandon my hiding place. With day dawning, I risked being spotted. On the other hand, my two birds of ill omen only came rarely during the day. So I got back to my uncle's house, which no longer belonged to him after all. I did not notice any change. The building was unoccupied and would surely remain so for yet a long time. The matters in hand were taking time and my disappearance was not likely to settle things. I went in unobtrusively, taking care not to be noticed. I wanted to retain my surprise effect.

I took advantage of the opportunity to explore upstairs, something I had not done up to that time. The room which served as an office was overcrowded with cardboard boxes, with administrative documents, so many things that did not interest me nor concern me. A typewriter, fairly new, an Underwood, was prominent on a stand. It was a fine machine and I gently stroked its keys. While I liked reading a lot, I must say writing also attracted me. Later, perhaps, when I got out of trouble... The other rooms were not deserving of interest. Nothing but the usual and especially, overwhelming, suffocating dust. In the attic, I found only antiques which would not even have found their places in the carts of Mr Tynderwearth or his pal Woodblock. A metal case intrigued me. It seemed rather new and stood out somewhat in this spot. I lifted its cover and discovered a firearm, a six-shot revolver, lying on a purple cotton cloth, along with a box of ammunition. My hand began to tremble; this object attracted and frightened me at the same time. A weapon! I was not a very great believer in them and hardly knew how to use them. However, without really thinking about it, I took the thing and slipped it into my coat pocket.

When it began to get dark, I set off again for the docks. It was generally at night that the two accomplices ran their dirty business. Perhaps I would be lucky to find them there.

The premises were surprisingly quiet. There was almost no activity on the wharves, and the place seemed deserted. I say 'seemed', as I had recently learnt not to trust appearances, which are very often deceptive.

The warehouse was no longer busy. The bales of merchandise were safe from the inclemency of the weather, but I did not observe any human presence. Furtively, hiding myself as best I could behind boxes and packing materials, I got as far as the little office, when a voice resounded behind me.

"A ghost! Is this possible?"

The man was standing quite near; he was wearing that evil smile which augured nothing good.

"Ron, get your ass here! Guess who's here!"

Ron emerged from the darkness and opened his eyes wide in astonishment.

"Not possible. But he was well tied up."

"Obviously not. Otherwise, how do you explain this?"

"Don't know."

"Bah, forget it. What matters is that he has come back, so we will be able to finish the job, this time."

Cold sweat ran down my back. These two characters were looking at me like two soulless beings who are going to crush an insect. The eyes of one reflected joy, those of the other brutishness. The talkative one took an object from his pocket and I heard the click of a flick-knife blade. Perhaps it was this same weapon that had killed Brackett? I felt lost; I had reached the end of the line, and there was not much more to be done.

In my pocket, I felt the weight of the weapon. Under normal circumstances, I would have hesitated to resort to such an extreme measure, but the instinct of survival can, without any doubt, make you take the plunge. As quickly as I could, I took the revolver from my pocket and squeezed the trigger. The deafening noise resounded in the warehouse and the knife holder looked at me incredulously. His look had changed, the evil joy giving way to surprise. Then came pain. He let go of the knife which fell with a sinister noise. Time was suspended for a moment. He bent double, holding his shoulder. Ron rushed for the knife and threw himself on me. I felt a burning sensation on my left side; the blade had struck me. I had at the same time squeezed the trigger once more and the noise, this time, was muffled by the proximity of the adversary. Ron rolled his eyes wildly, fell back and completely collapsed. He was motionless. The other man, sitting by a metal cask, was holding his shoulder and groaning.

I felt my wound. Blood was running rather profusely from it. All of that was inconsequential. I made my way to the wharf, as the place would soon be swarming with coppers. I was walking with great difficulty; the pain was intense and I did not think I could go very far. As I came out of the warehouse, a hand grabbed me by the shoulder. I turned my head, but my view was somewhat blurred. I made out a man's face, heavily bearded. A smell of alcohol made my nostrils twitch.

"Come here, my boy. You shouldn't hang around here."

Other arms grabbed me and I sensed that I was being carried. Then, there was darkness.

20

"He's coming round. All is well."

It was a woman's voice, this time. A hoarse voice, somewhat raucous, but filled with concern.

I opened my eyes. That made the second occasion on which, within a short space of time, I found myself at the edge of a precipice, then pulled back at the point of death by sympathetic arms.

My left side was aching. That confounded blade must have given me a good cut.

"Who are you?" I asked in a feeble, almost inaudible voice.

"I'm Carol; I'm taking care of you; don't be afraid."

"But the other man?"

I recalled the bearded face and the strong smell of alcohol.

"He's not far away. He's a friend of Cadell."

"Of Cadell?"

"Yes, he'll explain it to you. Rest yourself meanwhile. You've been damned lucky; the blade grazed your side. You'll recover quite quickly."

This short discussion had exhausted me; big drops of sweat ran down my forehead. I felt really tired. I absolutely did not know where I was, but that hardly mattered at the moment. I was comfortable there, safe and under the good care of Carol. Fatigue overwhelmed me and I quickly fell asleep again, sinking into a deep slumber, black and gloomy like a moonless night.

I spent the following days sleeping and eating. Carol was often at my side when I awoke and made me drink some herb-teas which she had brewed. She also put a sort of brown paste on my cut, so that the injury would not destroy my insides, she said.

When I was in better shape — I could sit down without feeling like my muscles were being torn apart — the bearded man came to see me. With this full beard, hardly anything but his prominent nose and two merry black eyes could be seen.

"Well, young man, I guess you're feeling better?"

He had a glass in his hand and held it out to me.

"Have a drink; that will do you some good. In any case, a lot more than Carol's herb-teas, okay!"

The drink was as disgusting as the one Cadell used to swig down. A kind of alcohol that burned your gullet and stomach.

"There you go! That will pick you up!"

"Certainly, sir."

"Sir? My name is Owl. When I was a kid, I used to climb trees, sit on a large branch and observe the landscape for hours… Hence the nickname."

"You are Cadell's friend?"

I recalled what Carol had told me.

"That's quite right. He and I are old pals; we've knocked about quite a bit. But that's a long story. In any case, he told me about you."

"About me?"

"Yes, that's right. He passed by a few days ago. He was worried and that's not like him. He was looking for you, but you had disappeared from the docks, vanished…"

"That's true, I had a bit of a hold-up, but I came back very quickly."

"Only to take a stab. Unbelievable!"

"I mean…"

108

"I know all that. We were watching you for a while. Murdock and Ron have the habit of taking on young men like you and make them do their dirty work. You aren't the first, you know. Those two are not much liked, but it would seem that you have wiped out one and damaged the other. Bravo for that!"

"I didn't want to do it, but I had no choice."

I felt my pockets.

"Don't look for your revolver; we hid it, you see. Supposing the coppers happened to barge in. Furthermore, you will need to take some precautions."

"Precautions?"

"You think the Police are going to give up? They are going to look for you again; you won't be safe anywhere."

"But I didn't do anything; they were going to kill me!"

"Go and explain that to Chief Merrit. To him you are nothing but a little criminal who killed one of his accomplices and wounded another. You are good for the colonies."

"The colonies?"

"Sure."

The information was hardly cheerful. However, Owl continued to smile.

"But if you are here, with us, then all that will be fixed. I'll explain it to you."

And Owl explained a lot of things that reassured me a little. The man and his wife Carol were some kind of street performers who travelled through the towns in the region. At market-places, they performed numerous juggling and conjuring tricks. That allowed them to earn some small change, just enough to survive, to have almost enough to eat and to dress warmly for the harsh winters. They lived, with other persons in similar circumstances, in disused warehouses, abandoned barns and dilapidated factories. These places were not in short supply and they were safe there. No one came and disturbed them there and the Police, who knew them well, gave them no trouble.

"You see, young man, you will be undisturbed here. But the policemen will soon come and search the premises and we are going to take our precautions. From today, you are Brad, a nephew from Harescombe. You live with us and we have taken you on in our group. Can you juggle?"

"Not at all."

"Well, you are going to learn. And then you are going to let those three hairs you have on your chin grow, just to change your appearance a little. For the moment, I don't see any other solution."

"Well, Mr Owl, all of that seems prudent to me. I will do as you say."

"Good! Let's have a drink!"

All of that, for me, could only be temporary. Allowing time for things to settle down and I knew that I would have only one desire, that of running to Cheltenham to kidnap Mary. I say 'kidnap', but undoubtedly, the victim would be compliant.

The warehouse that we were occupying, at some distance from the harbour, in a relatively neglected area, was visited by policemen. I had almost recovered from my injury and I was able to put on a good show. Mr Owl explained, as had been agreed, that I was a distant nephew, homeless and without any family, whom he had chosen to take in. I was in fact a nephew without shelter and without family, but my real uncle was only too rarely concerned about me. This provisional uncle seemed much kinder. After a brief discussion between Owl and a police officer, the latter wanted to question me all the same.

"So you are the nephew of this skinflint Owl."

"Yes, Mr Officer."

"Who were your parents, then?"

"Jane and Jack Teresson from Harescombe, a hamlet in the south of the town. You know it?"

The man seemed to be searching his memory.

"No, I don't think so. And what did they do down there, then?"

"It's a forest area, you know," — he did not know — "and my parents were coal-merchants."

The man frowned. He did not seem convinced by my explanations. But wasn't he a policeman and wouldn't this attitude be almost natural to him?

"So what happened to them, your parents?"

"My father had a nasty fall from a tree; he was killed. The following winter, we were penniless and my mother died from a terrible lung disease."

I had told this story, learnt perfectly with Owl, in the calmest manner possible, in a voice meant to be confident. I surprised myself by being able to lie like that with so much self-assurance. The prospect of prison was sufficient motive.

In fact, Owl really did have family in this hamlet. Jane and Jack Teresson had suddenly disappeared and their son had vanished into the wild.

"So you're working with Owl?"

"Yes, he took me on. I must admit that's a great relief."

"Hmm... Very well, young man. See you soon, maybe."

And the officer left the premises.

"Why 'see you soon'?" I asked Owl, worried.

"It's a way of speaking, you know. These policemen are always trying to frighten us. They are suspicious of everybody; don't worry about it."

I therefore decided to forget about this copper. Tomorrow was a big day; I was going with Owl and Carol into town. I was going to give my first performance.

21

That first outing was rather memorable. We had reached the city centre and we settled down on the square to perform our stunts. The passers-by, who were rather numerous on that market day, gladly gathered around to look at us.

But I was not yet very talented. Juggling was totally new to me and in spite of the training given by Mr Owl, my stunts with three balls were mediocre. The balls got away from me frequently, but I was introduced as a beginner in the profession and had a right to the indulgence of the audience.

Nevertheless, Mr Owl seemed satisfied with the outcome of that day's work. The money earned would last him a few days.

"You see, my boy, it's not so complicated."

"My stunts were mediocre. I really don't think I will be making a career out of it."

"You will, you will."

When we were back at the warehouse, Mr Owl told me:

"I was able to get some information."

Mr Owl and his wife Carol, by virtue of their endless moving around, knew a great many people and had the art and manner of loosening tongues.

"Really?"

"Murdock escaped from the Police. He's hiding out in the city or in its suburbs."

"So he hasn't spoken to the policemen."

"No doubt, but he must have a grudge against you. You have to be very careful, as this fellow is capable of anything."

I was well aware of that.

"He might try to get to you," continued the acrobat.

I felt my throat tighten.

"No… No… not me."

"How so? What do you mean?"

"Mary, he's going to attack Mary. He already wanted to hurt her, but this time, with Ron's death, he will take vengeance. I have to leave as quickly as possible."

"Leave? You don't mean that?"

"Yes, Mr Owl, I have to. He's going to kill Mary…"

I couldn't stay put any longer. Murdock could be making his way to Cheltenham at any moment, get into the estate — he had done it already — and attack Mary. I thought I was going crazy; I had to act, now, and prevent this tragedy, if that was still possible.

Mr Owl realized that he would not be able to restrain me. All the arguments in the world would not have changed anything; my decision was irrevocable.

He moved away for a moment, disappeared into one of the many nooks in the warehouse and returned carrying a canvas bag.

"Here, take back your revolver. I don't really like these devices, but you will need it. If someone has to die, I would rather it be Murdock."

Then, he turned to Carol.

"Prepare a knapsack for Jeremy."

So it was in the evening of that day, when the shadows were merging with the night, I set off. I was easily able to cover a distance of ten miles during the night. Carol had prepared a bag for me with some food and, besides the firearm, Owl had given me several coins — for my work, he had claimed. He did not despair of seeing me again one day and taking me on for good, but I had other plans. Our goodbyes were difficult.

I had used this route the first time my uncle had taken me to Cheltenham. How long ago that occasion seemed to me! In fact, it was barely a year.

So I arrived within sight of Cheltenham in the middle of the night. However, I had not taken the regular route. I could have had an unpleasant encounter or been observed and that was really not the desired objective.

I had therefore preferred to follow the forest paths or even the paths that ran through meadows. However, it was in one of these pastures that I stopped, hardly quarter of a mile from the manor. I knew where to find a shepherd's hut there and I was able to rest in it. A nap should not do me any harm; the coming day would certainly be eventful. Settled down in the straw, nice and warm, I had eaten several slices of smoked ham and fresh cheese provided by Carol. Owl had slipped into the bag a flask of his favourite whisky, but I had only swallowed a small gulp of it. I had also placed a beech tree log behind the door, thus jamming the latch. I would be alerted if an intruder turned up.

The morning found me fresh and in good form. I had slept a dreamless sleep this time. That had not happened to me for a very long time. Mary very often paid me a visit, but lately, above all, I lived over again the scene in the warehouse when I had to fire at my assailants.

I looked outside. Everything seemed perfectly calm. Some streaks of mist floated over the meadow and the enchanting music of a nearby brook could be heard.

Everything was going great. My morale was rather good, for today, after weeks of waiting, I was finally going to see Mary again. We would come up with a plan to leave this place and go and live our love in distant lands, in safety from all danger or from any nasty surprise.

It was still a little early and I decided to have something to eat.

Carol had put in the knapsack some biscuits she had made and some cheese still remained. Then, I decided to approach the manor. Cadell had to be already at work; I could then start there and try to make contact with him.

I moved slowly towards the estate, on the north side, this very bushy part that I knew so well from having worked there. Hidden by the shrubs, I cocked my ear. I could hear the noise of the pruning-knife, not far away, on my left. Cadell was busy pruning some lilacs which readily overran the ground. It was the ideal time, just after their flowering season.

I approached the spot, finding myself still, for the moment, on the outside of the property.

"Psst! Psst! Cadell, are you there?"

"Eh? What is it?"

I had recognized the raucous voice of the gardener.

"It's me, Jeremy"

We were not seeing each other, but we could easily hear each other.

"Young man, that's you? But what are you doing here?"

"You know it well, Cadell; I have come to see Mary."

"It's too dangerous at this time; you run the risk of being caught."

"I've taken my precautions, Cadell. Everything is fine."

The man grunted. He seemed to be unconvinced by my remarks.

"I absolutely must see her, you know; we have plans."

"You poor fellow, plans… What plans are you speaking about? So you don't know?"

"What should I know? Tell me."

"Lady Cheltenham and Sir Garmond have made a kind of arrangement."

"Yes, they are going to get married. But what does that have to do with Mary?"

Cadell was silent. What he had to tell me must be terrible. I heard some rustling of leaves and at last I saw the man coming nearer. He had a sad look that I did not associate with him.

"The arrangement is not the one you are thinking of. Mary has been promised to Sir Garmond's son. To Perdy! So, their estates will be linked up and that will settle matters for everybody."

I could not hold back a scream which rose to the tops of the trees. I was devastated; I sat down on the wet ground.

"Mary... Perdy... That's impossible!"

"Just as I say. But neither you nor I can change anything. This is not our business and we are not in the same league."

"And Mary?"

"She is like you, devastated. But her mother does not wish to hear anything."

My mind was racing. This news was upsetting my plans; the future was suddenly becoming very dark.

"In that case, so much the worse," I said then. "All the more reason!"

"What's that 'all the more reason'?"

"More reason to take Mary out of this hornet's nest. We're going to leave, both of us!"

"You poor fellow!"

Some noise could be heard in the vicinity of the stables and the manor, and we stopped talking for a moment.

"What's happening?" I asked.

"Milady is selling one of her horses. The upkeep of these animals is costly for her and she doesn't need so many of them."

That wasn't wrong, the more so because she herself hardly rode.

"It's Black One," Cadell resumed, before I asked the question. "A rich landowner from Portsmouth is interested; it seems he wants to make it into a racehorse. He is supposed to come today."

"Who is seeing about the stables?"

116

"A new man, one Nolan, unpleasant chap. I don't really like him. But he seems to do his work well."

"I'm going to have a look," I suddenly said.

"Don't do that, lad; it's not a good idea. I will stop you, if necessary."

Cadell had moved forward. He did not look threatening, but rather worried.

"I'm sorry, Cadell, I have to."

Starting to run, I went along the fence towards the western part, until I found myself on a level with the stables. That did not take me five minutes. At that sport, Cadell could not keep up with me. I was much faster than him.

I could now make out the buildings. There was, in fact, some commotion in front of the stables. A man, dressed in brown, whose figure was unfamiliar to me, was bustling about along the loose boxes. Black One had been brought out, held back by her tether to the hand-rail that closed off access to the stalls. But another figure had just appeared, at the corner of the building. Slim, nimble, seeming to fly rather than walk, wearing a garnet-red dress partly covered by a dark shawl; I immediately recognized Mary. My heart raced at once; blood was beating at my temples.

"Mary! Mary! I'm here!"

She turned her head, spotting me at the top of the hill.

"Jeremy, that's you! Jeremy!"

She changed direction to rush forward to meet me, her face lit up with indescribable happiness.

She was running, gasping for breath; in a few moments we would be in each other's arms and then nothing would be able to separate us.

But Cadell had appeared. He stopped Mary, preventing her from getting any further.

"No, Mary, you mustn't. The consequences would be terrible

for you and Jeremy…"

"Let me pass Cadell, let me, I beg you…"

She was shouting, crying and scratching the lawn with her fingernails, as she had fallen to her knees.

At the same time, two hands seized me by my coat collar and pulled me back.

"This way, young man! This time, we have you!"

Two policemen were dragging me towards a metal wagon, while Mary's heart-rending scream rose into the sky.

22

I had not seen the policemen arrive. Besides, what could I even have done? While Mary's screams continued to pierce the silence, I was pushed, unceremoniously, inside the wagon. The metal door clanged in a sinister fashion. Probably a sort of antechamber for the prison which awaited me. They quickly frisked me. One of the agents sat beside me, while the other one got the team going.

"Oh! A lovely toy," said the policeman, showing the revolver. "I think we made a good bet. You will tell us all that at the station."

And he finished his sentence with a big mocking smile.

The journey did not last two hours. When the doors opened again, I was in Gloucester, in the paved yard of the police station. I was led through various corridors before being put into a cell with a door that had iron bars. Depressed, crushed, without any hope, I sat down on the sole bench. Mary's screams still resounded in my ears and my heart was nothing but an open wound.

I fell asleep on my makeshift seat, not because of tiredness, but rather from lassitude. Mental lassitude, like a resignation, a surrender, a depression that had deprived me of all my energy. This time, that was the end of it, my future was laid out; I was going to go far away, to the colonies without doubt and I would never again see my native land nor my dear Mary, who was my only reason for living.

The lock, noisy, roused me from this drowsiness.

"This way! Hurry up! We have to talk!"

The policeman, ill-tempered, did not seem to be joking. For the moment, I had to keep a low profile. And tell the absolute truth. That was no doubt the best thing to do.

I went through some different corridors where a certain commotion prevailed. Along the walls, some fellows, young or old, looking haggard, waited for someone to attend to them. This place was very strange and gave me shivers down my back.

I was taken into a dark and dusty office. A single dirty window allowed light to penetrate this uninviting room. I recognized, behind the cluttered desk, the officer who had questioned me at Owl's place.

"I am Officer Merrit. Doug Merrit. I am in charge of your case. I think that it wouldn't be very lengthy, right?"

What could that mean? Was the man expecting immediate confessions that would have allowed him to close the case in record time? I preferred not to answer.

"You know that your situation is very disquieting?" he continued. "Do you know at least why you are here?"

"Not in the least. But above all I would like to know how I got here?"

This time, I had decided to speak, as this question was bothering me. Was it Cadell? No, that was impossible. He could never have done such a thing.

"It's not very complicated, you know."

As he said this, the officer smoothed his thick moustache and pulled an enormous cigar from one of the drawers of his desk. An acrid brown smoke began to fill the limited space in the room.

"Since this case of murder on the docks, we have been very attentive to everything that could shed light on it. Now, Ron, this species of Australopithecus, is dead from a bullet in his belly; his accomplice Murdock survived and believe me, he has been rather talkative."

I began to understand. This Murdock must not have hesitated to make me take the blame.

"He told us that you had tried to eliminate him, him and his accomplice, in order to steal their money and get their trade. I know that Murdock is no choirboy, but he has been very cooperative. According to him, at any rate, you were getting ready to do something bad again in the vicinity of Cheltenham and you would even be responsible for the death of the former groom, one Brackett."

"All of this is untrue," I exploded. "Let me meet this Murdock face-to-face."

"That will be difficult; he has managed to slip through our fingers."

That really was not good news.

"I'll sum it up," the policeman resumed. "You are involved in alcohol smuggling with Ron and Murdock. Brackett, from Cheltenham, must be also in the know and you eliminate him for some reason that I still don't know. You get the idea of going on your own and you try to eliminate your two accomplices. That failed with Murdock. So you lie low for a while and you reappear as a street performer, then you dash off to Cheltenham to fix another matter. All of that is clear. Moreover, we have the revolver which was used to bring down Ron. The judge will rule on that very quickly. Anything to add?"

"It's not like that at all, Mr Officer. I am a former Cheltenham worker and I came back to Gloucester to settle the estate of my uncle, killed by Murdock, by the way. These two pirates forced me to work for them because my uncle was indebted to them. They tried to get rid of me and Ron's death was accidental; I merely defended myself. As far as my uncle is concerned, you can check; go and see the solicitor, Sir Radcliff. And Lady Cheltenham will confirm that I was really employed at the manor."

"Nice story. But I doubt you would be able to convince the judge. And then a case settled so quickly is excellent for our reputation. As for Murdock, we will end up catching him or else he will end up like Ron."

"I am innocent. I swear, Mr Officer."

"I know; they all say that."

And Officer Merrit nodded to the policeman who was in the corridor.

"This is a mistake, I'm telling you! It's Murdock who caused all that."

"Brett, take him away; that's enough."

The policeman's firm grip compelled me to follow the path back to my cell. I was under the impression that I was not going to languish in there for very long. A judge was quickly going to determine my fate. Alcohol smuggling, two murders, an attempted murder... I was going to pay dearly and I had no means of clearing myself of blame. Perhaps Cadell could support me, at least concerning Brackett's death? I went back to my bench and was served a foul-smelling soup, along with a hunk of bread.

I spent the following days, five to be exact, in the prison in Gloucester. I had to wait there for my appearance before the judge.

As soon as I arrived there, I was subjected to a severe ordeal. The guards who received me were by no means kind and roughed me up, both physically and mentally. After a relentless search, I was moved on to the shower. A sort of wooden bucket of cold water which was poured over your head and which was supposed to wash you. The hairdresser cut my hair so short that I thought I was bald. I was given a grey outfit with white stripes, clothes which until then I knew about only from my diverse reading. A pair of clogs completed this basic gear. I was assigned to a cell, a room with limestone walls, twelve by eighteen feet, lit by a single small window with iron bars. A small table, a stool and a horsehair mattress placed on a wooden frame were the only furniture worthy of the name. A metal pail, in the corner of the room, was there for answering calls of nature.

A violent slap on my back propelled me into the room and the heavy door was noisily closed again. I heard the guard adjust the wicket, then the noise of his footsteps receded in the corridor.

Sitting on the mattress, my head in my hands, I replayed the last images of my visit to Cheltenham over and over. How was that possible? How, so near to happiness, did I find myself today, in this insane situation? Was there still a slim hope of turning back the events? I no longer believed it to be possible. The judge was going to condemn me without hesitation and my life would be lost forever.

My stay in this penitentiary went by rather quickly after all. I hardly saw my fellow prisoners except at the morning walk and when going to the chapel, which was not compulsory. But almost all the inmates went, a matter of getting out of their cells. These men, of all ages, carried all the weight of the world on their shoulders. They moved forward, bent, dragging their feet, with blank stares. Most of them perhaps would never get out of this place. I did not see any prisoner of my age. The youngest, a tall thin fellow, with a lanky gait, might have been about twenty years old, that is to say, three years older than I was. But I very quickly gave up on speaking to him; his wicked look was frightening, his smile on a toothless mouth even more so. Moreover, prisoners were not allowed to speak to one another. The rest of the time was spent in the cell. Dozing, having the three meals — porridge, potatoes and vegetable soup — and working, for those whose sentence had been imposed, which was not my case. They made shoes, clothing or even horsehair doormats.

So, on the fifth day, I was visited by a court assessor. He came to tell me that I would meet with the judge that same day and handed me a document to sign. I took advantage of it to ask for some writing materials.

"Of course, young man. I will get you what you need."

The man was affable and seemed rather sympathetic. That's how I was able to get two sheets of paper, a pen and some ink. I wrote a quick letter to Cadell. He alone could convey any information to Mary and he alone perhaps would be able to help me.

Dear Cadell,

I am at present being held at the county jail. I would say that I'm not being treated too badly, but it is the future that I am concerned about. The policeman in charge of the investigation has filed criminal charges against me. The death of Ron, which was accidental, and that of Brackett. I could not get him to listen to my version; he would have none of it, as I make the ideal culprit. I don't know what is going to happen to me. I am seeing the judge this very day. Do you think you could meet with Officer Merrit and tell him about Brackett?

Tell Mary that I am thinking about her every moment and if God allows me to get out of this hellish situation, I will meet her again and we will both leave. If that does not happen, tell her that in any case I wish her to be happy.

Tears fell on the paper. That was a signature suitable for the occasion. I folded the sheet of paper. I had to hand it over to the guard. I hoped he would not throw it away!

23

"Jeremy Page, born April 12, 1866 at Gloucester."

"Yes, Your Honour."

"You are here because you are accused of murders, in the plural, on the persons of Brackett Shinger and Ron Malavoy. Attempted murder on Murdock Longsdale has also been filed. We also have a record of active participation in alcohol smuggling on the Gloucester docks. Are you contesting these matters?"

"Yes, Your Honour. I am in no way responsible for the death of Brackett Shinger. As for Ron Malavoy, it was a matter of self-defence. Regarding the alcohol smuggling, Ron and Murdock forced me to do it to reimburse my uncle's debt."

"Forced? Then why didn't you inform the police?"

"They threatened to attack someone whom I like a lot."

"And who is that?"

I was still hesitant. Should I mention Mary? If all this got back to Lady Cheltenham…

"It's Mary Cheltenham, the daughter of Lady Cheltenham."

"I see. However, Officer Merrit transmitted the previously described charges; to him, the case is clear."

"He did not listen to my explanations and did not ask for evidence from Sir Radcliff or even Lady Cheltenham."

"Young man, you cannot call into question the decision of a

police officer. You know very well that he is conducting the investigation and refers directly to the court in transmitting his conclusions."

"But I…"

"That's enough, young man."

A man, dressed in a long black robe, wearing a wig and who had been appointed as my counsel, made signs to me to sit down and… to keep quiet. He asked leave to speak.

"Master Jones?"

"Your Honour. My client Jeremy Page is trying here to demonstrate that all the investigations have not been carried out. Perhaps we could hear from this Sir Radcliff, as well as Lady Cheltenham?"

The judge twisted the curls of his wig and leaned towards his neighbour, a man with the face of a crow. They whispered for a moment.

"We quite understand, Master Jones; however, your client, in any case, tried to hide away with this street performer, Mr Owl. Isn't this proof of his guilt?"

"In fact, Your Honour, Jeremy Page feared for his safety. Murdock could have tried to do away with him, having failed the first time."

The judge closed his eyes for a moment and finally responded:

"Very well, Master Jones. We are going to transmit this to Officer Merrit. When he has the result of these new investigations, we will then resume this hearing."

A bang of the gavel, loudly insistent on the piece of furniture placed in front of the judge, signalled the end of the session. I was certainly going to return to the county jail for a few days. But I was being granted a little time and the witnesses to come were surely going to help me to get out.

I was less worried from that time on. Before long, the police officer would have a different conception of this case, a different

126

light which would enable him to see it more clearly. He would finally understand that from being the culprit, I could become the victim and that Ron's death was due only to a reaction of self-defence. Everything was going to fall into place very soon.

All the same, I had to be patient for about ten days in my cell. Nothing important took place during this period, except for this disquieting young man who spoke to me during one of our walks.

"It seems that you wiped out Ron and almost killed Murdock? Bravo! Everybody here knows about it, you know. They gave us hell, those two; you did right."

"But I…"

"I'm going to get out of here in about ten months, finally, I hope. If we find ourselves outside again, come and see me, I have some work for you."

"You mean that…"

"Shut up over there!" intervened the warder on duty. "Otherwise, you are going back immediately."

Well, obviously, I was not interested in this proposition. The prisoners seemed to regard me as a hero, which I was not. But all this would soon be nothing but ancient history.

Finally, the assessor who had already visited me reappeared. He informed me that I had to go back before the judge in order to conclude this case. The new elements were available.

"Jeremy Page, on the occasion of this second appearance, we can now inform you about the result of the investigations which have been conducted."

He took hold of a grey cardboard file that his neighbour with the crow's face had just handed him. I noticed also, that this time, in the almost deserted courtroom, seated in one of the last rows, was Officer Merrit.

The judge opened the file and quickly glanced through several sheets.

"Young man, Officer Merrit, who is also present here, carried out the foreseen investigations. Could you, Mr Officer, give us an account of these inquiries?"

"Yes, Your Honour," replied the policeman as he stood up.

"We are listening."

"To start with, I paid a visit to Sir Radcliff, the solicitor who dealt with the estate of Sir Jenkins, uncle of Jeremy Page. The solicitor confirmed the situation with the business of the late Sir Jenkins. It turns out that Jeremy Page inherited some debts from his uncle and found himself, or rather still finds himself, in a difficult situation. So it is very probable that in order to seek to quickly make some easy money, young Jeremy Page may have, along with Ron Malavoy and Murdock Longsdale, got involved in this alcohol smuggling. It was a quick way to find the sums necessary to get himself out of trouble. To save time, Jeremy Page might have therefore wanted to go it alone and to eliminate, or at least try to eliminate his two accomplices."

I was going mad. So, the inquiries in regard to the solicitor, which should have been able to benefit me, were blatantly doing me a disservice. I wanted to intervene, but Counsel Jones put his hand on my arm, thus giving me a signal to wait.

"On the other hand," continued the officer, "Lady Cheltenham did not wish to testify. She indeed hired Jeremy Page at her manor, but she had to part company with him, as his behaviour left a lot to be desired. The work was not done properly and she thinks that the young man tried to abuse her daughter Mary."

"No! That's a lie! Mary and I…"

"Be quiet, young man, or I will have you removed!" shouted the judge, hitting his desk with a violent blow of the gavel. "Are you finished Officer Merrit?"

"Yes, Your Honour, that will be all."

My mind was working at full speed. How was that possible? Why these reversals and these lies? Lady Cheltenham must have heard about my relationship with her daughter and she was taking vengeance in this way, in order to get me out of the picture.

"Master Jones?"

"Your Honour, these testimonies are, to say the least, surprising and, I would even say, very audacious. Sir Radcliff describes a difficult financial situation, but one cannot conclude from it so easily that my client sought to obtain money by unlawful means. As for the remarks of Lady Cheltenham, they are very astonishing. I have here the testimony of the gardener of the manor, one Cadell Fortslaw. He was unceasing in praise of Jeremy and concluded that the mistress of the house was very satisfied with the young man's work."

"A gardener…? Master Jones, how can you doubt the word of a well-known and respected Lady, taking as your basis the statements of a mere gardener? That makes no sense."

"If I may be permitted," then intervened the police officer, "the other workers at the manor, the cooks in particular, confirmed the remarks of Lady Cheltenham."

I was alarmed. Cathy, Joanna, Lauren, all three were throwing me over. But I very much suspected that they must have been under pressure and were threatened with dismissal.

"Thank you, Officer Merrit, thank you, Master Jones."

"But, Your Honour…" ventured the counsel.

"That will be just fine. This time, we will be able to come to a decision."

The counsel sat back down, vexed.

The judge again consulted with his neighbour. That lasted several seconds.

"Jeremy Page, please stand."

I reluctantly obeyed.

"In light of the factors in our possession, following the investigations by the police services…"

Already I was not listening anymore. This nonsense on show was antagonizing me to the highest degree. Anger now roared in me, but I felt the hand of the policeman who was behind me become more insistent on my shoulder.

"Consequently, this Court condemns you to a penalty of twenty years of forced labour in one of our colonies. You will very soon be advised of the reserved destination. The sitting is closed."

The judge and his neighbour stood up, disappeared through a door in the wall and the policeman signalled me to follow him. Counsel Jones had already disappeared.

24

I did not stay a very long time in the county jail. As soon as the next day, two policemen came to look for me to announce my departure. I had, the day before, written another and perhaps a last letter to tell Cadell about the latest developments. I did not know if I would be able, later on, to continue to write and at any rate, I had to definitively write off this part of my life. I had to forget Mary. I knew also that was impossible.

I was taken to the docks. A boat of average tonnage was waiting, getting ready to sail. The two policemen escorted me on board. I supposed that they had to stay with me until my departure for the colonies. I could not get any information from them.

The boat, which was also transporting merchandise, reached the Severn estuary through the canal, then the port of Cardiff. It is there that the last loading was carried out.

Did I really realize what was in the process of unfolding? I was not so sure. This snap decision, this sudden conviction, I had the feeling of experiencing a bad nightmare. All that seemed so unreal to me that I had difficulty admitting its existence. And yet!

At Cardiff, still escorted by the two policemen, I was taken to the harbour. Here the boats were a lot more impressive and came from various countries in Europe. But I hardly paid any attention to them, as my mind was too engaged with my more than delicate situation.

Things then followed in succession rather quickly. We went aboard. A man in the uniform of captain of the civil marine received us and I had to confirm, verbally, my identity. There were some exchanges of documents, of signatures and the policemen disappeared. Their task was accomplished; the ship's captain was taking over.

"I am Captain Stark and here one goes straight! Especially dirty bastards of your kind. So don't bother trying to be clever. Boris is going to take charge of you."

Boris, whom I had not yet spotted, approached slowly. He was a mountain of muscles; his arms were thick like the trunks of young fir-trees. His head was buried between his shoulders to such an extent that he seemed to have no neck. The man was totally bald and his turned up lips revealed several gold-filled teeth.

At a signal from the captain, the man grabbed me by the arm.

"This way!"

His grip was frightening. I had the feeling that he was crushing my bones. So I followed him, carrying on my shoulder the meagre luggage that I had retrieved.

We took a staircase which plunged into the depths of the boat. Then came a rather dark gangway, then a door with a porthole which the man pushed open with a kick.

"Go in there. That's your lodging, oh! Oh!"

The hold, which had to occupy a good part of the stern of the boat, smelled of motor oil, urine, excrement and filth. My stomach heaved. In the rather pronounced darkness, I made out some other figures, perhaps about twenty. In the dark, I could see eyes as well as teeth gleaming. A dim paraffin lamp, hanging from a small beam, lit this unbelievable scene. The figures tried to approach, held out their arms, but were obviously impeded. I quickly understood the reason. Boris pushed me along the metal partition and slipped an iron on my left ankle. A chain linked this shackle to a ring fastened to the partition. This time I was really and truly a prisoner.

Boris went back to the gangway, leaving me to my fate. Pairs of eyes stared at me, hands tried to touch me and reflexively I curled up against the partition.

"Who are you?" asked a voice.

"What are you doing here?"

"You seem very young…"

"I haven't done anything…" I ended up saying. "I am innocent."

"Oh! Oh! Innocent… So are we, ain't that so lads?"

"Oh! Oh!"

These fellows clearly did not believe me.

"Where are we going to?"

"To Africa, it seems."

"If we get there. Maybe we all will be dead by that time."

"Don't worry, lad," continued another one. "Over there, at least there's sunshine."

That did not reassure me at all. What did this African sunshine matter to me if I had to live in chains far from the one I loved?

"Why Africa?" I asked again.

"They need our labour, for roads, bridges, in short, large-scale works. We will be still better off than within four walls in this country of rain and fog."

At that moment the metal floor began to vibrate. The whole boat seemed to wake up, roused by new energy which was going to make it move.

"That's it," remarked one figure, "they have started the engine. I hope you don't get sea-sick."

And imperceptibly, we felt that the boat was carrying out some manoeuvres to leave the harbour then reach the open sea.

My heart sank and tears ran down my cheeks. A kind hand was placed on my arm.

"It will be alright, lad, it will be alright."

25

Life in the bottom of the hold was not easy. As we moved on, the temperature continued to rise progressively, as much on account of the engines, which produced an infernal heat and because we were heading south.

Every day, at the end of the morning, we were entitled to an outing on the deck. Under the supervision of Boris, we were able to restore the circulation in our legs and breathe less polluted air. The sailors, busy at various tasks, hardly paid any attention to us. They were probably accustomed to being around this kind of passenger.

My fellow-travellers, on the whole, looked resigned. Perhaps they accepted the punishment that was inflicted upon them and as they told me, they preferred by far this fate, rather than to rot in a cell. As far as I was concerned, I still could not accept my situation. I did not feel I was liable for the accusations brought against me. Ron's death, I often came back to it, was inevitable. He would not have hesitated to kill me with his knife. I was not killed only because of a legitimate instinct for survival.

I had more particularly formed a connection with Big Boss, a middle-aged fellow, with grey hair and a drooping moustache. He had an enormous belly, distended by the pints of beer that he must have imbibed from a very young age. He was tall and could have rivalled Boris in strength, without a doubt. But he was rather quiet, likeable and very attentive to me. He explained that he had strangled, with one hand, the fellow who was sleeping with his wife. Usually so calm, he did not know what had come over him, but one evening, meeting the lover who was dashing through the back of his house, he had grabbed him by the neck and killed him without more ado. He had got twenty-five years of hard labour.

Another prisoner was successful in getting some information.

"Egypt! Egypt!"

"What about Egypt?" asked another one.

"It's there we are going. It seems that our dear government has drawn up some agreements with the local authorities."

"In that case..."

Egypt! That country, about which I had read numerous works, could have, in other circumstances, attracted me. Unfortunately, this was not the case. I very much ran the risk of spending twenty years of my life there, working like a madman under a blazing sun. All things considered, when I shall have served my time, I will be worn-out, crushed and exhausted and I will possibly live out my days lamenting over my ruined life... I almost wanted to throw myself overboard and put an end to it immediately. But that was impossible. Boris kept a close eye on us.

However, on the fourth day, a tragedy occurred.

Cumber, one of the prisoners, a frail, thin, tired and depressive individual, committed suicide. He had not accepted his situation and forced labour scared him. He was not eating, complained continuously and really worried us. That morning, at the time of our outing on the deck, he took advantage of a moment of inattention from Boris. The guard had been attracted by a crash of glass. One of the sailors, near the prow, had dropped one of those enormous glass buoys which exploded on the floor. Cumber made use of those two little seconds of inattention. He flew like lightning in front of a sailor who was busy straightening some kinds of spears with curved blades, boat-hooks or harpoons. The wretched man threw himself on one of these blades which slit his chest with a dull sound. Blood flowed, rapidly spreading on the floor in a wide, crimson red pool. Cumber fell to his knees before the dumbfounded eyes of the sailor, completely collapsed and did not move again. When Boris turned over the poor man, he was wearing a big, peaceful smile on his face.

This event did not seem to affect many people. Life went like this and like this went the fate of these human beings about whom no one, in the final analysis, really cared.

Cumber's body was placed in a coarse brown canvas sack. The opening was carefully closed with a sturdy rope and everything was thrown overboard, after which one of the sailors, who must have had some competence in religious matters, said a few words for the safekeeping of the unfortunate man's soul.

That day, we cleaned out our place of confinement with a lot of soap and water. With horsehair brooms, we rubbed the floor up to the point of restoring — almost — its original colour. That caused Big Boss to say that it surely would not be long before we reached our destination. If the harbour master or the British authorities decided to carry out an inspection surreptitiously, Captain Stark could boast of treating his passengers well. In fact, at the time of our daily outing, and also because it was necessary to make numerous return trips to empty and refill the pails, I observed, on the horizon, to the south, the darker outline of land. Birds came sometimes to meet us, additional evidence that the continent was not very far off. I also saw other ships, numerous and imposing, no doubt anchored along the coast.

"Soldiers," Big Boss told me. "We have gone again and poked our noses where we shouldn't and here we are into something that stinks."

"What is it about?"

"War, young man, war. There are some opponents of the Egyptian sheikh; our army has come to give him some help. I think that it's best to take control of the country and of the canal."

"War? But what about us then?"

"We will watch the shells passing by. Unless you get hit on the skull by any of them…"

I did not like this business very much.

In the evening, Stark paid us a visit. He was accompanied by Boris, of course, as well as two other sailors who were holding lamps at arm's length. The captain inspected us one after the other, wordlessly, and seemed satisfied.

The next day we were awakened earlier than usual. In fact, usually, it was not necessary to wake us up. The engines hummed at reduced speed and the crew was prey to great excitement. Boris made his appearance in the doorframe, where his massive silhouette stood out.

"We are in a hurry. On to the deck, slackers!"

These few words instigated us to take our time. Boris realized it, but could not, he knew, make us go any faster.

"They are waiting for you up there! We have arrived!"

This moment was both a relief and a concern. Freed from this stinking and uncomfortable hold, worried about a future still difficult to grasp. This forced labour, these colonies about which a lot had been heard, what was it really? How was one treated? Would the work be difficult? In fact, those who had come back and given a precise description of it were few. This observation was not encouraging.

"Line up here!"

They made us form two columns. Boris kept a close eye on us; Captain Stark was directing manoeuvres for entry into the port. The channel was not very wide; the place was occupied by a multitude of small fishing boats. It was necessary to clear a path to reach the wharf, made here of poorly assembled planks.

Along this floating jetty one could also distinguish troops, motionless, who seemed to be keeping watch.

138

We came alongside without mishap and a military man, bedecked with medals, climbed aboard and saluted Captain Stark. The two men seemed to know each other.

"Captain Stark."

"Commander."

"Everything went well?"

"A trip with no problems. We regret the loss of one man. He succumbed to a bad fever, but the man was already ailing. Here, this is a list of your flock."

If I understood Stark's words correctly, we were going to be under the orders of this Commander.

The officer perused the document.

"It's perfect. I'll handle it."

"Everything is all right then. They are all yours."

And so it was that I set foot on the land of Egypt. Yet there was little in the way I could have imagined. This time, I had an unfortunate role; I was not master of my own destiny.

On the wharf, soldiers surrounded us and we moved forward with them, to the tempo of their rhythmic step. We left the seaside, skirted for a while what I realized was the famous Suez Canal and passed through the little town. Men and women were coming out on thresholds, staring at us insistently. They did not seem hostile. Their faces reflected an amazing kind of indifference. They must have been accustomed to this sight, to this procession of evil human beings whom the British society was punishing by banishing them to this land. A land which no doubt would be our tomb.

26

We walked for two days and two nights over stony, dusty tracks. We moved forward, laboriously, by day under a blazing sun, by night in dreadful cold. The Commander seemed to be in a hurry to get us to our destination and made us go at a forced march. The stops were not frequent, but long enough to enable us to recover our strength. I must admit that I held out rather well. That was due to my youth, certainly, as well as the habit of outdoor life and the jobs I had performed at the manor with Cadell.

Finally, we reached our destination.

It was a camp of tents and huts in the middle of nowhere. Stones, sand, dunes and some clumps of palms. To the east, the ribbon of the canal and wooden roofs of a remote village.

The Commander made us form three lines, facing him and a group of soldiers.

"Here you are. This is the place where you are going to serve your sentence. The one that society has chosen to inflict on you with regard to the crimes you have committed. I am here to keep an eye on the proper application of this sentence and you can trust me to perform this task without fail."

We did not doubt it for one moment.

He surveyed the group, then continued.

"Your task is rather simple. To overhaul the railway track. It leads to the canal which you can see behind me. This one has been unfortunately damaged by unscrupulous persons hostile to our pacification policy."

Perhaps the Commander could have used the term 'colonization'. It was evident that the British Empire was seeking, by all means, to assure control over this canal. The English were taking advantage of the tensions between Egypt and rebels based on the border of Sudan to intervene and thus to obtain a hold over the country. But the Mahdists were putting up a strong resistance and the English army had to bring in reinforcements to repel them.

"You will have to carry out this job quickly, because this connection is essential for us. I will pass along the details to you. You will begin tomorrow morning at dawn. Cornwell will be charged with your supervision and with delivering instructions."

The Commander turned to the side and, with the horse-whip that he held in his hand, pointed out to us an officer with a surly appearance, blond, almost white hair, menacing eyes and an evil grin. And that fellow did not seem to be having a good laugh.

"Of course, the slightest deviation will be severely punished. So I advise you to go straight and everything will be all right. Cornwell!"

"Yes, Commander?"

"Take this vermin into the huts. Let them get settled in."

"At your service, Commander."

The lodgings, this name seemed a little inadequate to me, were cubes with poorly grouted planks. The roofs were in no better state. There were only two huts.

The interior was dusty. The ground was beaten earth and the dryness, inevitably, produced, at each step we made, a fine yellow dust which settled on everything. The furniture, spartan, comprised a single badly made table, two shabby benches and a dozen seamy beds.

"And here is your grand luxury suite," said the soldier mockingly. "You'll be in clover there. You have one hour before some grub."

We were divided between the two huts. Big Boss was with me and he picked a bed next to mine.

"We'll be comfortable here, you'll see."

"Hmm…"

"At any rate, still better than being in prison or in that wretched boat hold."

It was not the lodging that worried me, but rather the work that we were going to have to carry out.

Dawn found us awake. In spite of the tiredness due to the forced march, we were almost ready when Officer Cornwell came to alert us.

"Everybody in line in front of the huts! At the double!"

We had understood that it would be like this every morning. Except perhaps on Sundays? It's a question that we had not asked.

Cornwell called the roll. He scrutinized us one by one with his hawk eyes.

"Now, grub time!"

It was breakfast. The meal the day before, comprising boiled meat and broad beans, was already distant. This time we were entitled to a metal cup of insipid coffee, with two generous slices of grey bread on which some molasses was smeared. There were also oranges available to us.

After this quick meal, it remained for us to wash ourselves in front of some large tubs, which looked like troughs for horses.

"Go to the latrines! We won't come back here before midday."

The toilets were a shack built askew, located a little further off, at some distance from the huts. The air there was almost unbreathable, with a stinking smell and it must be noted that no one stayed in there for very long.

The last one to come out was Gallway, an Irishman evidently, who had been arrested on a night of drinking for having beaten to death two representatives of law enforcement.

"I say, you Gallway. Tonight you will empty the latrines," declared the officer.

We made our way to the construction site. In fact, they expected workmen's labour from us. The army was surely not interested in releasing any soldiers to carry out this overhauling. On the other hand, we were convicted prisoners and so they could use us for all the tasks necessary to the nation. These were part of them.

Cornwell briefly explained to us what it entailed. Squaring off, cutting and preparing the sleepers, arranging them on the ground and digging out the earth on either side, in order to make a slight mound. Two workers from the train services were there to direct us. We had at our disposal saws, hammers and pick-axes, all the equipment necessary for such an undertaking. We had to work four hours without interruption until midday. Between the time when the sun would be at its zenith and three o'clock in the afternoon would be the big rest-period, as it was more or less impossible to carry out this work under the blazing sun and the more than sweltering heat. We had water reserves and the midday meal was supposed to be copious. If they wanted to make us work, they had to feed us properly.

So, after the instructions and explanations, we began to work.

We had set off again along the track to be restored and each of us had a well-defined task. For my part, I had to saw some thick planks to the desired length, so they could serve as sleepers. That was not too difficult for me; I had already sawed enough wood when I was with Cadell. Obviously the climatic conditions were totally different, but it was especially from the sweltering heat that I suffered. It made the work much more difficult. Fortunately, we had as much water as we wanted at our disposal. The Commander needed us, so he had to pamper us.

In the space of four days, we had overhauled one-third of the line, but the Commander was showing impatience. According to him, we were not going fast enough and he found that certain members of the group were not doing their best. It was a matter of three of the prisoners, tired, frail, worn-out individuals, for whom this work was clearly not appropriate. Cornwell had received orders to 'shake' them up a little. Until that morning of the fifth day, when one of these three convicts, one Fergus, fell on his knees, exhausted, incapable of getting back up. Cornwell rushed up immediately.

"Good-for-nothing! Get back up! Get to work!"

Fergus was incapable of standing up.

Cornwell dealt him several blows with his horsewhip and blood could be seen staining the shirt of the unfortunate man. Big Boss reacted in turn by approaching the officer.

"Stop that!" he yelled.

"Stop that? You want some too?" replied Cornwell, who clearly was not expecting such a reaction.

We had all stopped working.

Cornwell, who did not wish to lose face, brought down his horsewhip on Big Boss' head. But the latter, with his arm, fended off the blow and grabbed the whip, wrenching it from the hands of its owner. Then he made a step forward and struck Cornwell several times with his huge fist. The officer, on the ground, was holding his jaw and his face, covered with blood, reflected intense hatred. His right hand grasped the revolver that he had at his waist and he fired three times. Big Boss, hit right in the middle of his chest, his eyes bulging and his expression incredulous, collapsed face down.

Some soldiers, armed with rifles, had come up and Cornwell, getting back on his feet, very quickly reassumed control.

"Take that away for me!" he said, pointing to Big Boss' lifeless body. "Three volunteers to bury him before the vultures sharpen their beaks."

We were in shock and were not even thinking about protesting. This occurrence, so sudden, had us flabbergasted. Here, our life was only hanging on by a thread. The Commander and Cornwell were the masters; the administration, no doubt, would never come and ask for explanations.

Three of us, of which I was one, carried the corpse in a metal wheelbarrow up to the camp. A soldier accompanied us and made a full report to the Commander, who did not even seem to bat an eyelid.

"Very well, put him aside, over there, near the latrines."

Rage overwhelmed me. This Commander was vile and odious. An irresistible desire to wring his neck was rising in me, but that would certainly not have suited my purpose or else, the soldier on guard would have put a bullet in my skull before I could do anything whatever.

With pick-axes and shovels, sweating profusely, we dug a hole, deep enough to put in the body of the ill-fated man. One of the prisoners made a cross with two small pieces of wood and muttered a few words before making the sign of the cross. The matter was closed. The Commander was watching us from his tent and shouted to us:

"Get back to work!"

We did so without complaint.

The work lasted about ten days until we had reached the canal. The Commander seemed satisfied and granted us a day of rest. We made good use of it, as the work had exhausted us.

The death of Big Boss was not forgotten. We did not say a word, but everybody was angry. And we also knew that we had to avoid bringing up that subject.

We spent that day sleeping and staying in the shade of the trees, doing nothing. Recovery would be slow, more difficult for some. Fergus, for example, had lost nearly twenty pounds, someone who already was not very well covered. I had the intention of requesting an audience with the Commander to try to convince him to give the poor fellow a break. I decided to attend to it over the next few days.

The next day, Cornwell announced the programme.

"Some new troops are going to join us very soon. They will be stationed here for a while and we are going to fortify this place."

Was it really necessary to protect the place or was it just in order to make us break up rocks and move earth? No one asked this question, as the foolhardy person would have received several blows from the horsewhip as a response.

Our mission was therefore to protect the southern access by raising an embankment a good six feet in height, reinforced by good-sized stones which could be extracted from a nearby uncovered quarry.

"You understood what it is about," continued Cornwell. "This work has to be carried out as quickly as possible. It would be in your interest not to be lazy!"

And the labour resumed, at the same rate as for the repair of the track. A curious fact moreover, this track, now that it was functional, had not yet received a single train.

The work, this time, was not any less difficult. It was different. Digging the ground, dry and arid, hauling earth to make a sort of mound with it, all that was not an easy thing and put our backs under severe strain. Moreover, the heat had reached record levels and was difficult for us to bear. Fergus, on the second day, fell full length into one of the trenches that we had opened and did not get back up. Carried to the shade of a palm tree, he stared at us for several moments with his washed-out eyes and stopped breathing. His body was unable to do it any more; it refused to continue like that and gave up. He was buried beside Big Boss, without the Commander being as much as moved. We imagined that when the losses became too significant in our group, other

146

convicts, having come from England, would come and join us. I really began, with uneasiness, to think that no one ever returned from these work camps.

We were on the job for two weeks when an unusual stir seemed to run through the camp.

"It seems that the rebels are not very far away," we were informed by one of the prisoners, by the name of White, with whom I had struck up a friendship.

He was about thirty years old, seemed quiet and meek, did not speak often and did his work without sulking. However, I suspected him of making plans to escape. Something told me he was playing a cunning game rather well and would not miss the opportunity to disappear if that happened to arise. He was tall, muscular and supple and his strong jawbone denoted a very resolute character.

"You're sure of that?" I asked him.

"Yes, yes. The soldiers continue to speak about it. They are expecting reinforcements and the Commander has doubled the night watch."

We did not have much information on the events. All we knew was that the English army had sustained several misfortunes in the south and that the Mahdist leader was not hesitating to launch attacks to harass our soldiers. The rebel leader had seized several cannons and machine guns which could compete with English arms.

"You think they will reach as far as here?" I continued.

"I know bloody nothing about it. They are interested in the canal, as well as that railway which, I believe, is soon going to be used to convey provisions and arms in transit. At any rate, if there is fighting and if it is going badly, I'm taking off."

So I was not mistaken. White was ready to take flight.

If White was right, we had to expect skirmishes. Was the Commander going to keep us safe and protect us or else were we going to serve as cannon fodder? I had no knowledge of any account in regard to such circumstances.

In the night, in fact, the guard was doubled. The officer had a heavy machine gun installed on the part of the wall that we had erected. It was a frightful weapon which could mow down about ten of the enemy in a few minutes.

It was like this during the following three days. The Commander was cursing and swearing because the reinforcements from Port Said, via the railway, were not coming. We continued the construction of the wall and had increased it to nine feet for greater security.

This was probably a good thing for us, as the real troubles began that evening.

We were concluding our day's work. A reddening sun was completing its plunge behind the dunes, flooding everything with a blood-coloured hue. I was putting away my tools when one of the guards raised the alarm.

"At six o'clock! Troopers!"

All faces turned to the direction indicated. A cloud of dust was rising about a quarter of a mile away and from its extent, we could imagine that the group was a considerable one.

The Commander had appeared, like a jack-in-the-box.

"To your positions! And get a bloody move on!"

He had grabbed a pair of field-glasses and was surveying the horizon. Further ahead, behind the parapet, Cornwell was doing the same.

The two men exchanged looks and the Commander nodded.

"Wait for my signal!" yelled Cornwell. "Wait until they get closer."

We began to make out the troopers. Mounted on fine, swift horses, the men, dressed in black, their faces wrapped in cloth, carried long-barrelled rifles slung across their shoulders. They were perhaps about a hundred, that is to say, three times more numerous than the soldiers of this camp. In the group, we could see wagons, also drawn by horses and on which more massive weapons were fixed.

"Machine guns!" shouted the Commander, who had also seen the weaponry. "Primary objective!"

And Cornwell completed this order:

"Fire! Open fire!"

The guns thundered, the machine guns — we had two of them — began to spit death. Some troopers were thrown under their mounts, but others continued on, shouting and widening their lines in order to form a semi-circle.

The horses were no more than about sixty feet off. The Commander, bent over and gesticulating, was giving his orders. All the soldiers were in action; they were defending the camp with fervour.

"Prisoners! To the munitions!"

We had understood what he was referring to. We had to provide the shooters with ammunition, reload a second gun, so that they could shoot without interruption. For the machine guns, we had to prepare the long replacement strips. Four prisoners were appointed to carry the cases which had been stored in one of the tents.

As they were passing in front of the parapet, the troopers began to launch some sort of explosive weapons, some sort of home-made grenades. The flaming oblong objects were hurled and after a few seconds exploded, releasing bits of metal which pierced the flesh. Other projectiles contained oil and the latter, as it spread, set fire to clothes and material.

The situation was critical. The troopers, swift and skilful, were escaping the soldiers' shots and were causing losses among them. The soldier whom I was providing with ammunition fell, hit in the face by a bullet which went through his forehead. He collapsed totally, on his back, his eyes turned towards a sky that henceforth for him was gone forever. He was not yet twenty years old. I grabbed his gun and began to fire on the assailants. I hit two of them in quick succession. Cornwell, who had observed the scene, did not interfere with me.

These exchanges lasted an eternity. In reality, not more than a quarter of an hour had passed. The Mahdists, since it really must have been them, put their machine guns into action. The infernal noise pierced our ear-drums. Bullets whistled, buried themselves in the earth of the hillock or mowed down my neighbours. Several prisoners were lying beside me, seriously wounded or dead.

"Damn!"

The Commander had been hit in the shoulder. That increased his rage tenfold. He grabbed one of the machine guns and began to shoot frantically. He created disorder among the assailants, but the latter, recovering, sent a group to attack us on the other side.

"Cornwell! Attend to the rear! Wipe out these scumbags for me!"

"At your service, Commander."

Cornwell took a group and dashed to the other end of the camp. They had taken grenades.

The situation stabilized itself for a moment, but the number of the troopers had to get the better of us. The soldiers were collapsing one after the other, and in spite of the losses, the troopers still outnumbered them. We heard Cornwell defending himself for a while, then there was silence in the direction of the northern sector. That greatly worried the Commander, who was well aware that the situation was slipping away from him.

The count was quickly made. There remained only about ten soldiers and hardly as many prisoners. The troopers were still about a good fifty or so.

"Regroup yourselves!" ordered the Commander. "Get your bayonets!"

This was quickly done. We were probably proceeding to hand-to-hand combat. But that was not the case. Some new projectiles spurted out, which claimed some new victims. A more significant device, perhaps launched by a sort of catapult, passed above us.

"A bomb! Hit the ground!"

The explosion was frightful. I had never experienced anything of the sort. The earth shook, cries broke out, and fire ravaged everything. Another bomb exploded, closer still, and I was propelled several feet backwards. Other bodies, dislocated, fell on me and I was, at that moment, as well as buried. Blood ran down my face; the man on me was looking at me with glazed eyes. It was White!

In spite of the humming in my ears, I could hear talking. It was not in English. The bodies on top of me were being moved and I heard the dull noise that a blade makes when it cuts through cloth and flesh. One of them pierced the already lifeless body of White and the point stopped a few centimetres from my right eye. The footsteps and voices receded. I could still hear the noises of the wagons and cases they were transporting, then the tread of the horses going away. Soon all that remained was the smell of blood, of fire and of death.

FRESH START

27

That made the third time that I came close to death. This series would finally come to an end.

When the footsteps, the voices and the horses had gone away, when the dust had settled and the smell of gunpowder was reduced, I gently moved one arm, then the other and finally my legs. The lifeless bodies which were on me seemed to weigh a ton and I had great difficulty sliding sideways to free myself from this human prison, this prison of corpses that were still lukewarm. I looked around cautiously, crawling slowly on the blackened sand.

I was not mistaken, the assailants had disappeared. Having completed their job, namely to sow death in this camp and to carry off the arms and ammunition, they had gone back to celebrate their victory.

So I decided to stand up. My limbs were aching, but I noticed with joy and astonishment also that I did not have the slightest scratch. Once more, I was very surprised by it. After the episode with the sack thrown into the canal, the stab in the warehouse, I really had to admit that a lucky star was protecting me. A lucky star which perhaps was named Mary. Without doubt, we were destined never to be separated and events could break loose around me, situations could be extreme, dangerous and almost fatal, I always ended up getting myself out of them. Destiny was no doubt laid down and I had to do everything to meet up with her again.

I had to act quickly. English soldiers were surely going to arrive shortly and then I would not be able to get away any more. For that was my objective. White was right when he said "if there is fighting... I'm taking off." But there it was, White was dead. Perhaps he would have been happy to know that I was going to put his plan into effect.

I glanced at the bodies which were strewn over this part of the camp. The soldiers were mixed up with the prisoners, the prisoners with some workers from the train who had remained. The ordinary soldiers, the officers, the criminals, all that now no longer had any significance. They were there, motionless, equal in death and unaccountable. For those who were believers, perhaps they had, at the last moments, hoped for a better world. Those had departed with a lighter heart, no doubt. The smell of blood and burnt flesh was unbearable. I vomited several times and was seized by fits of giddiness. I had to make an effort and struggle not to turn on my heels and immediately flee as far away as possible. But first I had to cover my bases.

I took off the small chain that I was wearing around my neck. On the end of it was a little copper medallion. My prison registration number was engraved on it. In this case, number 5214. We had to wear this medallion permanently. Otherwise, penalties could follow. They were very variable, going from the simple reprimand to extended punishment in the case of repetition of the offence. I had spotted, for a moment, a prisoner who was approximately my size and who was hardly much older than I was. However, we had not got on well. I found him among the dead, stretched out on his back, the left half of his face torn off by metallic splinters from the bombs. The unlucky man had fallen into the ditch that ran along the embankment. His wide open eyes expressed astonishment. At first hesitant, I plucked up the courage and undid his chain, replacing it with mine. When the English authorities came to inspect the camp, if they were not too particular, they would not notice the subterfuge. In this way, I had very strong chances of being declared dead. Great news.

"Thank you, old chap. Perhaps you are going to get me out of a bad situation," I murmured in honour of the young man.

Sadness then began to overwhelm me. Sadness, disgust and anger. An explosive mixture which I had to try to control; but was that possible? Could I hold out against that? Could I experience these events without becoming mad? Would I from now on be the same Jeremy Page? Wasn't I different now, to a point such that even Mary would not be able to recognize and accept me? I fell to my knees on the ground, striking the earth with my two fists and uttering cries which resounded in the unusual silence that had succeeded the murderous fury.

I thought the camp was deserted, abandoned by the troopers. Mistake! Two of the assailants were still there, charged with picking up watches, jewellery, money and other items of value. So they were searching the corpses, looking for everything that glittered or that could be sold. The warriors had been alerted by my cries. They were on the northern side, that same place where Cornwell had gone with a group of soldiers. The buildings and the tents had prevented me from seeing them. Convictions sometimes make one commit mistakes with far-reaching consequences. Of these men, covered in cloth from their heads to their feet, I could see only their eyes, black, shining and filled with visceral hatred. I had no weapon; I was still knocked out, and I was not a fighter. I therefore had no chance of escaping them. I raised my hands as a sign of surrender. But that seemed irrelevant, as one of the men, in one leap, was on me, brandishing a sabre with a curved blade. He made a circular arc with his weapon and I owed my escape to nothing but my recoiling quickly. The steel gashed my face from top to bottom, marking a long, blood-red tear from the top of my forehead to the right side of my jaw. I went backwards and fell on my back, at the mercy of my attacker.

"Goodbye, Mary; this time, it's the end…"

Two detonations sounded. The man with the sabre fell on his knees and collapsed in front of me, motionless. His companion executed a sort of spin and fell on his side, shaken by several final jerks. He had a hole in his right temple from which blood was flowing.

"Run, my boy, run quickly before I change my mind."

At the corner of the building, standing by the wall of planks, I saw Cornwell. He was standing askew; his left side was nothing but a large crimson spot. He was holding a revolver in his trembling hand. His face, chalk-white, betrayed intense pain.

"I can help you, sir…"

"Run, I say, run…"

And he was shaking his weapon.

I did not wait for any more. In the officers' tent, I found the Commander, his sword in his hand, lying on a thick rug. A curved dagger was lodged in the middle of his chest. Three assailants were lying beside him. He had fought to the end, not retreating before the enemy. In the drawers of a piece of furniture of varnished wood, I discovered some coins and some notes. I also took away clothes, water and a bag with some provisions, some bread, oranges and dried meat. A half-broken mirror allowed me to look at my wound. Luckily, it was not very deep, but I had to compress it for a while with some cloth in order to stop the bleeding. I took a last look at the camp. Cornwell was lying on the ground. He had saved my life.

The best thing to do was to walk towards the north. I needed to get back to Port Said to try to board a ship. We had done the outward journey in two days and two nights, but I decided to walk in the night and only a part of the day. Only early in the morning, because of the heat, but also in order not to be noticed. I had enough food, I had pin-pointed stops for water and I had, in my canvas bag, a six-shot Pond revolver for cases of dire necessity. I had become cautious with firearms. I remembered the troubles that use of the revolver had caused me at the time of the altercation with Ron and Murdock. But here, I could come face-to-face with Mahdist rebels and I was determined to defend myself.

However, this short journey passed without mishap. At night, I followed the track. In the morning, I walked on one side and the rest of the day, I found a corner in the shade both to conceal myself and to sleep.

So it was that the second day, from my hiding place, I heard the train which came from Port Said and reached the canal. The travellers, probably soldiers, were going to have a strange surprise. The discovery of the camp being imminent, it was therefore becoming urgent for me to leave this country and get back to Europe. However, I had no idea about how I was going to proceed.

On the third day — I had therefore made a lot of progress — I was getting near to Port Said. I then decided to avoid the city which could pose a risk. The English reinforcements were no doubt there and the city must have been swarming with soldiers. So I headed north-west, towards Damietta, which seemed to be a safer place.

Before reaching the city, I passed through a village by the name of Faraskur. I was only one or two miles from Damietta. The inhabitants, on their thresholds, busy sorting out seeds in large containers of earth, looked at me passing by without great astonishment. The unrest reigning in the country must have made them accustomed to meeting strangers. However, a European was approaching on the main street, coming to meet me. He seemed happy to come across me.

"I say, my friend, so where are you going?" he asked in poor English.

The man was about thirty years old, but showed pronounced fatigue on the features of his face. Purple rings emphasized his eyes, he had a bent back and his thinness was almost disquieting.

"That way," I replied, indicating the north.

"Excellent idea; get out of here as fast as possible."

He had no idea how right he was.

"There is going to be fighting," he continued. "The roast beefs" — in that I was to understand he was speaking about the English — "are arriving by the numbers. Big boats at Port Said, artillery, machine guns; the rebels have cause for concern."

From this announcement, I deduced several things. The man did not think I was English and I had done well to avoid Port Said.

"But tell me, you have a lovely decoration, there, on your face."

"Bah, a quarrel of no consequence."

My wound was beginning to close up; it was now a long, brown-coloured diagonal line. Luckily it did not seem to have any infection in it. I would get off with a nice scar. The man did not seem to believe my explanation, but he did not insist.

"And you?" I asked him.

"Oh! That's a long story. And I can't even leave, at least for now. These damned Frenchmen don't want to take me on board."

"Frenchmen?"

So the man was not French either. Perhaps Belgian or Dutch.

"Yes, at Damietta. They are the only ones over there. Explorers, soldiers and even fishermen. But they will go home very soon, there's no doubt about that."

I had heard about that at the camp. The French, finally, did not wish to be involved any more in this conflict and were leaving the British to sort themselves out with the rebels. That had a downside, because when the English regained control of the terrain, they would have ownership of the canal.

"Good luck to you. Perhaps you will be able to get a boat."

"Thank you, sir and good luck to you also."

"Bah…"

And he continued on his way.

These bits of information were very interesting. I picked up the pace and reached the port of Damietta within the next hour. It was the end of the morning and the place was rather busy. Besides the boats, all types actually, which were moored here or anchored a little further out to sea, traders were located on the wharfs. They displayed their products on trestles and a rather large number of buyers were moving around between the stalls. Each one was shouting in order to extol his fruits or his vegetables, his pottery or kitchen utensils. This atmosphere cheered me up; this contact with civilization tended to blur the last unbearable images which still occupied my mind.

I mingled with the crowd. No one particularly paid any attention to me. The place was frequented by Europeans; moreover, I noticed several fellows who looked like sailors. Dressed in short jackets of thick material, their caps pushed down on their heads, they also were coming to shop. I noticed a group of four men, who, standing in a circle, were having a heated discussion. I recognized the French language, which I spoke very little nevertheless. I was trying my chances all the same.

"Messieurs, Messieurs…" I said in my Gloucestershire accent.

The four faces turned towards me.

"Young man?" asked one of them, a bearded man with a ruddy face.

"Je cherche… un bateau."

I was also searching for my words.

One of the fellows smiled and answered me in very proper English.

"You're not a soldier who wants to escape?"

"Oh no, sir, not at all. I am not a soldier."

The man examined my dress. I had slipped on civilian clothes, but that did not mean much. My gash seemed to intrigue him.

"And that?"

"A dispute with a nasty fellow who was giving me some trouble. Nothing serious."

The men spoke in French for a while.

"You're not an old offender either who wants to hit the road? Because we see them from time to time, you know."

"No, no…"

Twice no. Not a very good idea. As if to confirm that the first was a lie. The man did not blink. After all, an English convict was not the concern of a French citizen.

"Go and look further along the wharf. You will see a red and white felucca. Ask for Marius and tell him that Marcello sent you. He will see what he can do. You have any money?"

"A little."

"Well, perhaps that could sort things out."

"Thank you, sir. I am going there directly."

The men continued their discussion and I left the market to go along the wharf in search of the felucca.

28

A footbridge enabled access to the boat. I went on to it without hesitation. The boat was rather quiet. One seaman, on the deck, was rolling up some thick mooring ropes.

"Monsieur, Monsieur…"

The man turned his head slowly, examining me from head to foot for a while. Perhaps from my accent and my appearance he had observed that I was not French, because he immediately expressed himself in rather correct English.

"How can I help you?"

"It's Marcello who sent me."

"Marcello? I see. You have money?"

"A little."

"Let me see it."

I took a few notes from my bag.

The man quickly pocketed them.

"Not much, but that will do. You will do the washing up and the cleaning. That's all right?"

What did washing down the deck and the gangways matter to me? As long as I could get back to my country… and Mary.

"Where are we going?" I was bold enough to ask.

"Toulon. Come back later. We get underway at three o'clock sharp."

"Understood."

And I got back to the wharf, happy with this arrangement that had been so easy. In two or three days, I would disembark on the shores of France.

At the appointed time, I turned up and met the four men I had come across at the market. The felucca took us to a bigger ship anchored quarter of a mile off the coast. It was a rather large fishing boat with nets, winches and pulleys, in short all that was necessary for this activity. The captain, by the name of Clin, showed me a cabin at the end of the gangway and sent me to the second officer, who was none other than Marcello, to let me know the tasks I was expected to carry out.

The trip proceeded uneventfully. The sailors were rather friendly and jovial. Nothing like the strictness and somewhat military coldness of the British ships. Here they spoke loud and clear, readily had a drink and patted one another on the back for the least thing.

These three days went by quickly. I cleaned the deck and the gangways and helped the cook in the kitchen. The latter questioned me endlessly and I had decided to remain rather evasive. I made up a story about a journey to Egypt for personal reasons and a sudden return due to circumstances. The cook seemed satisfied with these explanations and as he was a great talker, he passed on this story to the whole crew.

But the sailors did not concern themselves with my story. It mattered little to them. The captain was making a little money and the sailors escaped cleaning duties. I ate with them, in one of the steerage cabins. The food, in fact, largely comprised meat, but one of the sailors explained to me that due to fishing, he could no longer eat any fish… Not through compassion for these animals, but because the smell and the taste of these creatures sickened him. So we ate pork, beef and chicken, with which the ship's larder was well stocked. Wine also flowed freely, as those fishermen hardly drank any beer.

"Warm beer is good for the roast beefs," they liked to say.

I did not take offence at it. People's tastes and colours differ. In England, there was no lack of anecdotes about French sailors either, but I refrained. Although they were congenial, I had no desire to be thrown overboard.

The trip thus went by without any trouble. The sea was dead calm; the steam engines propelled the ship briskly. We saw some British ships going back to Egypt and some French ships heading for the port of Toulon.

"Oh! They prefer to go back home," Captain Clin remarked.

"Yes, but the canal? We are the ones who built it anyhow," responded a sailor.

"This story is not over!"

But the sailors had other things on their minds. Having left Marseille two months before, they had criss-crossed the Mediterranean Sea, sold their catch in Egypt and were bringing back spices, carpets and cloth, which they were expecting to sell over at a good price. They were also in a hurry to get back to their families.

"And you, my boy," Marcello asked me one evening, "don't you have a girlfriend?"

"Yes, yes, in England."

"And you went off like that, far away from her?"

"I didn't have any other choice. But I'm going to meet her again very soon and we are going to settle down."

"Good. You seem to be a decent chap. But that scar?"

"Bah, a minor matter. That's not important."

I thought about it. Would Mary still want me? This scar was not particularly pleasing to the eye.

"You will have to go across France. That's a long journey. Perhaps you could try to catch a train?"

The evocation of this steam locomotive brought back up memories that were still very fresh. Marcello must have noticed it.

"Is there something wrong?"

"No, no, Mr Marcello. Everything is all right. Just tired."

So, the third day, at the end of the morning, the captain anchored the ship. A launch enabled us, a few sailors and myself, to reach *terra firma*. I was not sorry to get back on dry land. In fact, I was not such a good sailor and the sea, this blue and infinite vastness, really did not attract me.

"There you are," Marcello said to me. "You can set about the continuation of your journey. Good luck!"

"Thanks, Marcello. Everything should be fine."

I left the seamen, who were in search of a tavern to quench their thirst. Now, I had to try to get to Marseille to catch the train there. The continuation of this journey seemed quite clear-cut to me. I would soon be at Cheltenham.

In fact, something else which I did not know, a railway line existed between Toulon and Saint-Charles station in Marseille, a godsend which would save me some time. Then the problem of foreign currency arose. With my pounds sterling, I was a bit worried about proceeding with the purchase of a ticket. Travelling without a passenger ticket had indeed crossed my mind, but I had no interest in being spotted. If I found the means of doing a little exchange, the matter would be settled, without taking any unnecessary risks.

The banking institutions, very few, did not entice me. I could be questioned and I really did not want that. In the vicinity of the station, a rather modest building, some suspicious individuals roamed about. They were not there to catch the train, nor were they awaiting friends. They leaned against the walls of the building or else were coming and going, pacing up and down in front of the entrance. They examined the passers-by sometimes in an insistent manner. I approached one of these strange characters, this time, using my mother tongue.

"Change?"

The man thought for a moment, staring at me slowly.

"Course, sir. Pounds?"

"Yes, forty pounds. Is it possible?"

He must have been accustomed to it, because he responded without thinking this time. I must say that the pound sterling was a recognized international currency and was dominant on the market. It therefore easily attracted covetousness.

The man searched in his pockets and put a wad of notes in my hand. They were francs, very obviously.

"Right like this?"

"Okay. Done. Thank you."

I was incapable of knowing if this sum was correctly valued. I did not know the current rate of exchange. But I suspected that the character had to pick up a more than sufficient margin in the process. I was simply hoping that this sum would be enough for me to travel across the country.

At the station I bought a ticket for Paris. It was a ticket for third-class, the cheapest one. The carriages were open-air and the seats very crude. I was lucky; a train was ready to leave. The usher was moving around on the platform, announcing the imminent departure and helping the first-class ladies to get into their carriages. The signalman had checked and put the train's red tail light into operation and the pantry-man had confirmed the stocking of his restaurant-car. At the front, the mechanical engineer had finished greasing the moving parts of the connecting rod assembly. He had also checked the water level. The driver was keeping his boiler ready for use.

I was settled on a wooden seat in one of the carriages at the back. On my right, a farmer probably, was holding on her knees, in a metal cage, a russet hen which clucked incessantly. On my left, was a man dressed completely in black, his top-hat screwed down on his skull, with a hatchet face and shifty eyes. In his hand, he held a bible with a thick leather cover.

The whistle sounded and we were shaken by the start-up. I heard the regular hissing of the locomotive, the roar of the steam, like the breathing of a giant. It was the first time that I was taking a train. England was rather well equipped with railway lines, but I had never had the opportunity to take them. In Gloucester, important works were underway to develop this means of transportation, but that was warranted by economic and industrial reasons. The transportation of goods was a lot faster by it than by road or the waterways.

The train picked up speed. I had never been moved at such a pace, close to seventy kilometres per hour, it was said. It was a strange, intoxicating sensation. The breeze whipped my face and my eyes began to water. We could smell this chimney odour, of burning coal and that quickly became unpleasant. My neighbours had pulled up a sort of scarf on the lower part of their faces, in order not to breathe in the fine particles which flew about. The phenomenon was amplified when we went through a tunnel, the Mussuguet. There, for close to two miles, while the train had slowed its pace, billows of steam and smoke were blown back directly on the carriages. Obviously now, the carriages without any roof were filled with smoke during this crossover.

In the carriages, the passengers were coughing and spitting. Our eyes red, we got a little fresh air when we left the tunnel. The train had picked up speed again and the smoke now passed above us.

The rest of the trip, up to Marseille, went a little better. I had become accustomed to this new environment. After the meadows and the hills, the woods and the pastures, the cliffs, the rocks and the view of the sea, the train entered Saint-Charles station. With my ticket for Paris, I simply had to change trains and I decided to take a seat in a second-class carriage. The latter was covered and closed, so the smoke would not be able to trouble me. If I had to respond to a check, I could always play on my status as a foreign traveller and make it clear that I had not understood the system of classes very well.

Settled in this new train, for a journey through Lyon and Dijon, I did not wait for a very long time. Departure was quickly set in motion. My neighbours, here, were different. Dressed more elegantly, the middle-class status of the passengers was noticeable. Many of them were reading, with a detached, almost arrogant appearance. Nevertheless, I must have been out of place, with my shabby clothes, my fifteen-day-old beard, my long hair covering my forehead and this scar across my face. I could see beautifully dressed ladies looking at me often, with worried expressions.

The train had taken on its cruising speed. Through the fixed window-pane, I was looking at those lovely landscapes of the Rhone valley. France was a beautiful country. Verdant, sunny, and with a booming economy. That is why I was seriously considering settling there with Mary. We would certainly be very happy there.

At Valence, the train filled up with water. A wooden tower, equipped with a voluminous tank, discharged the amount necessary for the continuation of the journey. The mechanical engineer again did a meticulous inspection of the driving part and the driver took the opportunity to wash his face, because it was already covered with coal dust.

The journey resumed, without mishap, in a rather quiet atmosphere, in spite of the noise from the rotation of the axles and the continuous vibrations. In the end we were lulled and fell into a sort of drowsiness, up to the moment when suddenly, the door of the preceding carriage was forcibly opened. Two individuals, their faces half-hidden by scarves of beige cloth, their heads covered with woollen caps, burst into the carriage. They each held a long, menacing cutlass and one of them began to shout:

"My good people! Just keep quiet and everything will be fine. Open your bags wide and take off your jewellery, your chains, your rings, your watches... Hurry up, hurry up. My friend is going to pass around to collect them. Oh! Oh!"

The travellers were terrorized. They had already heard about this kind of attack in trains. That did not happen very often, very fortunately, but once was enough. Policemen would sometimes move around in the trains, but not in a systematic manner. The two crooks must have known that this train, at least between Valence and Lyon, was not watched. The ladies, trembling, got their jewellery ready. The men offered their signet rings and their watches. Wallets, well-stocked for some, were also part of the haul. Everything happened very quickly. The criminals seemed to be professionals.

"And you, young man," the one who was passing between the rows asked me. "You didn't hear?"

"What? I don't understand..."

"You're screwing with me! No need to speak French to understand what we want."

Then, turning to his accomplice:

"Eh LeBoeuf, that one is taking us for a ride."

"Teach him French, oh, oh!"

I realized that the thief had *carte blanche* to make me obey. Hitting me or perhaps even running his cutlass through my body. I had undergone too much suffering of this sort to be able to accept this new ordeal. Ron and Murdock, the attempted drowning, the brawl in the warehouse, the war in Egypt. No, this was not possible any more. My mind, my body, all my fibres rejected this situation. I thrust my hand into my bag and brought back out the Pond revolver. I stuck the barrel against the nose of the aggressor, pushing up his nostrils.

"Stop, my boy, stop! Hear what I'm saying. We won't get

pissed off."

"Get the hell out! Hurry up!"

My expression must have frightened the thieves. My expression, as well as the revolver.

"Through here! This way!"

"No, no, that's not possible."

"Everything is possible. Move it; put down your bags."

The crooks obeyed without a word. Then, I led them up to the door that opened on to the track. Three men from the carriage had come to lend me a helping hand and had taken away the knives.

"No, no… if you please…"

He was now addressing me politely.

I had opened the door.

"You are lucky; the train has slowed down. It's this or the police."

The two men jumped, rolling over and over on the embankment of the track. They would escape with nothing more than a few nice bruises. I saw them get up and raise their fists in a threatening manner.

All that had happened very quickly. Perhaps I had reacted somewhat brutally by making those men jump from the moving train? Perhaps I rather ought to have informed the inspector? But my reaction had been visceral, I knew; this situation had compelled me to act without really maintaining control over my actions.

Immediately, the passengers surrounded me, heartily thanking me for my bravery. With a revolver, it was not too heroic…

"Thank you, young man, thank you indeed."

"What courage!"

"You are English? I'm not surprised. It is said that English people are very brave."

"So where are you going to? To Paris?"

"You did very well; they did not deserve anything less."

"We should inform the Police when we stop in Lyon, don't you think?"

This suggestion drew me out of my torpor. Inform the Police? Who would come and interrogate me, of course; who would ask me questions about the revolver. That was not a good idea.

"I'm getting off at Lyon. That's where I'm going."

"Very well," said one of the travellers, a very tall man, wearing a soft felt hat. "We will go together to see the station's policemen. My name is Sabre, Pierre Sabre, like the weapon. And you know, what is strange, is that I am from a family of armourers. And you?"

I was caught unawares; I had not thought about the question.

"White. Benjamin White."

"Pleased to meet you. So I will direct you, when we arrive."

And while everyone recovered their valuables, the train continued on its way. No one in the other carriages had noticed anything and we did not see any inspector.

The train finally arrived at the Lyon-Perrache station. It was hissing and spitting steam. On the platform, an usher announced the stopping of the train for a good half-hour, time to refill with water and coal and to check the machinery.

So it is there that I was supposed to get off. That was not in my plans, but staying in this train exposed me sooner or later to an inevitable encounter with an inspector or policemen. The travellers who were continuing the journey, particularly the women, gave me some big waves. I went down on to the platform, following Pierre Sabre, who seemed to know the premises well. He was slipping through the crowd easily, glancing behind from time to time to see if I was following him.

"It's not much further. Over there, on the left. There is an office where we can find policemen."

"All right."

I let Sabre get a little ahead. When we were separated by some

170

travellers, I deliberately changed direction towards the right. The doors opening on to the street were there. I slipped through, beginning to run to get outside. The embankments of the Rhône were nearby, about a hundred yards away at most. Behind me I heard someone calling. "Mr White! Mr White!"

I reached the embankment, going north on it. I had reached the city limits. They would not come to look for me here; moreover, Pierre Sabre had no doubt abandoned the idea of informing the police. The principal actor in the events had taken flight.

The houses were more scattered and the clamour of the city had disappeared. Lyon was a large metropolis and the little that I had observed had impressed me. A lively, noisy, busy city, a sort of hive that hummed with activity. The proximity of the large river, the road, the railway, the famous textile mills, the businesses, all of that greatly contributed to the growth of the city.

Evening was falling. Noticing some isolated shacks, surrounded by meadows, I spotted a gardener's shed. It would do for spending the night. Tomorrow, I would consider the continuation of my journey. But one thing was certain, I had to disappear as quickly as possible, leave this city, by road or by the river.

29

At the crack of dawn, I was on the way.

I proceeded on this rather well maintained road which led away from the city of Lyon. But contrary to England, where one McAdam had invented a new type of surfacing, here, in France, the roads were made with cobblestones or large stones. Regular maintenance was enabled by very good organization and many roadmen. I passed horsemen, merchants' or farmers' wagons, as well as pedestrians. Stagecoaches were a lot rarer since the growth of the railway, like the mail coaches, the service of which had been suppressed.

While I was walking at a good pace for more than two hours and there was almost no traffic now, I heard, behind me, the trotting of several horses, as well as the noise of metal-strapped wheels. A stagecoach!

The team comprised five horses: three in front and two in the second row. The coachman, on his seat, spurred on the horses, as the road sloped up slightly. From inside, however, four travellers had got out in order to lighten the carriage, while the three ladies sitting in front, in the *coupé*, had not left their seats. I raised both my arms.

"Halloo! Halloo!"

The coachman, too busy getting the stagecoach to move forward, did not seem to be concerned about me. As the vehicle was now on a level with me, I questioned one of the travellers who was walking on the side.

"Do you have a seat for me?"

The man hesitated for a moment.

"You need to check with the coachman. I am only a traveller."

"Of course. I understand."

I repeated my question, intended for the driver, this time.

"Where are you going to?" he asked me.

"To Paris."

My appearance must not have reassured him too much. He scrutinized me for a moment.

"And where are you coming from like that?"

"From Lyon."

"With that accent?"

"Yes, with that accent. I am English and I wish to return to my country."

"You have any money?"

"I think so. A little."

"For Paris, that's one thousand, three hundred francs and a three-day journey."

I glanced at my money. The amount was there. As for the delay, I hardly had a choice.

"I have what's needed."

I climbed up on the drawbar and handed over the agreed amount.

"All right; take a seat in the back."

The stagecoach had reached the top of the slope and the travellers took their seats again. Taking a quick look, I observed that there were six persons, men and women, inside. I had counted three female travellers at the front. With the two others already seated in the back, that made a total of twelve passengers, that is to say thirteen persons including the coachman. The roof was loaded with trunks. For my part, I still had my bag, which I kept on my knees.

I slipped on to the back bench. My two fellow travellers, middle-aged men, with sullen expressions, nodded slightly at me. Both dressed in long, thick black cloaks, their faces half-hidden by bushy beards, top hats on their heads, they seemed to be twins.

"Good day," I said smiling, in order to break the ice.

"Hmm…" said one of them.

I was forgetting how I looked, which must have worried them. Perhaps they did not want to engage in conversation.

"Nice weather for travelling, isn't it?"

"Hmm…"

I did not think I would get two sentences from these oddballs. I decided to give it up. Tossed about at the will of the terrain of the road, I immersed myself in contemplating the scenery, very lovely indeed, and I even ended up dozing.

It was the coachman, by his repeated shouts, who dragged me out of this drowsiness.

"Stop! Stop!"

I turned towards my neighbours.

"Where are we?"

"Around Dijon, I think," one of the crow-men deigned to respond.

I was not a real expert on the geography of France, but I had seen several maps of the country before. We had therefore covered close to ninety miles. This stagecoach was moving well. I must admit that the team was up to it.

The day was drawing to its end. The coachman had stopped the stagecoach on an esplanade of beaten earth. Some yards away loomed the outline of an inn. Probably a reconverted posting-house and from then on the property of companies that exploited these transportation services.

So it was there that the horses would be replaced, that we would go to have a meal and spend the night. I was boiling with impatience, in fact, and I was not too happy with this compulsory stop. Would I have been able, with a horse, during the night, to reach another inn further north and take another stagecoach? The matter seemed difficult for me to negotiate, all the more because innkeepers and company officials were reluctant, not to say refused, to hire out their horses for travel at night. There were still on the roads, and generally at night, bands of armed robbers who attacked vehicles and robbed the passengers.

However, the night passed very quickly because I slept straight through, in a dreamless sleep. The place was quiet, the bed comfortable and my roommates — the same ones who were my back seat neighbours — slept like logs.

The following two days of travel passed by without any surprises. The fine weather was part of it and in this month of September, the days were very pleasant. We did not have to put up with heat, which was a change for me from my stay in Egypt. The halts were regular. Quenching our thirst, stretching our legs, relieving ourselves in a meadow, behind a clump of trees, admiring the scenery. Inside, in the *berline,* there were loud and robust discussions and people laughed a lot. No one seemed to be concerned, just like at the front, in the *coupé*, where the three ladies seemed to be having a lot of fun. It was only here, at the rear, on the *rotunde,* that the atmosphere was gloomy. My neighbours did not utter a word.

However, the trip went quickly. In the evening of the third day, after a night spent in the vicinity of Troyes, we saw the towers of Notre-Dame. I already had admired this building on several paintings and I recognized it very quickly. The first houses in the suburbs were appearing and the traffic was suddenly becoming heavier.

"Do you know where the terminal is?"

"At the Luxembourg, young man. At the Luxembourg."

"The Luxembourg? So what is that?"

175

"Oh! Oh! He does not know about the Luxembourg!"

It was the first time that this man was laughing in the space of three days. But he was laughing because he was making fun of me. I adopted a casual tone of voice.

"No, sir, I don't know the Luxembourg. Is that a crime?"

His neighbour, the second crow-man, leaned forward, turning his emaciated face towards me.

"It is a large, magnificent garden. The Senate is located there and Parisians enjoy walking about in it. Several weeks ago, the first electric streetlights were installed there."

"Thank you, sir."

The traveller had suddenly become talkative. He must have been a Parisian. Evoking his city loosened his tongue. So I took advantage of it.

"You seem to know the city well. Do you know the easiest way to get to England?"

"I would recommend the Saint-Lazare station if you prefer the train. Then, go to Le Havre; there you will certainly find a boat."

At that moment the stagecoach stopped.

We had entered the city, through the Boulevard de Port Royal, a magnificent avenue, bordered by hundred-year-old plane-trees. A steam-powered bus had stopped in front of us. Travellers went on and others came off. All around me was nothing but movement, bustle and noise. The very wide roadway was getting rather heavy traffic. There were wagons there, vehicles of all kinds, drawn by mules, horses or even by hand. I observed also steam-powered vehicles which, like this bus, were transporting people in the city. There was a rather large crowd on the pavements. All that was a great change for me from my Gloucestershire countryside, but I immediately loved this city.

30

The stagecoach had let us off in front of the wrought-iron entrance gate of the Luxembourg garden. I paid my respects to the passengers, as well as the coachman, and I then decided to visit this park. I also needed, I think, to take stock of my situation.

The situation with my plans and the situation with my finances.

Taking into consideration the amount that had been required for the Toulon-Marseille train and the Lyon-Paris stagecoach, I should have just enough to get back to my island. In the worst possible case, I could find a job for a few days to earn a little money. Seated on a bench by one of the magnificent paths of this garden, I observed the walkers. A certain zest for life was prevalent. The men, middle-class for the most part, sported beautiful suits or long, wide cloaks and wore their top hats with pride. There were many who held canes, more for style than through genuine necessity. The women wore embroidered dresses in rather bright colours and hats with very wide brims. Their gloves reached up to their forearms and I saw very often small watches hanging from the umbrellas or the parasols they were carrying. On the other hand, I saw very few children.

All these beautiful people strolled about with the greatest unconcern and Paris seemed to me a city where it was good to live. I saw myself, walking with a nonchalant gait, with Mary holding my arm. We would walk along the ponds, admire the fountains and nothing would obstruct our happiness. I drove away these images. They were making me sad. Because, while I had only very little doubt about the reality of seeing Mary again in the near future, the plan for marriage to Perdy presented itself. An insane and inconceivable plan.

The afternoon was drawing to its end. I left the garden, going through it diagonally. Getting information regularly from friendly passers-by, I found the Odeon, went down towards Boulevard Saint-Germain and reached the embankments of the Seine. There, opposite me, majestic and proud, stood Notre-Dame. There also, as in the Luxembourg garden, a rather large crowd thronged the forecourt. Strollers admired the building and many were going in to visit.

Some street vendors were located on one of the sides of the large square. I thought again about those two nice men, Tynderwearth and Woodblock, who followed no other trade but that. Criss-crossing the roads of Gloucestershire and Wales, they moved in like that, from place to place to sell their stuff. I noticed one of them who offered food.

"Fresh bread! Farmhouse *pâté!* Fresh bread..."

On some placards hanging from the posts of his stall, the vendor certified that his products came from established farms along a river called the Bievre, south of Paris. This claim attracted a number of women, probably housekeepers of middle-class homes, but also strollers attracted by this appetizing food.

I had a little loose change left. I chose a quarter pound of a brown bread, which had a strong smell of cereal, as well as a thick slice of *pâté* with herbs and spices.

"You won't be disappointed, little fellow! When you eat it, you'll come back!"

I did not understand much of this language, but I understood that his products should be exceptional.

"Thank you, sir. I will taste them."

And I moved off, biting heartily into this improvised meal.

With my elbows on the low wall overlooking the river, I finished my modest, but tasty meal. Daylight was fading, the sun, iridescent on the surface of the water, reflected orange coloured flashes according to the movement of the waves. Some barges, heavily loaded, powered by steam engines, were going down the river. I followed the majestic curve of the watercourse with my eyes. Downstream, on the right bank, the Louvre and the Tuileries garden. Further on, as I moved away from the embankment, by all logic, I had to be heading for Saint-Lazare station. I knew, that for several years now, at least that was the case in England, the trains ran at night. Trips by stagecoach, on horseback, or even by boat were no longer possible from the end of the day. I had nothing to lose by making inquiries.

Some passers-by showed me the way to go. I took advantage of it, all the same, to go through and admire the Tuileries garden, after having skirted the Louvre. And to think that I had never even visited London, the capital of my own country, which also had to have a thousand treasures hidden away. I promised myself, after my return, if events allowed me, to go there, with Mary, of course.

At present, I had to, once again, change a little money. This time, the station had a window available which offered this possibility. I still had enough pounds sterling and this exchange would easily allow me to pay for my train ticket as far as Le Havre. I must say that I had, in the Commander's tent, laid hold of a rather significant sum. The Commander no longer had any use for it and society indeed owed me that for having condemned me while I still considered that I had acted in self-defence.

The clerk pointed out to me a placard placed on the flap of his window.

"Closed, young man. You need to come back tomorrow, from eight o'clock."

"Sorry, sir... I am... sorry... but..."

Perhaps my ploy would work?

"I must... how do you say? As soon as possible... catch the train. Please, sir..."

The man, who had stood up, hesitated for a moment, hung back up the jacket he had taken from a coat-rack and sat back down.

"Very well, young man. Know that this is exceptional; normally, we don't..."

I put down a wad of notes on the flap, which silenced the fellow. He abandoned his explanations.

He scratched a series of numbers on a sheet of paper, murmured a set of calculations and circled a result. He recorded these numbers in a large notebook with blue-tinted lines and applied a rubber stamp in a box below the writing.

"Here, young man. That makes six thousand, two hundred and forty-four francs for you. Good evening to you."

He closed back his window with a tap, grabbed his jacket and disappeared through a door located behind his tiny office. His affability left a lot to be desired, though, but he had, nevertheless, agreed to change the money. That is all that was important.

Happy with this successful transaction, it now remained for me to find a train and the ticket to go with it.

Night trains were fewer, obviously.

In the night, there are a lot less travellers. But Le Havre was an important destination and two trains did the journey. While first-class offered compartments with beds, second-class had unpadded seats for this night trip. Passengers very often brought blankets with them — because it was never very warm in these carriages — as well as thick cushions to alleviate the discomfort of the seats. I had none of all that at my disposal, but my objective made me forget these inconveniences. Finding Mary again was the priority. I could endure and put up with a lot of things to achieve this goal.

31

A train was getting ready to leave in an hour. A stroke of luck! I only had to settle myself quietly in one of the second class carriages and have a little patience. The journey was to last three and a half hours. Inwardly, I was therefore beginning to bubble. Le Havre, the boat, the disembarkation at Portsmouth — probably — and I would not be more than a few miles from Mary…

In the half-hour preceding the train's departure, the passengers, rather few, came and settled in. These coaches being only feebly lit by a yellowish ceiling light, some people had brought their own candlestick in order to read during the trip. As far as I was concerned, I had no need for any. I was going to take advantage of this journey to sleep and recuperate a little. I had a feeling that I would need all my strength and all my lucidity for the coming days.

An usher crossed the platform and made his announcement:

"Departure for Le Havre, departure!"

He checked the closure of the doors. A strident whistle sounded and the train started to move. The irregular exhalation of the locomotive was heard and thick plumes of steam and smoke mixed together spread over the platform where a few men and women were waving goodbye.

The train left the city of which, in the darkness, only the

indistinct shapes of houses could be seen. Soon, the latter disappeared, giving way to a countryside dimly lit by a new moon. The rhythm of the engine became more rapid and more regular. We were moving on at a good speed. In the carriage, some men were dozing, others were reading the newspaper. There were only two women who were, however, accompanied. I then closed my eyes; I needed to sleep. This journey passed without any major incident, except for a prolonged stop at Les Andelys to put back water in the engine's boiler. But I only opened one eye at that moment, having been alerted by the shouts of the usher.

That is how I reached Le Havre and when I set foot on the platform, I took a huge breath of fresh air. I had, all the same, travelled a long way from Egypt and this hell which still haunted my mind. Cornwell, the Commander, Big Boss, White, Fergus... all these characters who seemed almost unreal to me. Sometimes I wondered if I had really experienced these events. So many things had happened since my departure from Cheltenham manor. My scar was there to bring me back to reality. I was going to make a fresh start, but I had not yet determined my plan of action. I should not forget that I was an escaped prisoner — even if the authorities might have thought that I had died in Egypt — and that Mary was betrothed to Perdy. So many obstacles which were not going to make my task easy. I had to think seriously about all that in order not to plunge headlong into a situation which I would no longer be able to get out of.

It was still dark. In Le Havre station, a restaurant was open in the welcoming hall. It was not a big establishment, but one could eat several simple dishes there and quench one's thirst, which I did without hesitation. The coffee was not as good as Cathy's, but it was a while since I had drunk any and I really appreciated it.

It was still a little early, but I decided to go to the docks, which were located just at the exit of the station. Indeed, the number of travellers continued to increase and those who wished to embark for the United States were more numerous each day. But my focus was on the boats of small or medium size which connected the British Isles. Among the impressive number of ships anchored here, I should no doubt be able to get lucky.

Day had dawned. Activity was still rather quiet on the docks and along the piers. I strolled about, calm and collected, turning up my jacket collar, because the wind from the open sea had grown stronger. It brought with it odours of seaweed, kelp and obviously, fish. These smells that are only found in these particular places.

Going along the warehouses, for a short half-hour, I had the strange sensation of being watched, indeed of being followed. Some bandits up to no good were looking for an easy prey, a traveller to relieve of his possessions? I was gripping the revolver in my bag. I had no intention of using it, but it would be a very dissuasive item in case of a difficult situation.

I looked behind me. Some furtive shadows glided along the walls and I heard the noise of footsteps with erratic rhythms.

There was no doubt. I was well and truly being followed. Not wanting to take any risks and not wishing direct confrontation with these marauders, I sped up the pace, heading towards a more busy section where I would be safe from any attack.

But some other figures, two to be exact, loomed in front of me, cutting off my path. Behind, three shadows approached. Undoubtedly, I had the gift of attracting trouble. I dashed to the left, slipping between warehouses, barrels, boxes and carts. Behind me, the shadows had begun to run.

"Stop, you son of a bitch!"

This voice, behind my back, was familiar to me. No, that was not possible!

I wheeled around.

"Murdock!"

"Yes, Murdock," the voice began again.

The man had approached, and I could now make out his face. There was in his dark eyes this profound hatred which transforms man into a savage beast that nothing could stop.

"You don't believe your eyes? What did you think? That I would rot away in Gloucester waiting for the coppers to catch me? I quickly slipped away here; that wasn't too hard. I even got a job. And then, this morning, I see you land there, out of the blue. What a surprise…"

"Job? Smuggling, you mean."

"Call it what you want. It doesn't matter. Soon, all that won't concern you any more."

I began to get worried. My situation was not great, all the more because the shadows, Murdock's accomplices, were grouped behind him. There were five of them. It was not an equal match.

"I'd like to tell you once again that it wasn't me who informed the police."

"Rubbish! You are a nasty snitch. And you know what happens to snitches?"

A cold sweat began to run along my spine.

"And as for Ron, I didn't want to, but…"

"You're concerned about Ron; he was a fool, anyway. But no more chit-chat, as they say. I'm going to settle the matter."

I quickly pulled out the revolver and shot into the air, to show that I had no intention of taking this lying down. If Murdock came close, he had to think that I would not hesitate to take him down. Which was not true, because I did not want to repeat the events at Gloucester. Murdock must have sensed it.

"No, no, you won't do that, because this time it won't be hard labour, but the hangman's rope… Besides, I don't know how you managed to escape."

I shot in the air again.

The other men, behind, did not dare to come closer. Murdock, himself, continued to move in.

Then, I turned round and began to run. I zigzagged between the warehouses, until the moment when a metal ladder appeared. It was attached to the wall of a brick building. Perhaps I would be safer on the roof of the latter. I climbed the twenty or so rungs. This roof was almost flat and I ran across it. Behind me, Murdock had just appeared at the top of the ladder and launched himself after me, with a long cutlass in his hand.

These warehouses adjoined others of the same kind and their roofs were separated only by twelve to eighteen feet. So, with a leap, I crossed to the following roof and Murdock, suddenly speeding up, was getting ready to do the same. He was determined not to let me get away and I did not care to use my weapon.

I had reached the last warehouse. There was not, this time, to all appearances at least, any further means of escaping. I turned round, facing my pursuer.

"This story ends here, you dirty little brat. I don't know why, but from the beginning, I knew that you would bring nothing but bloody trouble. And as you have an annoying tendency not to want to die for good and all, I'm going to finish the job now."

I had aimed at Murdock.

"You won't shoot. You will end up alerting all the dockers, as well as the police. What are you going to gain from that?"

Murdock was not wrong. I knew it. And he knew that I knew it. Then an idea came to me. A dangerous idea, but an idea. I took a leap, running at full speed towards the side of the roof, which overlooked empty space. Murdock took up the chase. At the very moment the edge drew near, I threw myself flat on the roof, sideways, stopping my slide a few inches from the edge. Murdock was surprised and opened his eyes wide with astonishment at this unexpected trick. I stretched out one of my legs, hooking him by his ankle. He lost his balance and swung forward, cursing.

"Damn!"

A dull noise alerted me that he had fallen to the ground.

I leaned over towards the wharf.

Murdock was lying on his back. He had ended his fall on some metal spindles pointing towards the sky. One of them had gone through and through at the level of his abdomen. A large bloodstain extended over the material of his jacket. He was shaken by some jolts. Then he stopped moving, his eyes having lost all brightness. I was finally rid of this crook, although I was not really happy with this tragic end. I would have preferred to see him end his days behind bars and, especially, convey to the Police, the exact truth of the events in Gloucester.

I found another ladder to climb back down. But on the wharf, Murdock's accomplices were rushing forward, shouting and I heard the strident police whistles.

I had little chance of escaping. I stopped for a moment, tightened my bag firmly against me with the strap provided and plucking up my courage, I dived resolutely into the black water.

32

The water was cold. My bag and my clothes were not really making it easy for me to swim. I moved forward quietly and went around a boat. I held on to the hull, listening attentively.

"But where did he disappear to?" asked one voice.

"He can't be far."

"What a little bastard; we have to find him."

"We'll skin him alive."

"Let's not stay here; the police will come."

"Let's separate and search the warehouses."

"You, Le Sec, deal with the boss. Hide the body."

The voices moved away. These men were accomplices of Murdock, who therefore seemed to be the boss. He had formed another team of gangsters, here, in Le Havre, and must have been running his usual little business. But this time, for him, the exploit had ended. If the Police had to come, it was better that I move away. Moreover, staying like this without moving, I was rapidly getting cold. I resumed my swimming, as quietly as possible, slipping from boat to boat. So I went a rather long distance from the scene of the incident and I was able to climb back on to the wharf. The wind had strengthened again and I began to shiver with cold. I needed to take shelter quickly or find a ship. Going back up along the estuary, I noticed a merchant ship of modest size. About one hundred and twenty feet long, fitted with two strong sails and a metal chimney, it seemed to match what I was looking for. Further, its name, *Adventure*, gave me confidence. Compatriots!

I crossed the access bridge and called out several times.

"Hello! Is anyone there?"

I repeated my call and was patient for a moment. Finally, some footsteps were heard on the stairs of the passageway and a man appeared. Tall, rather thin, a cap on his head, he stared at me with his small, very light eyes.

"That's any way to wake up people?" he said, obviously annoyed.

"Sorry, sir, I'm looking for a ship, to get to England. I have some money."

He quickly inspected me from head to foot. His face relaxed.

"You are soaked. You swallowed water?"

"You mean..."

At that point, some whistles sounded on the wharf. The man turned his head a moment, then stared at me again. My scar must have intrigued him.

"Troubles?"

"Some thieves. They tried to rob me."

"That's rather frequent here. You shouldn't stroll around alone, so early in the morning."

The whistles drew near.

"Go down and hide yourself. I will take care of the rest."

I did not have to be told twice. I went down the stairs two at a time, went along the corridor and into the cargo hold and I hid behind some wooden boxes. I took off some of my clothes, which were soaked.

I heard the seaman talking with some policemen on the wharf for a while. I could not catch the whole conversation, but it was an issue about a fugitive and a man found dead. The seaman gave some responses that I did not grasp very well, but the tone of his voice was one of astonishment. The voices finally fell silent and footsteps moved away.

"Psst, my boy, you can come back up."

The man was waiting for me on the deck.

"Sulliver. Nathan Sulliver. I am the skipper of this boat. Two other mates are still asleep. Last night they were in town and scoured all the taverns. I don't even know how they managed to find their way back. Oh! Oh!"

"Benjamin. Benjamin White."

"Very well, Benjamin, you seem like a good fellow to me. And these Frenchy bandits trying to give you trouble... Well, welcome aboard. We are getting ready to sail in an hour for Portsmouth."

"Portsmouth? That's more than I hoped for."

"That's where you're going?"

"Yes, exactly. I couldn't have found anything better. It's extraordinary luck. You need to tell me how much I owe you."

"Nothing at all, my boy. Helping a compatriot in trouble is a duty. You don't owe me anything."

"I don't know how to thank you."

"Then don't thank me. I think that in such a situation, in my place, you would have done the same. Am I wrong?"

"No, you are right."

"Well, that says it all. Make use of the trip, but you will see, it won't be very long. I have a new engine which makes this barge as fast as the wind. Go to the cook and he will find something for you to eat and give you some dry clothes. You look tired."

In fact, the latest incidents had turned me upside down. This encounter with Murdock, this tragic end, the fear of being caught again...

I spent the following hour in the company of the cook. He was not a full-time cook, because the crew on this boat was rather limited. He was a seaman whose culinary talents had earmarked

190

him for this supplementary duty. He was a Scotsman with a guttural accent, a solid gait and an honest look. He loved to cook fish, in all shapes and forms. While working at his stoves, McGlevet spoke to me incessantly about his native Highlands, the Isle of Skye, Portree in particular, where he had lived for a long time. It is there he had acquired a liking for navigation and for fish. I made the acquaintance of two other sailors, Trent and Blackmore, two Welsh nationals, somewhat rough men, but in fact very friendly. This ship was a true condensation of the United Kingdom.

The trip lasted only about twelve hours. One hundred and forty miles separated us from Portsmouth and the boat, at a steady pace, covered the distance rather quickly. The October sea was a little rough; a south-west wind rushed into the Channel, but the crossing was on the whole fairly calm. During the voyage, we met quite a number of warships.

"Nasty business," Sulliver confided. "This business with Egypt is not over. It seems that the Mahdist rebels are rather tough."

"That's what I have heard as well."

The army was therefore still dispatching reinforcements because the situation was going on and on. But, to tell the truth, this did not bother me. The vague desires of our leaders for distant foreign lands had really never interested me. There was so much to be done in our beautiful country that I did not understand these outlays of money and of human resources for these particular causes.

"Here we are at home, my boy. Look at these magnificent coasts."

The cliffs of chalk stood majestically several miles away. A cool breeze had begun to blow, but had dissipated the clouds which were trailing above the earth. Some sea-gulls, taking us for a fishing boat, had approached.

"And now, what are you going to do?"

"Some business to settle, Mr Sulliver. And then get married, no doubt."

"Oh! Oh! My congratulations! A pretty fiancée?"

"The most beautiful, Mr Sulliver, the most beautiful."

At Portsmouth, the authorities did not give any trouble. Sulliver was well known and the disembarkation took place without incident. The port officers barely took a look at the boxes placed in the hold, which the sailors were now going to carry on to the wharf, then into the warehouses.

We said our goodbyes.

"Goodbye, Benjamin. If you need a hand or if you are looking for work, you can count on me. Don't hesitate. Unless you're leaving this region?"

"I don't know yet, Mr Sulliver. But I will not forget your offer."

And I went into the town to find a bite to eat.

I was going to make a fresh start.

REVELATIONS

33

Night had fallen, but the taverns in the town centre were open. Behind the yellowish window panes the lights of paraffin lamps gleamed. It is in one of these establishments that I gulped down hot soup and savoured some chicken breasts. I had settled myself in a corner of the large smoke-filled room. Dealers, craftsmen, and some dockers came there, at nights, to spend some time chatting among friends and drinking ale. I preferred to remain circumspect, not attracting any attention. Here, no one knew me and all the same, I was depending on my appearance for avoiding any unpleasant encounters.

I found lodgings in an unprepossessing hostel, at some distance from the town centre, opposite the docks. The establishment was neat; the concierge, an old, baby-faced woman, rented me an attic room on the second storey. The hostel was not very full; I saw two travellers or travelling salesmen who were talking, leaning on the bar, and drinking Irish whiskey. I greeted them quickly and disappeared into the room. I intended to leave very early. I had paid in advance.

The sun had barely risen when I was already on my way. In this season, the days got shorter rather quickly and I was determined to cover as many miles as possible each day. According to my calculations, I should be able to reach Cheltenham in the space of five or six days, at the rate of about twenty miles per day. I preferred not to take stagecoaches or the train which linked Portsmouth to Gloucester. A journey on foot would be longer, but a lot safer. Moreover, I was not following the busy main roads, but cut through paths in the woods or meadows, keeping a north-west direction as my aim.

Leaving Portsmouth, I quickly traversed a countryside of pastures with widely scattered housing. Here, there were deserted footpaths and a very low population density. Then came a lovely forest of beech and birch trees. I was beginning to come to life again, having come close to death several times... These trees were life. These smells, this undergrowth, this scent of leaves mingled with mushrooms and the gentle singing of the brooks running beneath the moss... Soon, at the end of the road, Mary, who would open her arms to me and with whom I would leave for other shores.

I reached Winchester, at least its vicinity, in two days. I had taken deserted paths, gone through meadows and woods. I had even skirted the villages of Sheffield and Waltham. It is only at Owslebury that I risked entering a farm to buy a little food. The farmer, quite happy to earn a little money, provided me with home-made bread, cheese, some eggs and duck *pâté*. I was at ease for a while.

So I avoided the town and continued my journey towards Swindon. There again, I skirted the hamlets each time that was possible. The terrain was less wooded and hillier; I was more exposed. But I was not worried, however, because no one in this area knew me. Still I might have been recognized.

I held my course, I kept up my pace and I was not tired. The harsh climate of Egypt and the rough jobs had toughened me up. And my will was directing me, now a permanent pressure in me that guided each of my footsteps. The weather was merciful. In spite of it being the early days of November, the temperature, strangely, was rather mild and the rain had spared me. At night, I always found a barn, or a shack in which to take shelter. I got a well-deserved rest there and I slept straight through, with no dreams or nightmares.

After Swindon, I had two more days of walking. Once again, I avoided the villages, left Cheltenham in the south and went around the north of Prestbury. From having worked in the woods adjacent to the manor, I knew how to find several shacks to make a final stop there. These woods belonged, partly, to Lady Cheltenham and it was even possible that I would find Cadell there, getting the wood ready for winter. That is what we had done together the previous year.

I found such a shack. The rickety door was not closed. Inside, were several foresters' tools, a big jacket hanging on a nail, a small pile of wood for preparing a fire and a few bottles of cheap whisky which I recognized immediately. I smiled in the dark. This good man Cadell, what a surprise I was going to give him.

In the first place, though my plan was not quite worked out, I would contact the gardener. He alone should be let into the secret. I knew I could count on him. I should, for the time being, indicate my presence to him alone. Cathy, Lauren and Joanna should not know. As for Wickney, that idea had not even crossed my mind.

It was late. I had a bite to eat and decided to get some sleep. Sleep on it, they say. I would roughly put together my plan the next day, with a clear head.

It was the rays of light, through the poorly joined planks, that woke me. I had slept like a log and the night had not brought me any new ideas. I first had to get some fresh air and breathe deeply while taking a walk outside.

I walked for a few minutes in the vicinity, taking advantage of magnificent nature. Each morning is a new birth, like a new life taking its first steps. Each morning is the beginning of a new story. I was going to have to write it and take it to its conclusion.

Some noises, at first faint, then more precise, were heard.

Leaves crackling under footsteps, branches being pushed aside by a hand. Cadell? Did I have it right? I was getting ready to go and meet the newcomer when something held me back. An apprehension, a suspicion at first indescribable, but which gained momentum. I took shelter behind a clump of trees and waited. A man appeared. He had a stern face, framed by long black hair. He was of average build and was wearing a long, very thick grey cloak. He was moving forward with a determined step. I decided not to move. I did not know this individual. Who could he really be? He was aware of the existence of this shack, so there was a great possibility that he was coming from the manor or that in some way, he was working for Lady Cheltenham. Perhaps it was this famous Nolan, the new stableman, about whom Cadell had spoken the last time I passed through the estate.

The man had gone into the hut. I vaguely made out his figure through the little side window. He seemed to be bustling around the fireplace. He did not stay inside for very long. He came back out, a smile on his lips this time, and left as he had come. Strange visit. And I did not like this expression he had when he was coming out. His expression was that of a person who was preparing a dirty trick and who is pleased with it. I had to clarify that because I felt trouble coming.

The visitor having gone away and having disappeared from my sight, I checked the shack, particularly around the fireplace. At first sight I did not notice anything particular until my eyes were attracted by one of the stones at the base of the hearth. It was not really in place, as if it had been displaced, taken out and then put back. I gently lifted it. There, under the groove for this stone, a cavity of a few inches, I spotted a small metal case. I was very intrigued.

What was it then?

I took the case from its recess and opened it. A ring, apparently gold, fitted with an emerald green stone, lay in it.

197

I tried to understand what could have really driven this man to come and hide this ring here. A thief who would have hidden his loot? It was a possibility. A little too simplistic for my liking. There was something there which was still escaping me or which I did not dare to think was true. No, it was not possible! This shack was used essentially, not to say solely, by Cadell. Placing this piece of jewellery here could be an attempt to have him accused of a theft that he had not committed. This stranger was no doubt the famous Nolan and perhaps he was trying to have Cadell dismissed. But then why?

Decidedly, there were some strange things happening at the manor. From now on it was a necessity; I had to alert the gardener before he fell into this trap. I took the box and hid it outside this time, in a little hole at the foot of a beech tree that I could easily identify. The stranger would be wasting his time.

I waited until evening to take action. This incident had persuaded me to act as quickly as possible. Cadell was in danger; I had to give him some help.

When night fell, I set off. These woods were half a mile from the estate; ten minutes would be enough to get me there.

I entered the grounds through the north side. Through the lawns, staying parallel to the main garden path, I was going to see the gardener's lodgings very soon.

A strange sensation then overwhelmed me. Finding myself again in these grounds, after an absence of six months, more than a year after I was employed, really affected me. I had spent some good times here, in the company of Cadell, Cathy and her friends, Lady Cheltenham, who had always been kind to me and with Mary, obviously, who always occupied my mind and my heart. To see her again filled me with joy and also anxiety. Would her feelings towards me have changed? Would she accept my new appearance with this frightful scar across my face? Would she take the risk of sharing life with a convicted prisoner who had escaped from his gaolers? Would her love for me be stronger than all that? I was scared, I really had to admit to myself.

I saw the stables. The adjoining lodging was faintly lit by a paraffin lamp. Nolan was awake. An angry growling was audible and I heard stirring in the stableman's lodgings. The latter must have enlisted the services of a dog for surveillance of the premises. That would not have been easy to negotiate. In fact, Lady Cheltenham had got rid of the ones her husband used for hunting. Nolan certainly must have insisted on having one with him.

I quickened my pace. I really was not looking forward to an encounter with a mastiff. In the vicinity of Cadell, nothing. The shack was plunged into complete darkness. I approached stealthily and discreetly opened the door which, luckily, did not squeak on its hinges.

I waited for a moment on the threshold, catching my breath and letting my eyes get accustomed to the dimness. Cadell had not gone to bed; his bed was empty. Strange. I had no time to think about this problem; I felt the cold metal of the barrel of a rifle placed on the nape of my neck.

"Don't say a word, don't move. Go forward slowly."

Cadell's rough voice was commanding. He would not hesitate for one instant to blow my brains out.

"It's me, Jeremy. Jeremy Page. Cadell…"

There was hesitation, an imperceptible movement of the weapon, the pressure of which relaxed slightly.

"Jeremy? Jeremy is dead! So what are you telling me?"

"Cadell, I'm back. It's really me."

I took a big step forward and turned around. Cadell had lowered the rifle, lit a lamp and feverishly brought it closer. He ran the beam of light several times in front of my face. I had lifted up a lock of my hair.

"For Christ's sake! It's really you! How is this possible?"

"It's a long story, Cadell; it's a long story."

And the man squeezed me in his arms as a father would do to his son. Tears ran down his cheeks.

We spent part of the night telling our stories.

For my part, I told him everything. The solicitor, the alcohol smuggling, the trial, the departure for Africa, the hard labour, the attack by the Mahdist rebels, my escape to Europe, the train, the stagecoach, the death of Murdock and my arrival here.

"There, Cadell, it was a long journey, but here I am."

"I gave up hope. Owl, whom you met, had sent me some information. According to the last news, the prisoners and the soldiers in the camp in Egypt had all been killed, well almost. There was one survivor, an officer, one Cornwell, I think."

This information worried me. Cadell must have noticed it.

"A problem, laddie?"

"This Cornwell was the officer who supervised us. He saw me leave the camp. So he knows that I survived. I thought he was dead. This is not such good news."

"But he let you leave. So why would he set the police after you now?"

"That's right, Cadell, that's right."

That comment gave me hope again. Cornwell perhaps had decided to forget about me.

"And here, Cadell? How is Mary?"

I had not yet breathed a word to him about Nolan.

"Mary is not doing too well. Since you left, she has been hardly recognizable. Sad, has lost weight and is ghastly pale. She is often ill and doesn't always go to school. The prospect of her upcoming marriage to Perdy hasn't helped."

"I absolutely must see her."

"That is not very advisable. If you are caught, this time, it will be the hangman's noose…"

"I know. I'll take the risk. And this Nolan?"

200

"No good. A strange fellow, shifty and sly. I don't understand how Lady Cheltenham hired him. But I gather it's on the recommendation of Sir Garmond."

"Well, Cadell, the problem is more serious than that."

"What do you mean?"

"I saw this Nolan this very morning, at the shack. I think it's indeed him."

A brief description of the individual confirmed that it was really the stableman.

"He came by to hide a piece of jewellery under one of the fireplace stones," I continued.

"A piece of jewellery?"

"A gold ring set with an emerald. No doubt a piece of jewellery belonging to Milady."

"To Milady?"

"Yes, Cadell. This is only an assumption. But suppose for a moment I saw right. Who will be accused of this theft?"

In spite of the feeble light dispensed by the lamp, I saw that Cadell was livid. He swallowed a good swig of his whisky.

"Damn! I will make him pay for that!"

"Don't be hasty, Cadell. I think that it's better to let it take its course. I have moved the ring. If Nolan wants to carry out his plan, it could well be that it may turn against him."

"I say, laddie, there's something inside there," remarked Cadell, tapping my head.

"But, all the same, I would like to understand why this Nolan is so intent on getting you dismissed."

Cadell thought for a moment, his forehead creased by a big wrinkle.

"You know, laddie, it's an old story that I had somewhat set aside, but with what you just told me…"

I was all ears, intrigued and concerned at the same time.

"That goes back more than two and a half years, now. Mary's

father, Lord Cheltenham, had a bad fall from his horse and was killed. It was a terrible tragedy here, even the newspapers made it their headlines."

I remembered this article that I had caught a glimpse of when we were working in the grounds.

"And?"

"I have always thought that it was not an accident. Lord Cheltenham was an excellent horseman. He had served in the army as a Light Dragoon; he knew how to stay up on a horse, believe me. It is pretty much at that time that Sir Garmond appeared. He took advantage of the widow's distress to endear himself and to establish connections. Sir Garmond owns lands, forests and recently some plots where the subsoil seems to conceal coal. No doubt he wants to increase his domain and this marriage between his son Perdy and young Mary is an unexpected opportunity."

"You don't think, however, that …?"

"We can think anything. I had told Wickney about it in confidence, but he didn't take me seriously. So I am the only one here who believes that Lord Cheltenham's death is not an accident, but a murder. The perpetrator, through a third party, could well be Sir Garmond."

I was astounded. But that seemed so credible. That could also explain why Nolan was trying to get Cadell dismissed. This same Nolan who had been hired on the recommendation of Sir Garmond.

"You need to get some sleep now, laddie. I will wake you up before sunrise."

"No, Cadell, I'm going to pay Mary a visit. Now."

"But…"

"See you later, Cadell."

I had already crossed the threshold of the shack.

34

A glance at the stables reassured me. The light was out. Nolan had to be asleep this time. On the contrary, Cadell would surely have difficulty closing his eyes. I heard a horse neigh, but this time, the dog did not reveal itself.

I quickly slipped up to the back door. It was locked from the inside, but I knew how, by sliding the tip of my penknife between the sixth and seventh planks, to fly the latch, a trick Cadell had shown me. That made just a slight 'click' which did not run the risk of waking up anyone. But I remained cautious. I passed in front of the kitchen. My heart sank for a moment. Cathy, Lauren and Joanna had been so nice to me. Although they had not supported me during the police investigation, I did not bear any grudge against them. They had surely been forced to express a prescribed version of the facts.

I quickly cleared the corridor, moving forward stealthily and listening attentively. The building was completely silent. That was striking, almost alarming. I made a stop at the foot of the staircase. I was almost in sight of my goal, still a few yards to go... I climbed the steps, making several pauses to listen to this heavy silence. Nothing, still nothing. It was almost as though the house was deserted.

On the landing, I went by the door to the library on my left. On the right, a corridor, identical to the one on the ground floor. This time, the doors gave access to the bedrooms, Lady Cheltenham's and Mary's, the others being unoccupied. Mary's was the very last, at the end of this long dark corridor. Luckily, the moon, almost full, diffused its soft light through the large windows that overlooked the main courtyard.

I stopped, my heart pounding. I felt like I was out of breath, although I had not made any particular effort. My hands were trembling, my whole being was quivering with a strange sensation of happiness mingled with fear. I believed for a moment that I was going to make an about-turn.

Taking a deep breath, trying to measure the risk that I was taking at this moment, I gently turned the handle and moved forward in the semi-darkness. A paraffin lamp, almost turned down to its lowest, shone on an occasional table. The half-drawn curtains allowed a little moonlight to come in. The large bed was facing me. I heard the steady breathing of the young girl and my heart vibrated even more intensely. I drew closer and gently seating myself on the edge of the bed, I contemplated the lovely blonde curls, which looked like a river of diamonds. I gently caressed her pale cheek.

"Mary, Mary, it's me… Jeremy."

She stirred slightly, uttered a sigh and turned her face to the other side.

"Mary, Mary…"

"Hmm…"

"It's Jeremy; I'm back…"

"What…?"

This time, she raised herself halfway, opened her big, drowsy eyes wide and, in spite of the semi-darkness, tried to make out my face.

"Jeremy? But you…"

"No, no, I'm really here, very much alive; you aren't dreaming."

Mary oscillated between astonishment, fear, joy and stupor. I was seeing it in her eyes. I continued to caress her cheek gently and kissed her on her forehead.

"I came back; it's finished Mary, the nightmare is over. We are together, again."

Mary was scrutinizing me. My hair, my beard, my cut. I realized then that I had taken an insane risk. Mary ran the risk of not recognizing me and could, at any moment, begin to yell and alert the household. But her eyes softened, a smile lit up her face and she kissed me on my lips.

"Jeremy, you're here. I knew it; I have dreamed about this scene so often. We're not going to be separated any more this time."

"Yes, Mary, we will never leave each other any more."

And she dropped her head against my shoulder, her body shaking with sobs. All the nervous tension that had accumulated in her for months had just suddenly subsided. Happiness, though accompanied by tears, was taking its course. The desire for us to embrace there and then, to merge our bodies, deprived of love for so long, was strong, but there was a great risk of being caught.

We remained like that for a while, savouring these moments of completeness, of sharing and rediscovered joy.

Mary started to speak again.

"But how did you do it? Everybody thought you were dead. And this scar, my God."

"That was the price to pay. I had escaped from this confounded camp and I had to defend myself."

"That doesn't matter, you know; scar or not, you are still Jeremy, the one I love so much."

"Oh Mary, I was so afraid."

This time, it was my turn to relieve myself of all this nervous tension and I began to sob.

"You must have lived through some difficult times."

"Worse than that, Mary. Worse than that. All the more because I did nothing but defend myself. Those two nasty characters wanted to get rid of me and I had no choice, you know."

"I believe you, Jeremy, I believe you."

I don't know how long we stayed like that, against each other, looking through the window at the moon going down on the horizon.

It was Mary who roused us from our delightful torpor.

"You need to leave. Wickney will be up at the crack of dawn, like every day."

"I'll be on my way. But we have to decide on a place to meet again. I have some important, serious things to tell you."

Mary raised an anxious face.

"You're scaring me, Jeremy."

"What I have to tell you is important. You're not going to school now?"

"No, I was too weak and my mother preferred to keep me here for some time."

"Can you at least go outside?"

"Yes, I'll pretend I have to get some fresh air. I will say that I'm feeling better and walking in the grounds will do me some good."

"Agreed, that's an excellent idea. Let's do that then."

And we agreed on a time and place to meet again.

35

I had passed back to see Cadell and had left him before morning. I had a lot of trouble restraining him because he wanted to wring Nolan's neck, immediately. I had to fight hard to explain to him that confusing Nolan would bring about a better result than doing away with him. Cadell would have spent the rest of his life in prison and nothing would be settled. Concerning the dog that I had heard barking, he explained to me that it was a watchdog, specially trained for that. Nolan fed it red meat exclusively to get it accustomed to the taste of blood and he had trained it for attack. It was necessary to be on one's guard against this dog, which could prove to be dangerous, just like its master. Lady Cheltenham was not very favourable to the presence of this animal, but Nolan had insisted, arguing that this beast could keep a thorough watch over the estate and ensure the security of the property.

"I don't like that dog," Cadell had told me. "It has a shifty look. Beware of it and above all, never turn your back on it."

I had spent the morning in the shack, which served as a shelter and a hiding-place for me. I was on the lookout for the slightest noise, because Nolan could turn up at any moment, for one reason or another. In short, I was not at ease.

It was at the beginning of the afternoon, after a quick meal made from some provisions supplied by Cadell, that I set off for the grounds. Well beyond the lake, at the north-east end of the property, in a less accessible area, I was to meet Mary again. Images of the night before came back to me. What happiness in this reunion! Nothing more from now on could separate us and prevent us from living our love.

I met Mary as a blazing sun lit up the meadows, still white with the morning's frost. We were at the end of the grounds, logically safe from any unpleasant surprise. Sitting on a blanket that I had brought, our collars turned up to protect us from the chilliness, I was still hesitant about how to address the issue.

I told her, in detail, about my misadventures which had occurred since my departure for Gloucester, at the time of my uncle's death.

Mary only knew this story in a very general way. So she was most attentive when I gave her a very detailed account.

"But, your uncle, what then?" she asked me.

"Murdock and Ron."

"As with Brackett."

"Yes, as with Brackett. But those two won't harm anyone else any more."

"And this camp in Egypt?"

I told her about my life in the camp. She was upset by it.

"But all that is terrible."

"That's the word, terrible. The work was hard, under overwhelming heat. The officers were inflexible and moreover, the Mahdists attacked us. I was the only survivor, well almost."

"Almost?"

"According to Cadell, who gets his information from his friend Owl, whom I mentioned to you, one officer survived."

I had forgotten Cornwell and there he was coming up again. My anxiety resurfaced.

"You think that he…?"

"I don't know. Anything is possible, the best and the worst. I don't know what to think. That's why, for the moment, I have to remain very discreet."

I talked about my journeys by boat, by train, by stagecoach, on foot and my arrival here, at Cheltenham, the previous day.

"But you, Mary, you haven't told me much."

"You know, since you left, nothing much has happened. Nolan replaced you, Sir Garmond came here several times and my mother has arranged my marriage to Perdy for next spring…"

At that moment, Mary began to cry and snuggled against me.

"This marriage will not happen, Mary. Trust me."

"But what can be done? We can't compete, you know that."

"We have to get away, far, very far."

"But I can't leave my mother, Jeremy."

"All the same, she is forcing you to get married and she didn't support me at the trial."

"I know, Jeremy. But we can't blame her. It's this Sir Garmond, which whom she is infatuated."

"Exactly. I wanted to speak to you about that."

The time had come. I could not keep my doubts to myself any longer.

"It's about Sir Garmond," I continued. "I have discussed it with Cadell. You know that he is always a wise counsellor and is rarely wrong about people."

"That's true. In spite of his bad temper, I have to give him that."

"Cadell thinks that your father's accident was not one."

Mary turned ghastly pale. Some little nervous twitches quivered her left cheek. She was waiting for me to continue.

"Cadell thinks that it was murder, premeditated, of course. Sir Garmond gets rid of your father, appears as if by magic and gets close to your mother."

"That's not possible! You're lying!"

Mary began to beat on my chest. For a moment, I allowed her time for her anger to subside.

"Mary, these are only assumptions, but they could explain certain things."

"I don't believe it, no, that's impossible."

"Your father was an excellent horseman. How do you explain his being killed like that, during a simple ride?"

"I don't know, I don't know. I don't know any more."

"And Sir Garmond who appeared at just the right moment? And this marriage? Sir Garmond is increasing his domain. Don't your mother's woods contain coal? That would be an excellent operation for this businessman, don't you think?"

Mary had regained her composure and was now thinking about the situation more lucidly.

"But even if there was an inkling of truth in all that, nothing can be proved, you agree."

"That's not so certain."

"How so?"

"Cadell intends to make Nolan talk. This strange stableman surely knows a lot more about it than he makes it appear. You know that he prepared a trap to get rid of Cadell?"

Mary opened her eyes wide. All this information, all at once, was a lot.

I then told her about the matter with the piece of jewellery concealed in the shack.

"Cadell is waiting until he is accused. That won't be long. Then the trick must be foiled and it must be demonstrated to your mother that Nolan is conspiring and acting on behalf of another person, Sir Garmond, in this case."

"All that seems dangerous and risky, Jeremy."

"We hardly have any other means. When this first phase is settled, I could finally reappear and regain your mother's confidence. In this way our love will no longer be impossible."

"Jeremy, hope to God you're right!"

We embraced for a while. Our lips met and time, once again,

seemed suspended, putting us in a safe place, out of the world, there where nothing could affect us.

Some footsteps could be heard at a lower level, behind a clump of nut trees.

"Someone is coming," whispered Mary.

"Well, let's not stay here."

We left the spot, slipping discreetly into the undergrowth.

"Search! Search!" uttered a voice. "Search!"

"Belzebuth!" Mary said to me.

"Belzebuth?"

"Nolan's dog. Let's run."

Behind us a stampede could be heard. The dog was rushing forward at full speed; soon it would be upon us. And suddenly, I saw it. Muscular, with an enormous square head, gaping jaws, from which protruded fangs sharpened like daggers. A mass of more than one hundred and twenty pounds against which nothing could be done. The animal made a leap in the direction of Mary, who had turned her back to it. In a few moments, it would be on her and would tear her to shreds if no one intervened. Nolan was not visible at that moment. He had to be lower down, near the gravel path. I did not take time to think. I had taken the revolver out of my bag and fired in the direction of the beast. The animal, hit in the head, collapsed all of a sudden, was shaken by some erratic movements and stopped moving. I grabbed Mary by the hand and dragged her as fast as possible far from this place. It was essential that Nolan should not see us.

36

Wickney was standing as straight as an arrow in front of the sitting room.

"My Lady?"

"Wickney? A problem?"

"Nolan is here, My Lady. He wishes to speak to you."

Lady Cheltenham put her book down on an occasional table covered with an embroidered doily.

"Very well, Wickney. Let him come in."

Nolan was standing slightly behind, his woollen cap in his hand and looking contrite.

"Come closer, Nolan, come closer. To what do I owe your visit?"

Nolan had moved forward and stood in front of Lady Cheltenham. Obviously, he did not know where to begin.

"Well then, My Lady, there is a problem, in the grounds."

"A problem? Nothing serious I hope."

"You will judge for yourself, My Lady."

"Tell me, Nolan, tell me."

"One or more strangers tried to enter your property, this afternoon."

"Well, it's good of you to call my attention to it."

"I was making a round when Belzebuth..."

"Oh yes, that dog."

Lady Cheltenham did not like that dog.

"Belzebuth detected the presence of people. He has a highly developed sense of smell, you know, a watchdog. Besides, I train him…"

"Come to the point, Nolan, please."

"So he dashed into the undergrowth and I couldn't catch up with him at the time."

"And your…Belzebuth found something."

"No, My Lady, he's dead."

"How did that…?"

"The individuals shot him with a revolver. Belzebuth was killed instantly."

"This story is unbelievable."

"That's why I wanted to talk to you about it, My Lady."

Wickney, who had remained near the entrance door, could not believe his ears.

"You did well, Nolan. So there are some people trying to get into my estate. I really wonder why."

"Perhaps I have an idea, My Lady."

"Go ahead."

"Perhaps that has some connection with Cadell."

"Cadell? What does he have to do with this matter?"

"I suspect him of associating with some unsavoury people."

"That's very astonishing to me. Cadell has been on my staff for over eight years and I don't have the slightest reproach to make against him. He is a hard-working man, efficient, discreet and does not cause any problem whatsoever. I have a lot of confidence in him."

"I understand all that, My Lady, and yet…"

"Explain yourself, Nolan. Don't speak in riddles."

Lady Cheltenham was annoyed by this situation, but she could not ignore what her stableman was saying. After all, even if the man seemed strange to her, she had to admit that he did his work properly and that the loss of his dog must be painful for him.

"Now, My Lady. I suspect Cadell stole one or more pieces of jewellery belonging to you."

"How so? That accusation is serious, Nolan, you know? On what basis are you making this assumption?"

"I came up on Cadell unawares. He was hiding a gold ring, set with an emerald, in his lodgings. I was very astonished by that. I remember having seen you, I don't know on what occasion precisely, wearing that piece of jewellery."

Lady Cheltenham remained open-mouthed for a moment. That piece of information dumbfounded her.

"It's true. I have a ring like that. I haven't been able to put my hands on it for a while."

"Since when, My Lady?"

"That goes back about a fortnight, I think."

"It's that, My Lady. It's that time I caught out Cadell."

"I thought it had been mislaid, telling myself that I would very well end up finding it sooner or later. But what you're telling me is flabbergasting. I can't believe it. Are you sure about what you're saying?"

"Yes, My Lady. I'm sure of it."

Lady Cheltenham dropped herself on a nearby seat. Cadell, her appointed gardener, this trustworthy man. How was that possible? There must be some explanation. She quickly collected herself.

"Very well, Nolan. I thank you for informing me. I am going to take the necessary steps. I'm sorry about your dog."

"My Lady."

Nolan left.

Lady Cheltenham waited until the stableman had moved away and signalled the major-domo to come close.

"Wickney, we are going to have to pay a little visit to Cadell."

"I understand, My Lady."

"I will ask you to serve as my witness."

"Of course, My Lady."

"Well, let's go right away."

Within the following quarter of an hour, Lady Cheltenham and Wickney turned up at Cadell's lodgings. It was almost midday and the gardener had just come back home.

"Oh, My Lady. A visit?"

"Yes, Cadell. A somewhat peculiar visit, I must admit. I got a bit of information that you won't like."

"You're making me anxious, My Lady. What is it about?"

"How should I say this? I was told that you were guilty of a theft. Theft of jewellery. I have simply come to verify the truth of these remarks. I hope, of course, that they are only slander and lies."

Cadell's face turned purple. Not from fear or shame, but with anger.

"But, My Lady, you know well that I would never do anything of the sort. For all these years that I have served you..."

Lady Cheltenham was very upset. This accusation obliged her to take insensitive actions against the gardener, but she really wanted to get to the bottom of this.

"You understand, Cadell, that I have to check."

"I understand, My Lady."

"Wickney, do your work."

And Wickney, obeying the orders, set about searching Cadell's lodgings. He examined, like a real weasel, every inch of the shack. That took more than two hours, during which Cadell had gone out and sat on the front steps. When Wickney thought that he had left nothing to chance, he simply declared:

"Nothing, My Lady. No trace of the smallest piece of jewellery."

Lady Cheltenham was thinking. Cadell was probably innocent or else perhaps he had time to get the ring into the hands of a receiver, who would deal with making some money from it.

"Cadell, you can see that I'm reassured," she said, meeting up with the gardener again. "This experience must have been painful for you, but it was the only means of clarifying this matter."

"Yes, My Lady, but can I ask you a favour?"

"Go ahead, Cadell."

"So, who told you this unkind rumour?"

"It's Nolan, the stableman. But I suppose that he is mistaken and I will ask him to kindly apologize to you."

"Very well, My Lady."

The mistress of the house had Nolan summoned as quickly as possible. The latter, without question, made his way into the building to see how things were going.

"Nolan, we have checked your allegations. Cadell does not have this ring in his possession."

"My Lady, but I am very sure I saw it in his hand. It's probable that he has hidden it somewhere other than in his lodgings. He goes into the woods in the northern section rather often now."

"Obviously, Nolan, there is wood to be prepared for winter."

"Isn't there a shack in these woods? Cadell has made it a sort of shelter, I think."

"Yes, that's right. What are you getting at then?"

"Perhaps he has hidden the piece of jewellery in that shack, My Lady."

Lady Cheltenham had not thought of this possibility. Although Cadell's guilt seemed improbable to her, she should, once again, check the place.

"Thank you, Nolan. You can prepare yourself. I am going to think about this matter. If I have to go to this shack, with Wickney and Cadell, then I wish you to accompany me."

"Of course, My Lady."

37

As agreed with Cadell, because the plan seemed to be working wonderfully well, I had hidden myself not far from the shack.

So I saw the group arrive. Lady Cheltenham, who for the occasion was wearing some big leather boots, Wickney, Cadell and Nolan. The latter was smiling, which said a lot about his state of mind. Cadell was managing to maintain his composure, because since we had put our strategy in place, his nerves had been severely tested. Nolan thought he had control of the situation; it was quite the contrary. He was following his plan: denouncement... search of the lodgings... visit to the shack... In fact, we had virtually provoked this succession of events.

I was completely concealed in a thick clump of nut trees and holly bushes. Some young fir trees helped to perfect this hiding place and the needles of some and the foliage of others allowed me to see without being seen. I could hear the verbal exchanges perfectly.

"Let's do this, if you don't mind."

Lady Cheltenham was conducting the operation; Wickney, no doubt, was going to proceed with the search of the premises.

So Wickney went in first. When they all were inside, I drew closer. Through the wooden partition, I could hear the words exchanged. Taking a furtive look now and then through the little window, I could distinguish the figures. I knew the inside of this shack well, so I could easily know where each of them was and what they could do there.

For a while, I heard nothing but the noises caused by the search. It was rather quick, because there was not much furniture and there were not many possible hiding-places. Wickney finally gave a shout.

"My Lady, I have something."

"Yes, Wickney?"

"There, under this stone in the fireplace, which seems to me to be strangely positioned. I'm seeing a case, My Lady."

"Well, Wickney, then take it out of there. Don't keep us in suspense."

"Here, My Lady."

I was all ears.

"Nolan, what does this mean?"

"I don't understand, My Lady, I would have sworn that…"

"A pebble, a mere pebble. All this business for a pebble."

"But I swear to you, My Lady that…"

"However, you had mentioned a gold ring. Confusing a green stone with this pebble of a similar colour is one thing, but gold?"

"I don't understand, My Lady, really."

"Cadell, I am really sorry for all this. I should not have doubted you for a moment. As for you, Nolan, we will need to get to the bottom of this. Right now, get lost."

I had heard enough. I went back to my hiding place and saw Nolan moving away very quickly, brandishing his fist in a sign of vengeance. Then came the rest of the group who returned to the path to the manor.

This phase of the plan was a total success. Cadell was cleared of all suspicion. Nolan was becoming suspect in the eyes of Lady Cheltenham. Cadell was going to move on to the next step, interrogating the stableman, in his own way. Up to then, Mary had remained outside of all these events. I did not wish to involve her, in one way or the other, in all of this. There would still be time to lay down all the cards on the table.

At the end of the day, I had got close to the stables and hidden myself near the water tank. There was enough junk there to hide oneself easily. I did not have to wait very long. In spite of the increasing darkness, I saw Cadell's figure going down the steps of his lodgings. That was the time when Nolan, having finished his duty, would normally check the closure of the loose boxes. He did not see Cadell come up. The gardener seized him by the collar of his coat and dragging him at arm's length, took him to the lodgings. Nolan was no match for him. Much smaller than Cadell, puny, he was not up to the task. Moreover, he did not try to defend himself. That would have been useless, as Cadell could have killed him with a mere punch.

Stealthily, I moved forward right up to the lodgings and took my place on the threshold. The door was half-open.

"So, my good fellow, you're confusing emeralds with common pebbles? You wouldn't make a good goldsmith."

"I don't understand," stammered the stableman, "I don't understand. What do you want from me?"

"I want to know why you made up this whole story."

"I didn't make up anything, I…"

I heard the sound of a rather hard slap.

"Don't hit me, for pity's sake…"

"Of course, I'm going to hit you, until you spill the beans."

A second slap sounded.

"So, Nolan, your memory's coming back?"

"I don't know, I don't know anymore. I was compelled…"

"Compelled?"

"Yes, compelled. I risked losing my job and my sister…"

"Your sister? You have a sister?"

"Yes. She has the use of a patch of ground, you know."

"No, Nolan, I still don't understand."

"I can't say anything, Cadell. Or else…"

There was silence. Nolan seemed really terrified.

"Who? Just give me a name."

"I can't, Cadell."

"Sir Garmond, perhaps?

"No, no…"

Cadell realized that Nolan would not say any more.

"One piece of advice, Nolan. Tonight, pack your bags and disappear as fast as you can. If I see you again tomorrow morning, I swear to you that I will rip you apart, piece by piece."

"Yes, Mr Cadell, I will leave."

And Nolan left Cadell's lodgings to go back to his own.

Through the partition, I heard the gardener.

"Come and have a drink, laddie."

38

Lady Cheltenham was upset. This issue had caused trouble. Clearly, Nolan had wrongly accused Cadell. For what purpose? In whom could she confide and ask for advice? Her daughter Mary was outside of all this and would have no opinion on the matter.

She was occupied with these thoughts when Mary turned up.

"Mother, can I speak with you for a moment?"

"But of course, Mary. How are you today?"

"Better. These daily walks in the grounds are doing me a world of good."

"Indeed, you look better. But I am worried because some prowlers tried to get into the property and killed Nolan's dog. I would far prefer that you go out with someone. Perhaps Cadell could keep your company. You'll be safe with him."

"Yes, mother, that's an excellent idea."

"Good. So we'll do that. But what did you want to speak to me about then?"

"It's about this issue, with Nolan…"

"You know about it?"

"There's nothing secret here, mother, at least… almost."

Lady Cheltenham did not see the mischievous glint that lit up her daughter's face for a moment.

"I wonder if the intention was not to discredit Cadell and make you dismiss him," the young girl continued.

"I indeed thought about that, but why then?"

"Cadell has serious doubts about father's accident."

Lady Cheltenham remained thoughtful for a while. That had already crossed her mind.

"He told you so?"

"Yes, he has implied as much to me."

"What did he say exactly?"

"That father was an excellent horseman and that this fall, on a route without any obstacles, seemed very astonishing to him."

"You know, Mary, an accident is just that. It's always something that no one expects, even in a familiar and *a priori* risk-free situation."

"I agree with you, mother, on this principle, but all the same. And then there is…"

Mary stopped. Going any further was risky.

"Yes, dear?"

"Sir Garmond."

"What does Sir Garmond have to do with this matter?"

Lady Cheltenham had slightly raised her voice. This was a sensitive topic.

"He appeared right after this accident. You were in a period of distress, of weakness and he, how should I put this… took advantage of the situation."

Lady Cheltenham had quickly moved closer.

"Little fool! How dare you?"

Her hand was already raised, ready to administer a slap on this brazen girl who was attempting to call into question Sir Garmond's integrity and reputation.

But her arm could not come down. A strong hand had grabbed it, preventing this unfortunate action. Cadell had appeared and intervened.

Lady Cheltenham was rolling her eyes crazily.

"Cadell, how dare you?"

"Don't do that, My Lady. There is a strong chance that your daughter is right."

"How is that? No, no…"

"Nolan, can you tell me who recommended Nolan to you?"

"Sir Garmond, of course."

"Well, you can see. Nolan is working for Sir Garmond. He tried to have me driven out because he knows that I have serious doubts about your husband Lord Cheltenham's accident. If you had dismissed me, undoubtedly, I would not have been able to speak. Or else my remarks would no longer have had the same weight. I would have been accused of slanderous words, dictated by vengeance and bitterness."

"Cadell, that's not possible. Sir Garmond is so charming and attentive."

"Isn't he considering marriage between his son Perdy and your daughter Mary?"

"That is arranged, in fact, for spring."

"Abandon that plan, My Lady."

"Cadell, you're overstepping your duties. I could dismiss you immediately for such behaviour."

"I know that, My Lady, but you won't do it."

Lady Cheltenham was at a loss. Mary brought a chair so her mother could sit down.

"With this marriage, Sir Garmond merges the estates. Your huge forests form part of his patrimony, somehow. He will profit from it because it's very possible that the subsoil of those woods conceals coal."

"My God! What can I do?"

"Cancel the marriage plans, to begin with," replied Cadell.

"Yes, mother; this marriage will not happen. I have other plans."

"How so, what are you talking about?"

"Things that mean a lot to me and about which I'm soon going to speak to you."

"But what is happening in this house," whispered Lady Cheltenham. "What is happening?"

"My Lady, with all due respect, invite Sir Garmond to another party. The situation will then become clearer."

Lady Cheltenham got up, approached the gardener and looked at him intently. Could she see into the soul of this man, with this rough and uncultured appearance? Could she trust him? Wasn't Cadell hatching some sort of plot to avoid appearing guilty of things she did not suspect? Was he making accusations in order to better exonerate himself? In his tired eyes, tinged with sadness, she discerned sincerity, candour and kindness. Cadell was a good person; she could depend on him.

"Agreed, Cadell. I'm going to prepare the invitation."

39

The buffet, this time, had been placed in one of the large rooms on the ground floor, just opposite the small sitting room. Cool drinks or hot tea, French wine and Scotch whisky, savoury cakes with bacon or cheddar, everything was foreseen to satisfy the guests, despite their small number. With regard to the Cheltenham estate, there were only Lady Cheltenham and her daughter Mary. In respect of Sir Garmond, he had come with Perdy — John being absent — and two couples of his neighbours and friends.

Cathy and Joanna were responsible for the service. Wickney kept an eye on the proper order of the party.

Discussions, on the men's side, related to the situation in Egypt.

"After all," said Sir Deville, a friend of Sir Garmond, "our brave soldiers were right about these pillaging and rebellious Mahdists."

"Control over the canal will be total. The French only have to behave themselves now. They will be forced to negotiate," responded Sir Garmond.

"Don't they want to make it an international issue and ask for arbitration?"

"Yes, I've heard about that. What nonsense."

On the ladies' side, the discussion was also well under way.

"My dear Eleanor, this grand estate, how marvellous, and these magnificent grounds," Lady Turner was saying. "But this must require a lot of work."

"I'm in good hands, you know. My people are very conscientious and hard-working."

"How lucky you are with that. When I think that my husband does not want to leave the city. He even talks about going to settle down in London."

Mary was listening to all this only with one ear. Seated on a chair, she was sipping a raspberry syrup prepared by Cathy. A real nectar. Luckily, she had avoided Perdy, who had asked his father's permission to go into the grounds to visit the horses. But she knew that sooner or later, in the afternoon, she would have to meet him and speak about the marriage. She did not feel ready for this ordeal.

Around four o'clock, the Devilles and the Turners went home. They had things to do and the follow-up to this occasion did not concern them. Sir Garmond and the mistress of the house had serious things to discuss.

Lady Cheltenham settled herself in the little sitting room with her guest. Mary was present; Perdy still had not returned.

"This unruly chap always does only as he likes," remarked Sir Garmond.

"Would you like me to send for him?"

"Well, perhaps…"

"Wickney"

"My Lady?"

"See if you can find young Perdy. Tell him that his presence is desired."

"Understood."

"You have indeed, my dear friend, a peerless major-domo. That's an important element in a large house like yours."

"Indeed, Sir."

Sir Garmond had moved closer. His eyes shone with a very

peculiar brilliance as he looked at the young woman, so beautiful in her pretty dress with violet-coloured flounces.

"Sir Garmond, we have to discuss some important things."

"Of course. Time is going by and the marriage of our two children is approaching very quickly."

Mary stirred on her seat. A nervous tension overwhelmed her. Sir Garmond must have noticed it.

"Well, Mary, are you satisfied with this plan? You know Perdy. He is a little wild, but he's not a bad lad."

"You mean, Sir Garmond…"

Lady Cheltenham cut off her daughter's sentence and intervened without beating about the bush.

"Sir Garmond, this marriage will not happen."

The businessman remained open-mouthed, surprised by this sudden announcement.

"My Lady, what is happening? I don't understand. Some specific obstacle? An occurrence that would compromise the plan?"

"You couldn't have said it better, Sir. Certain concerns about you compel me to review this issue."

"How is that, My Lady? Explain yourself."

"Sir Garmond, some strong suspicions weigh against you. It seems that you are no stranger to the death of my husband."

Sir Garmond, obviously offended, leapt up.

"This is a very serious accusation, My Lady. How did you arrive at such a disparaging assumption?"

"The recent shenanigans of your right-hand man Nolan aroused my curiosity and my suspicions. Moreover, one of my employees has argued in favour of a murder rather than an accident."

"Nolan? So, who is this Nolan?"

"How so? Wasn't it you who recommended him?"

"Not so, My Lady. I don't know this character. Who is he then?"

"My stableman. Hired eight months ago at that, on your recommendation."

"But that is impossible"

Lady Cheltenham tried to remember. Thinking about it, Nolan had been recommended indirectly by Sir Garmond. Someone else, in fact, had vouched for him. Was that possible, she thought.

"All right," she replied. "You don't know this Nolan."

Mary opened her eyes wide. This assertion was disconcerting her.

"And my woodlands, which abound in coal, it seems?"

"Oh no, My Lady, these forest areas are free of coal, I can assure you. But I don't understand very well what you are getting at."

In truth, Lady Cheltenham herself no longer knew which way to go next.

"And Perdy?" Mary intervened.

"Perdy? Your major-domo went to look for him; I hope he will soon turn up."

"That's not what I mean," continued the young girl, with a malevolent look. "Do you know that he tried to rape me, last summer? That without the intervention of one of our workers…"

Sir Garmond looked shocked.

"Perdy? I don't believe it for one second."

"And yet, Sir Garmond, that is indeed the case."

Lady Cheltenham, who did not know about this matter, looked at her daughter in astonishment.

"I don't believe it…"

"Perdy is a worthless, violent person. His behaviour has revolted me. You understand that for that reason, I can't bring myself to marry him. I don't love him."

"Miss Mary, this incident was no doubt a momentary lapse on the part of my son. He has matured since, has certainly thought it over and will be for you, I have no doubt, an excellent husband.

228

Besides, I am going to commit him, as soon as he gets here, to offer you his most sincere apologies."

"Sir Garmond," Lady Cheltenham intervened, "you realize that these events, as well as the grey areas hanging over the death of my husband make it so that I cannot, now, envisage this marriage. I am so sorry for you."

"My Lady, know that I am innocent of the suspicions that you have about me. Since we met, I have not stopped thinking about you and I would never have tried to cause you the slightest harm. I thought that this marriage would have brought our two families together and would have allowed me to see you more often."

"Let us forget this idea, Sir."

At that moment, Wickney reappeared.

"My Lady, young Perdy cannot be found."

40

I was waiting, impatiently, for the end of that day. Mary would not fail to come and give me a report about it. The weather was rather mild; the wind had dropped and the clouds frequently parted to allow a little light to come through.

I heard the rustling of leaves and the cracking of twigs. Mary's figure stood out between the trees. She moved forward quickly, nimbly, driven by a powerful desire. She threw herself against me.

"Jeremy!"

"Mary, here you are! Everything went well?"

"Yes. My mother did not beat about the bush. I hardly recognized her. She must have great confidence in Cadell."

"She can be confident. And Sir Garmond?"

"He denied having incited anything whatever. It's strange, but I had the impression that he was sincere. I am a little bewildered, at the moment."

"But then, we haven't got any further."

"The only thing that is very clear now is that this marriage will not take place."

"That's wonderful. Finally, I'm going to be able to come out of hiding."

"Yes, Jeremy. And it's necessary for my mother to decide to accept the facts. It is with you that I want to live."

We remained entwined for a moment, continuously searching for each other's lips. Mad desire was mounting in us, irremediable, inevitable, submerging us like an equinox tide.

"Come, Mary, the shack."

We left the grounds. In ten minutes we had reached Cadell's little shack. In no time, we were undressed, lying on the cloth mattress which served as a makeshift bed. After this time spent far from each other, we had the feeling of rediscovering our bodies and we spent a long time on delightful and magical caresses. We were just one; we vibrated in harmony, in rhythm, like a tuning-fork releasing its tinkling note.

The door opened noisily, silhouetting a menacing shadow in the fading light of the opening.

Mary was covered with a cotton sheet, while I tried to find my clothes again.

The shadow moved forward a few steps. In his hands the barrel of a rifle glinted.

"Well, my lambs, you're having a good time?"

"Perdy!" shouted Mary.

"Yes, Perdy! Perdy the reject, Perdy the unloved, Perdy the madman, the violent, the uncontrollable... Perdy whom you reject and whom you don't want as a husband... What a pity..."

From strong and biting, his voice had taken on an unctuous and ironic tone. It was not, however, any less disturbing. This pointed rifle frightened me. Perdy was capable of anything, especially of the worst.

"Perdy, put down that rifle," I asked him without raising my voice.

"And why would I do that? Can you tell me? Mary is rejecting me and throwing herself into your arms. I surprise you both here, in the process of fornicating. And you think that puts me in a good mood? You think that makes me want to put down this rifle?"

"Perdy, don't be an idiot. Your father is going to be mad; have you thought about that?"

"My father? He doesn't care about me. It's only your mother he is interested in. For so long, he has been thinking only about her. Your father's accident was an opportunity for him. Just before that happened, he intended to go far away, to try to forget Lady Cheltenham."

These remarks immediately raised questions for me. If Sir Garmond had decided to leave the area, he therefore was not thinking of getting rid of Lord Cheltenham. That corroborated what he had been saying and the impression that Mary had at the time of the recent conversation.

"I don't believe it," Mary intervened. "Your father loves you, even if he doesn't really show it. I know that."

"That's all rubbish."

We needed to buy some time and I had to find a solution to get us out of this.

Mary continued to speak and was trying to calm down the young man.

"Perdy, Perdy, I will marry you if you want…"

"It's too late, now. You slept with this confounded stableman and you don't love me, I know. I prefer to get it over with."

The tension had gone up a peg. Perdy's finger was tense on the trigger.

He seemed to change his mind.

"I have a better idea. Something much more amusing. Move to the back."

We obeyed, because the threat of this rifle was very real.

"That's perfect. Two pretty little turtle-doves… Don't move any more now."

And Perdy quickly backed out, slamming the door behind him. We could hear a noise of boards, as well as some dull thuds struck on the shutter. I got up and discovered that the door was blocked on the outside. No means of getting out for the moment. Then some other blows were heard on the side of the little window. Perdy was in the process of blocking the opening with some small planks. He was nailing them with a sledgehammer and some long steel nails.

"He's shutting us in, but for Christ's sake, why?"

"I don't know, Jeremy. So what is his plan?"

We were happy that we had not been shot like common rabbits. To be locked up in this shack was not as dramatic as that, after all. But we were quickly going to change our tune.

Wisps of smoke began to creep insidiously under the door. Grey, thick smoke, which stung our eyes and irritated our throats. Then the spirals increased and the first flames could be seen consuming the planks of the walls.

"My God," Mary shouted. "Fire. He wants to burn us alive, in this shack."

At that precise moment, I thought that all was lost.

I squeezed Mary in my arms. Then we closed our eyes.

41

The flames had burnt the walls and the roof. In a few moments, it would be all over. We began to suffocate and tears from our reddened eyes ran down our blackened cheeks.

In spite of the angry roaring of the fire, I heard several detonations. Gun shots, no doubt. Then, suddenly, someone pulled out what remained of the door, that is to say, a heap of planks in flames.

Through the smoke, I made out a familiar figure.

"Cadell!"

I dragged Mary towards the exit. She could hardly stand up. Outside, we lay down on the bare ground, deeply inhaling fresh, life-saving air.

"How did you do that, Cadell?"

"I was watching that one."

"But, your arm?"

There was a red spot on his shirt at the level of his left arm.

"A scratch, my boy; don't worry about that. Old Cadell is used to those. Instead, take this and catch up with that raging madman."

Cadell handed me his rifle.

"But where has he gone, then?"

"I have no idea, but he has to be found. Perhaps around the manor. He could be attacking Milady or even his father. Hurry up, lad, hurry up."

Mary had got back some colour and was smiling.

The shack continued to burn. Luckily none of the nearby trees had been affected by the flames.

"Let's go," I said to Mary.

And we dashed off towards the manor. This time, we reached there in record time.

"Look," Mary said to me, "the horses!"

The loose boxes were open. One of the horses, Filou, was missing.

"The road," she further said to me.

We grabbed the reins of two of the horses, Azurea and Moonlight, two fast, frisky mares.

Very quickly, we had reached the main courtyard, passed the main door and took the road to Prestbury. We set our horses at a gallop. As we passed by the building, I noticed Wickney, on the landing, his eyes wide open in astonishment.

The noise of the hoofs resounded on the stony ground. Clouds of condensation escaped from the horses' nostrils. The animals were giving it their all, but we had to be careful not to exhaust them or cause any muscle damage.

As we came out of the woods, before that long descent leading to the village, we halted the horses. Mary examined the ground. She had a certain knack for tracking.

"That way," she shouted confidently.

A border path went off to the left. Indeed, rather recent hoof marks were visible in the friable soil.

"He took this path. But where can he really be going to?"

"Does he himself know?"

And we followed this track, the only link that connected us to Perdy, this young man who had become uncontrollable and capable of anything.

Mary had become an excellent horsewoman. She managed

Azurea with ease, avoiding the snares that could arise at any moment. The ground, grassy and soft, did not facilitate our progress, but we could not allow ourselves to be outdistanced, on the contrary.

The path ran through a beech grove, went up a mossy hump and opened on to a rather wide pasture. A few hundred yards away, we spotted Perdy, lying on his horse's neck and dashing along at a good speed.

"Go! Go!" shouted Mary, urging on Azurea. We were going to catch up with him.

And the race resumed worse than ever. The horses were at their best; sweat began to run down their necks; we needed to end it quickly, as exhaustion could be awaiting them. That would be a disaster. Both for the horse, which risked not recovering from it and for our man-hunt, which would end then.

We were gaining ground considerably; Perdy seeming to be in difficulty. His horse also must have been feeling tired. Finally, conscious of the impossibility of his escaping, Perdy made his horse do an about-turn and faced us. He had shouldered his rifle. Out of caution, we stopped.

"Perdy!" shouted Mary. "Don't be an idiot; lower that rifle! I know you're acting in a fit of anger and jealousy. Pull yourself together!"

"Sorry, Mary, that's not on the programme. I am going to let you…"

"What's he doing?" I asked Mary.

"I don't know. I don't like this at all."

Perdy had put the barrel of the rifle under his chin. With his right arm extended, he just reached the trigger and was no doubt going to squeeze it, in a final gesture of madness mingled with despair.

Quick action was necessary. I shouldered Cadell's rifle. I had to be careful not to hit the horse. Mary looked at me, alarmed.

"Jeremy, what are you doing?"

I squeezed the trigger. Perdy, hit in his leg, uttered a cry, pivoted on the saddle while letting go of his weapon and fell on to the grass. In a few seconds we were over him. His wound was not critical; the bullet had cut into the outer part of his thigh before ending up in the meadow.

"It's over, Perdy," I told him. "We're going back."

Perdy did not struggle. He did not put up any resistance. I succeeded in putting him in front of me, on Moonlight, while I led his horse by the leading-rein. We were going to return at a walking pace.

Everything seemed to be working out for the best. What could have been a tragedy had taken a turn for the better. Moreover, the young man's remarks came back to me and implied that Sir Garmond had nothing to do with the death of Lord Cheltenham. Mary had also understood those words.

When we arrived at the manor, there was some excitement in the courtyard. Lady Cheltenham and Sir Garmond, Wickney, Cadell and two other persons, whom I did not know, were there. Cathy and her friends were not there.

We dismounted. Lady Cheltenham, at first surprised by my presence, stared at me for a while before exclaiming:

"Jeremy, Jeremy Page, how is this possible?"

In her voice there was strong emotion, as well as unconcealed joy.

I respectfully greeted the persons present, while Perdy, in pain from his leg, had seated himself on the paved ground. Sir Garmond was looking at him coldly.

"Jeremy," resumed Lady Cheltenham, "you're alive?"

"It would seem so, My Lady. It's a long story, you know…"

"You will continue your tale at the station, young man," intervened one of the two men whom I did not know.

"How so?"

237

"It's the Police, Jeremy. They have come to arrest you."

Mary gave a blood-curdling scream and threw herself against me.

"Jeremy, no... I don't want to lose you again."

Lady Cheltenham was staggering from one surprise to another. She remained speechless before this spectacle which she would not have imagined for a single instant.

One of the policemen took the rifle from me and grabbed me by the arm.

"Don't give any trouble; that would be better."

Cadell was boiling inside. I thought he was quite capable of overcoming these two policemen by himself, but that would have complicated matters instead of settling them.

"Leave it alone, Cadell, leave it alone. I will explain myself to these gentlemen."

Mary was crying and had snuggled up against her mother who, understanding her deep distress, tried to console her. Perdy, in spite of his pain, managed to smile and rejoice at this situation. Perhaps he thought he was regaining the upper hand. His father was saying nothing.

The sequel went rather quickly. A carriage was waiting near the entrance. I was taken to it and the team started to move. I was going back to Gloucester prison. I was sick at heart when I saw the lofty outline of that building that I loved so much receding.

Unfortunately, I knew the penitentiary establishment, and so I was not really out of my element in returning to one of its cells. Some former prisoners were present, others had disappeared and some new ones had replaced them.

This time, I hardly had hope about my future any longer. It would probably be the hangman's rope. Lying on my pallet, eyes fixed on the ceiling oozing with pervasive moisture, I thought about the recent events. Mary and I, we were so close to happiness. We had succeeded in avoiding the worst with regard to

Perdy; we had even escaped death in that shack. All the same, I questioned myself about the presence of those two policemen in the manor courtyard. Who could have really informed them? It must have been someone who knew about my presence. Except for Cadell and Mary, no name came to my mind. Finally, I saw again Lady Cheltenham's face when she had recognized me. It was a joyful face, filled with happiness. How could Lady Cheltenham have denigrated me at the time of the first trial and show her joy when I returned? Something definitely did not fit. But these thoughts were unimportant now. I was very soon going to swing at the end of a rope and the world, continuing to turn without me, would end up forgetting me.

Master Jones came to pay me a visit the very next day. Things seemed to be progressing without delay. Would he be able to fight for me again? However, he was wearing a broad smile. The smile of a counsel who is trying to make you confident even in the most hopeless situations.

"Good morning, Jeremy."

"Good morning, Master Jones."

We were seated in a little room provided for this purpose. A warder, standing near the door, was keeping an eye on us.

"So, what happened, Jeremy?"

"If I tell you this story, Master, you are going have trouble believing me. But I am tired and I have the impression that there is not much we can do. Leave me. The die is cast, anyhow. The court will send me to the gallows, there's no doubt about that."

"Why resign yourself, Jeremy? Perhaps there is still a glimmer of hope?"

"I don't believe so, Master. There is no more glimmer, no more light. I'm moving forward in the dark…"

"Please, Jeremy. Tell me. A second opinion, sometimes… a detail, a word."

This counsel did not want to abandon me. I could not blame

him; he was doing his job. However, he was really taking my case to heart. For that, perhaps I should make the effort to not disappoint him. If not, he also would end up losing faith.

I therefore gave him a detailed account of the events since our last meeting, which is to say at the time of the trial in the preceding spring, which had sent me to Egypt. Gradually, as I progressed with my story, the counsel opened his eyes wide. The episode in Egypt particularly struck him, as well as Murdock's death or again the fire at the shack.

"Jeremy, it's not possible that you overcame all those ordeals to get here."

"That's what I sometimes tell myself and yet, I have to accept the inevitable. Fate is going at me furiously and will emerge the big winner."

Nevertheless, I finished my story. All through this long, virtual monologue, Jones had not stopped taking notes in a large notebook with lined pages. He put down his pen and began to think.

"There are some details that bother me," he finally said.

"Which ones?"

"This Sir Garmond, who doesn't seem guilty and Lady Cheltenham, suddenly happy to meet you again after having accused you. That's paradoxical at the very least."

"That's what I also thought, but at the moment, that doesn't get me anywhere."

"Allow me, young man, to do some research. If the matter is restricted to the circle of persons occupying the manor, we will get around it quickly. I don't want to forget anyone. Give me a few days."

"Do it, Master, do it. I hope your investigation will bear fruit or bring in some new elements."

"It would be useful for you. Because the judge, instead of being content with changing your punishment, to stiffen it, probably, would have to reconsider the whole file. That is somewhat like if the case is taken up again from its very beginning."

"You don't give up, Master."

"It is necessary for someone to do this for you. Shut up in this prison, you cannot do much and I feel that your fighting spirit is at its lowest point. Let me do it."

Master Jones had restored my morale. After his departure, I thought about his plan. There was no harm in trying. I tended to agree with his theory. If it was a case of someone in the close circle, from then on, I saw only one person acting as the mastermind. Looking at it more closely, it was not an impossibility.

42

At the manor, there was consternation. After Jeremy's departure, Lady Cheltenham and her daughter had a long conversation. A sensitive issue as that of forbidden love, and lack of respect for rules and customs. But Lady Cheltenham had an open mind. She listened to her daughter and understood her happiness and her pain.

"My poor darling, why didn't you tell me anything?"

"I didn't dare, mother. You know well, these middle-class rules... Jeremy, a mere stableman... And then, you had planned this marriage, with Perdy. What could I say or do?"

"That plan was a mistake, I admit. I thought that you would get along well with this young man. I did not know him well enough. And it is true that it would have brought me closer to Sir Garmond. I acted out of egoism, I now think."

Mary was extremely lucky. Most of her friends, at school, could not say the same. Their parents were inflexible on this issue and in similar situations, her friends would have been subjected to severe reprimands. Those things were not regarded lightly in families of the British aristocracy. Lady Cheltenham was perhaps an exception. Perhaps her childhood, lived in a family of traders, of limited means on the whole, from the city of Gloucester, had filled her with these principles of tolerance which she had been able to retain. And, she indeed had to admit, she liked Jeremy a lot, this gentle, nice young man, hard-working, polite and affable. Perhaps he was a little like the son she had lost at an early age, well before Mary's birth? She was also very attentive and gentle.

"And what about Jeremy, now?" she asked.

"They are going to hang him, for sure."

"We need to stake everything. I have the feeling that something is escaping our notice."

"Yes, mother. Perdy implied that Sir Garmond was not responsible for father's death. And as far as Jeremy is concerned, your testimony condemned him at the time of the trial."

"How is that?"

"Jeremy told me. He explained to me how you had stated that you were not satisfied with his work and that he had even tried to attack me."

Lady Cheltenham was on the verge of venting her anger.

"But that is the total opposite. I never stopped praising him. I explained how he had saved you at the time of that fall from the horse. I recounted in detail his work here, at the manor, more than satisfying…"

"Mother, did you write down all that?"

"No, Mary. It was only verbal. It's Wickney who went to Gloucester and was responsible for reporting my testimony, as well as those of the servants."

"Wickney! My God! Wickney! That's why we have been going round in circles from the beginning. I would never have thought…"

Both mother and daughter were having difficulty believing their own deductions. However, that could fit the bill. The motive remained. Why? Or else for whom? Sir Garmond seemed to be clear of suspicion; Perdy was nothing but a wasted scamp who had transgressed the rules, but who had no knowledge of this matter. Jeremy was a victim; someone had tried, and succeeded in having him condemned by crushing him and Cadell was trying to see things clearly.

"Mary, let's not waste any time."

They left the room. This time, it would be Cadell taking them into the city. At the bottom of the staircase, they stopped suddenly. Wickney, with an evil smile on his lips, was standing at the bottom of the steps, with a rifle in his hand.

"Not another step, My Lady, and you neither Miss Mary."

"But Wickney, what are you doing?" asked Lady Cheltenham.

"What I should have done a long time ago. All this is your fault!"

"My fault? What do you mean?"

At the end of the corridor, Cathy had discreetly pushed her head through the kitchen door. Wickney could not see her, having his back to her. So Lady Cheltenham decided to buy some time.

"I don't understand, Wickney."

"It's simple, however, My Lady. Since I got here, a good ten years or so now, I see only you, I live only for you…"

"Wickney, how could I have known?"

"You couldn't; you didn't even see me. To you I was nothing but an obedient and zealous servant who was doing his work…"

"That is indeed why I hired you, Wickney, and besides I have never had to complain about you; quite the contrary."

Lady Cheltenham had regained a self-confidence that astonished her daughter. Her mother was able to keep cool in the most hopeless situations. Mary also understood the strategy, which consisted in buying time. She had seen Cathy disappear through the little back door.

"Well, all that is over, my dear Lady. I had begun by eliminating your husband, that thief…"

"A thief?"

"Yes, lands that belonged to my family, once upon a time, and which he bought off dirt cheap. And then, he stole you, you who were destined for me…"

Wickney was beginning to get worked up. His face was gradually getting a purple tint, his hands were trembling and twitching on the rifle butt.

"My husband; so that was you?"

"Yes, My Lady, I'm not afraid to declare it. Some straps cut with a penknife, a bad fall, a good blow on the head to complete the job."

"Wickney, you are a monster…"

Wickney was not listening to her; he continued.

"And then there was this young rogue, this Jeremy who could have got in the way. He was getting along too well with Cadell, who had some suspicions, I knew… I pulled some strings."

"All these issues; so it was you, Wickney, every time."

That was the moment that Mary chose to fall to the ground, giving a little scream. She was lying on the floor, as if lifeless.

"Mary, Mary," her mother asked, kneeling next to her. "Answer me, what's happening?"

This incident disconcerted Wickney, who let his guard slip and lowered his rifle for a short moment.

From the end of the corridor, a dreadful explosion resounded. Wickney, hit on his thigh, collapsed with a cry of pain. Cadell, his arm wrapped in a large cloth, a gun still smoking in his hand, came up quickly and disarmed the major-domo.

43

Counsel Jones came to see me again two days later. In my dark, damp cell, I was beginning to stamp my feet in impatience. It had to end. Whatever the future verdict may be, I was in a hurry for this matter to come to a close.

"My dear Jeremy, I bring you a piece of blue sky."

I remained hesitant.

"I have some news coming out of Cheltenham. Some things that you are going to like, I'm sure of it."

I was all ears. Was the light going to come back on?

"As I had told you, I carried out some research on the occupants of the manor. They have, believe me, each one of them, an interesting past. That allowed me to see things more clearly."

"And?"

"One individual caught my attention."

I already had a pretty good idea about that.

"It's Wickney, the major-domo."

"I had indeed thought about it, but we did not have proof of any sort."

"From now on it's done, Jeremy. Proof and confessions."

I could not contain my joy. What could be better than this?

"The major-domo has been exposed. They came close to a tragedy at Cheltenham, but your friend Cadell intervened just in time. Before these events, I had received some information about

246

the individual. I found some connections with a solicitor, one Radcliff, himself rather influential with the judge. If you understand what I mean."

I could not believe my ears. Everything was therefore connected. Wickney, Radcliff, the judge. Wickney, who had certainly made things worse for me and had got some of his acquaintances to intervene and send me far away.

"Has he been arrested?"

"Yes, Jeremy. He is, at this very moment, on the premises of the Police. It is Officer Merrit who is heading the investigation. Things should be making good progress now."

"Thank you, Master Jones, for this extraordinary work. How could I ever thank you?"

"Thank me by recovering your good nature. The judge will not be long reacting, in order to complete this case."

"The judge…?"

"Set your mind at rest; this time, it is Sir Templeton, someone very upright, very serious and known for his incorruptibility. Have faith."

When Master Jones had left, I tried to put a little order into my ideas. The person whom I would not have suspected for a shade of a second was the one who had fomented this horrible plot. I re-examined Wickney, at each one of those moments or circumstances in which I had met him. His bearing, his efficiency, his discretion, nothing in him had allowed who he really was to become known.

Lady Cheltenham must have been very astonished, and disappointed. Another concern haunted my mind. How was the mistress of the house going to react when she found out what united us, Mary and me? I feared the worst. Jones had not mentioned that to me, but perhaps he was not aware of this secret affair.

I had a very feverish night. A night filled with rather pleasant dreams and with disquieting nightmares. No doubt, my mind was very disturbed and it probably needed time before recovering some serenity.

The warder woke me up.

"Page! Get ready! The judge is expecting you this morning. You have one hour!"

In an hour, I had time to get dressed and to drink the infamous prison coffee. I was also able to go for a walk for a quarter of an hour in order to drive out the last mists that floated around in my brain.

Like the previous occasion, I was then taken into the session.

The court seemed to me to have more people than at the time of the first trial. Besides Judge Templeton, three other persons, with grim faces, were seated next to him. On my right, Master Jones, standing, was awaiting me, with a smile on his lips. Some people whom I did not know occupied a bench in the back.

The policemen who accompanied me made me sit down. A heavy silence reigned in the room. The judge was consulting some documents that he had placed in front of him and from time to time, his neighbours spoke to one another in low voices.

Then Templeton spoke.

"Jeremy Page, please stand."

I quickly obeyed. It was in my best interest to remain discreet, calm and even docile. I was waiting to see how this hearing would turn out.

"We come back today to the matter which was judged by my colleague. If we are reopening this case, it is because some new elements necessitate its re-examination. The fact that you escaped from your place of detention also justifies this new arraignment."

I acquiesced with a nod.

One of Judge Templeton's neighbours then spoke.

"Today we therefore return to the charges for which you had been initially tried. To wit, the murders of Brackett Shinger and

248

Ron Malavoy, as well as attempted murder on the person of Murdock Longsdale, to date at large. You had also appeared on charges of alcohol smuggling in the city of Gloucester and its vicinity. You had, after judgement, been condemned to twenty years of hard labour. That's right?"

"Yes, Your Honour."

The man had a smile. He was not the presiding judge and I did not have to call him 'Your Honour', but in fact, I did not know what to call him.

"Could you explain your presence on British territory?"

"I escaped, sir. I left the camp in Egypt."

"Can you relate the circumstances of it for us?"

I then recounted the conditions of work and the circumstances of my escape. I also spoke about Cornwell, who had refused my assistance, but had let me leave. I was counting on the possibility that the judge did not know that I knew the officer was alive.

Judge Templeton, after my account, resumed speaking.

"We have the officer, Matthew Cornwell, here; he will enlighten us."

I feigned surprise. A bailiff opened the door and Cornwell, in his officer's uniform with the breastplate shining with medals, made his entrance. At a slow and stately pace, he reached the stand.

"Please state your name."

"Matthew Cornwell, officer of the British Army, in the service of Our Majesty the Queen."

"Officer Cornwell, do you here swear, on your honour, to tell the truth, the whole truth, in order to enlighten this court in the case before us."

"Yes, Your Honour."

"Very well. Officer Cornwell, were you in fact stationed in Egypt at the camp of El Salahaia from May to September 1883?"

"Yes, Your Honour."

"Did you have, at the last moments of the existence of this camp, a prisoner by the name of Jeremy Page, present here in the dock?"

Cornwell glanced in my direction. He made an attempt at a slight smile.

"Yes, Your Honour. He was, moreover, the only survivor, along with me, after the attack by the Mahdist rebels."

"What would you say about this young man?"

"He was an exemplary prisoner. Hard-working and obedient; I never had any problem to report against him. Perhaps I even owe him my life."

"How is that, Mr Officer?"

"Jeremy was alive. Miraculously, he had escaped from the massacre. He involuntarily diverted the attention of two of the enemy forces. That allowed me to take them down and also save myself. It cost him the scar that you see on his face."

"And so you allowed him to leave? You did not try to stop him?"

"No, Your Honour. My weapon was empty. I had no more ammunition; I had just used my last cartridges. Moreover, my strength was deserting me. I was seriously wounded and then..."

"Yes?"

"Jeremy had participated in the defence of our camp and had taken down several of the enemy."

"Very well, Officer Cornwell. The facts that you have related to us, those concerning you more particularly, will be, you know, examined by a military court."

"Yes, Your Honour, I know that."

"I thank you, Officer Cornwell. You can stand down. We will call you back, if necessary."

I felt like a weight was being lifted off me. Obviously, Cornwell had not accused me, but had drawn a rather positive picture of my character. Regarding his weapon, I was, on the contrary, very certain that it still had some cartridges.

The judge considered Cornwell's remarks for a moment and spoke in a low voice to his neighbours.

"Jeremy Page," he announced, "Officer Cornwell's testimony has impressed and surprised us. It will certainly be taken into account when making our decision. Master Jones? Any comments or questions?"

"Your Honour, Officer Cornwell's statement clearly shows that Jeremy Page is not the murderer that has been described to us. He defended the camp and tried to help an officer. I sincerely hope that this court will take these new elements into account in its forthcoming decision."

The judge gave a slight nod.

"We are now going to address the complaints brought against your client, my dear Master. As I mentioned in my preamble, new elements cannot be ignored. You have requested the appearance of several witnesses, essential, you say, in this case."

"That is correct, Your Honour. Recent events, statements and confessions throw new light on this complex case. I have therefore drawn up the list of these witnesses, a list which you have been able to review."

The judge gave a signal to the bailiff who was standing near the door. He opened it. I then saw Lady Cheltenham, Mary and Cadell moving forward.

44

Lady Cheltenham was called to the stand. She was wearing a gazelle-coloured jacket over a dress with the drape trailing on the ground. A round hat adorned with pale pink ribbons covered her hair, which hung down in waves on the nape of her neck. She made a strong impression on the court by the presence emanating from her person. Mary and Cadell had seated themselves on a bench in the back and both of them were throwing me encouraging looks.

Judge Templeton regained his self-control very quickly. The beauty of this woman had, it seemed, deprived him of his faculties for a moment.

Ritual reclaimed its rights.

"Please state your name."

And Lady Cheltenham soberly introduced herself.

"Eleanor Margreth Cheltenham, widow of Lord John Cheltenham, owner of the manor of the same name."

"Very well, My Lady, could you tell us what induced you to come and testify before this court. Did recent events urge you to do so?"

"Your Honour, I did not personally appear at the initial trial concerning young Jeremy Page. I had conveyed my comments to my major-domo, Wickney Blunt, but today I doubt that my remarks were faithfully reported."

"What do you mean by that, dear Madam?"

"I mean that the statements made by this man were not at all consistent with the reality and so I have come here, before this court, to correct this error."

The judge consulted his documents.

"I see here, that you had said, or someone had said, pardon me, the following: '*His behaviour leaves a lot to be desired, the work is not done properly and I suspect him of having tried to abuse my daughter Mary.*' Is that right?"

"That is what the major-domo, Wickney, said. My opinion is that Jeremy Page is an excellent worker, hard-working, polite, helpful and devoted. He does not mind what the task is and his work is excellent. He has never tried to assault my daughter, but saved her when she suffered a fall from a horse. I have never had to complain about him, on the contrary."

"But then, My Lady, how do you explain the major-domo's remarks?"

Master Jones then requested an intervention.

"Master Jones?"

"If I may be permitted, Your Honour, as well as you, My Lady, I would like to develop my argument on this precise point."

"My Lady?" asked the judge.

"Of course."

"I wager," began the lawyer, "that Mr Blunt's attitude was part of a series of manoeuvres which he used, not to say misused, and which hide an astounding truth. I therefore dare to declare here, that Mr Wickney Blunt killed Lord John Cheltenham and deliberately worked on sending young Jeremy to prison for many years."

One of the persons sitting at the extreme right of the judge then exclaimed.

"We are not here to try Wickney Blunt. This statement is inadmissible."

The judge frowned.

"It is true, Sir Windberg, that we are here to come to a decision on the fate of Jeremy Page, but the facts that relate to Wickney Blunt cut across our case. That, we cannot ignore."

Sir Windberg, disappointed, made a sour face and scowled.

"The session is suspended," Judge Templeton then announced, violently rapping the piece of furniture with his gavel.

The justices having retreated through a door cut directly into the wall, the wait seemed endless. I could not speak to Mary, or to Cadell; I had to keep still on my bench, without turning my head. This moment was particularly difficult.

When the court reappeared, we had to stand again.

"After careful consideration, the Court decides to temporarily suspend this trial."

Mary uttered an 'oh!' of astonishment.

Cadell grunted.

Lady Cheltenham remained silent.

"The Court believes, in view of these recent statements, that this trial cannot be continued until the light has been fully shed on the case of Mr Wickney Blunt. So, as soon as the Police communicate the results of their investigations, we will proceed with the trial of Wickney Blunt. It is only then that we will be able to come back to the case at hand. Until that time, Jeremy Page remains in prison."

The gavel came down again, sounding the return to the cell for me.

I had time to see Mary's misty eyes, Lady Cheltenham's smile and Cadell's expression which implied, as always, '*it will be all right, lad, it will be all right.*"

45

I went back to my cell. I had high hopes that it would not be for very much longer. The judge seemed to be in a hurry to finish it. As soon as Wickney's case was settled, I would no doubt be able to regain my freedom and finally think about my future, about *our* future, the one that I wanted to live with Mary.

At the end of the afternoon, as usual, I took advantage of the walk. It was the only time that I could really stretch my legs and breathe air fresher than that in my cell. It was also one of the only moments when I got close to the other inmates.

The weather was almost cold, in spite of brilliant sunshine. A nasty wind was blowing in the little yard and I had turned up my jacket collar. The other prisoners were stamping their feet and clapping their hands.

"Damn! Not warm today," said one of them.

"We'll catch our death!"

"You just have to complain to the warden; perhaps he'll change the weather, ha! Ha!"

This type of joke was common. These exchanges enabled them to keep up their spirits somewhat.

I had got near to the high enclosure wall, the one facing north. The brick wall cut down on the wind, which was becoming biting. Alone, in my corner, I contemplated, over and over again, the recent developments in this matter. Everything constantly brought me back to Mary. We loved each other, and this love, stronger than anything, would necessarily get the better of all the obstacles that might appear. At least that is what I wanted to convince myself of.

"So brat! You're back?"

The lanky man who stood in front of me did not look friendly. I examined his face in vain; I did not know this man.

"You remember me?"

"I beg your pardon, I don't think I know you."

"Mister is making nice and speaking like the nobs... What are you thinking?"

This fellow looked dangerous, but I still did not understand why he was speaking to me.

"Seriously, I don't understand."

It was then that my gaze caught his forearm, as he had turned up his sleeves like a boxer getting ready for a boxing bout. I saw a tattoo, an eagle with its wings spread. My mind began to work. That tattoo... Innsworth, that house in the suburbs of Gloucester, where I used to go to deliver the alcohol loaded on the docks. This fellow was one of the two hooded men who received the goods.

"You tried to take out Murdock, so it seems? And you wiped out Ron. Murdock is on the run and we don't know if he'll come back, so I'm going to finish the job for him."

This accomplice of Murdock's, who had ended up being caught, was looking to avenge his partner. It was just my luck to run into him in this prison.

As if by magic, a piece of glass appeared in his right hand. A piece of a broken mirror or something like that. It was triangular, about ten inches long and its pointed tip was as dangerous as that of a dagger. This fellow definitely intended to wipe me out.

I grabbed his wrist, preventing him from bringing this improvised weapon any closer. The work in Egypt had further developed my muscles, particularly those in my arms and I was able to block my adversary's movement. My attacker was not expecting that. He probably thought that he would get the better of me without any trouble. His face, leaning over me, expressed hatred. His distorted mouth formed a sort of diabolical grin.

The man was exerting all his strength, but he was not making any progress. I even succeeded in making him move back. If I could twist his wrist, the matter would be quickly settled. But he used another strategy. He dealt me a violent blow to my head on the ridge of the left eyebrow. The impact was terrible; I saw stars dancing before my eyes. So I relaxed the pressure of my hand and the blade of glass managed to move slowly, but surely, towards me. A few more inches and the tip would pierce my stomach. It was only a matter of seconds.

The grin had turned into a broad smile.

"Oh! Oh! You filthy brat, I'm going to kill you..."

But that did not happen. The man jerked backwards. An arm had grabbed him by his neck and pulled violently. A fist came down repeatedly on his skull and he collapsed like a puppet.

"Well, that was a close one!"

In front of me stood that disquieting young man whom I had seen at the time of my first stay in prison and who had spoken to me during a walk. He was the one who had, as it were, congratulated me for having killed Ron and attempted to do away with Murdock.

"Thank you. Indeed. He wasn't easy to deal with. Without you..."

"Bah! I recognized you. That fellow was one of Murdock's hirelings and you know that I can't stand those people. If he tries to give you any more trouble, don't hesitate to let me know."

He picked up the piece of glass and slid it into his pocket, as a warder was approaching.

"What's going on here?"

"Nothing, warder. It's our friend Hale; he wasn't feeling well, the sun maybe."

The warder was not fooled. Disputes among prisoners were frequent. Hale got up slowly, looking haggard. The warder did not observe any apparent injury; he turned round and went to the other end of the yard.

"You, Hale, it would be better for you to stay in line. The next time I will calm you down for good," my rescuer yelled.

The man grunted and moved off, rubbing his head.

Counsel Jones brought me news about Wickney's trial. The judge did not invite me to the hearings. Perhaps that seemed useless to him.

"My dear Jeremy, we are nearing our goal."

I was eager to hear more about it.

"Wickney has confessed. He fully understood that he could not lie and that it would be better to make a confession quickly."

"What did he say?"

"Everything, from the beginning. An unbelievable story. When he arrived at Cheltenham, he fell under the spell of the mistress of the house. Madly in love with Lady Cheltenham, he became insanely jealous and decided to get rid of her husband. That was not solving his problem, but it would seem that he had an aversion for the individual. Lord Cheltenham did not, however, ill-treat his major-domo, but Wickney could not control himself any longer. He's the one who concocted the riding accident in the grounds and who finished off his master with several blows on his skull. Nobody had imagined that it could have been a murder. Who could really have had a grudge against Lord John Cheltenham?"

"Moreover, Wickney, the obliging and zealous major-domo, was truly safe from any suspicion."

"Wait, Jeremy, the sequel is instructive, even though you may anticipate it. Wickney took a rather dim view of your arrival at the manor. Cadell had some doubts about the riding accident; he had confided in Wickney himself about it. Given your amicable relationship with the gardener, the major-domo was afraid that you might stir up this issue again. In short, Wickney was uneasy."

"Yet I was miles away from being concerned with that story."

"That didn't prevent Wickney from taking you down."

"The solicitor, that's it?"

"Yes, Radcliff. The solicitor had a hand in some shady business. Moreover, we will need to re-examine the situation with your uncle's business… Wickney, I don't know through which go-between, was aware of it and set about blackmailing the solicitor. That's how Radcliff, threatened by Wickney, influenced the judge at the time of your first trial. No extenuating circumstances were applied and my attempts to review the position of the court were swept aside, you remember that?"

"Yes, perfectly, Master Jones."

"That's how you were hit with a heavy penalty. With you in Africa for twenty years, it only remained for Wickney to get rid of Cadell. By having him wrongly accused in order to get him dismissed. That's when he had recourse to the services of Nolan who, moreover, has disappeared and whom we won't see any more, I think."

I remained flabbergasted. I had been very far from imagining all that. I had indeed almost paid a heavy price for it. But I still had to appear before the judge.

"It will be all right, now," Jones declared. "We are going to plead self-defence for Ron's murder. For the alcohol smuggling, you were forced to do it. Those two gangsters were threatening you. The judge will take that into account."

A question was on my mind.

"And Mary, have you any news about her?"

"Mary? Yes, of course. She is fine; she has recovered her

259

appetite and her smile."

"Lady Cheltenham told you…"

Master Jones smiled.

"She is anxiously awaiting your return."

46

Master Jones was right to be optimistic. My trial took place just two days later and was smoothly conducted. Wickney's confessions and sentence — he was sentenced to twenty years imprisonment — had an influence on my destiny.

The judge accepted the self-defence and shut his eyes to the alcohol smuggling. After all, my own trial had enabled a murderer to be unmasked. My conviction had led to the arrest of Wickney. The major-domo's Machiavellian plot had finally turned back on him.

The solicitor Radcliff was not forgotten. Study of his businesses, of his bank accounts, which were numerous and hefty, revealed embezzlement of funds, swindles and other less than laudable schemes. He was sentenced to six years in prison and reimbursement of the sums he had stolen, that is to say, embezzled. It could thus be discerned that he had swindled my uncle by making him believe in the poor profitability of Stock Exchange investments, while in fact he had kept the money for himself. I was therefore able to recover a rather tidy sum, which allowed me to pay off my uncle's debts.

Perdy was not troubled by the courts of justice, because no complaint was lodged against him. But his father, Sir Garmond, sent him off to France to some distant cousins. The worthy man would pay for his food and studies, but he really wished his son to leave the country and move away from him.

Officer Matthew Cornwell was arraigned before a military court. I was asked to testify in it and I was questioned about the behaviour of the military at the camp in Egypt. I told the truth. Cornwell was dismissed and struck off the Army lists. He evaded prison, but found himself penniless and on the street. While I did not forget the valuable testimony that he had formulated concerning me, I could not remove from my memory his violent attitude at the camp and notably the murder of Big Boss.

I was released from prison on a fine sunny morning. The air was fresh, the sky clear; it was good to breathe deeply. In front of the door of the penal institution, Lady Cheltenham's barouche was waiting for me. On the coachman's seat, Cadell, a broad hat on his head, smoking a varnished pipe, awaited me.

"Well, laddie, are we going home?"

"Oh yes, Cadell! And quickly!"

47

It seemed like a spring morning. The temperature, very mild from sunrise, had put the whole household in a good mood.

I must say that it was a festive day.

Tables were set up on the grounds, on the lawn which had already assumed its seasonal colours. Owl busied himself with the arrangements, while his wife Carol helped in the kitchen. Soon, no doubt, Owl would take on the duty of major-domo, while his wife would back up the servants.

Since my return to Cheltenham, I had resumed relations with the cooks. Cathy had cried her eyes out when she saw me again. At the time of the trial, when her testimony had been requested, she had been unstinting in her praise for me, but Wickney, of course, had totally distorted what she had said.

"How you have changed!" she had said to me, squeezing me tightly against her. "And this scar, my God!"

I had told her about my exile to Egypt, the camp, the war and my return... It was, no doubt, all that which had changed me.

Lauren and Joanna were also beaming.

"We are happy to have you back, Jeremy. We missed you, especially in the mornings, for breakfast."

Cadell had prepared a fire to cook some joints of meat. Roe deer, he explained, which he had hunted himself for the occasion in the Prestbury woods.

Mary was spinning around with happiness and kept on laughing out loud. She glowed with beauty in a pretty champagne-coloured dress. Garnet-red pieces of embroidery enhanced the outfit and her straw hat with a beige ribbon had a most beautiful effect. I had eyes only for her and I kept on feasting my eyes on her. Never would I have imagined, just a short while ago, such a scene.

Lady Cheltenham appeared. Sir Garmond was holding her by her arm and they moved forward in harmony, with a stately gait. Their faces reflected a definite picture of happiness. That day would be one of announcements.

"My friends," said the mistress of the house, "what a splendid day!"

"For a splendid outcome," I dared to respond.

"Indeed, Jeremy. It couldn't have turned out better. You paid a heavy price to achieve this happiness, but I must emphasize that you never gave up."

Lady Cheltenham was aware of the profound motivation of my determination to survive and to have the truth revealed. But in the final moments, without the help of Cadell and Jones, I would have, no doubt, given up the fight.

Before starting off the festivities, Lady Cheltenham requested everyone's attention. Ears became attentive and eyes curious. Movements were suspended.

"Before we dine, I wish to make an important announcement to you. Or rather, two announcements."

She paused and turned to Sir Garmond, who was standing slightly behind.

"Sir Garmond and I are thinking of getting married."

"Oh!" exclaimed the cooks.

"It will be next autumn, no doubt, because, earlier, another important event has to take place and that is the object of my second announcement. Mary, my dear daughter, is going to marry

Jeremy, in the coming spring. It's not possible to do otherwise."

Everyone began to laugh.

"Even without my consent, they would get married all the same. But that is not the case; I am happy with this upcoming marriage. Jeremy is a young man who can be relied on; if not, I know very well that my daughter would not have chosen him…"

More bursts of laughter. Lady Cheltenham was in great form this morning.

"There, everything has been said."

And Milady embraced her daughter. Some tears, of joy, no doubt, ran down her rouged cheeks. Cathy and her friends also embraced me, each in turn; Cadell gave me a slap on the back which could have knocked over an elephant. Sir Garmond soberly shook my hand.

"Congratulations, young man. I wish you all the happiness in the world."

"Thank you, sir."

"Call me George."

Cadell informed us that the cooking was done and that we should not delay tucking into the animal, which promised to be excellent.

We did not have to be asked twice, evidently. The meal took place in high spirits. After the terrible events that had affected everyone, and some more than others, it was good to meet up again and enjoy being reunited, around this big table.

Today, there was no more My Lady, cook, gardener or stableman. We were like a family, united, relieved, reassured and confident. That was priceless.

After the meat, which was indeed succulent, the vegetables prepared with care by the three partnering cooks and Cathy's delicious apple pie, Mary and I disappeared for a horseback ride.

Azurea was in great form and Moonlight was giving signs of wanting to stretch her legs. We saddled the horses and went in the direction of Prestbury. That was the most interesting route. Leaving the road midway, we found superb grasslands in which we were able to give our horses free rein. Trotting, galloping, passing by streams, the edge of forests, magnificent paths bordered by oaks, it was sheer ecstasy. Animals and riders were at one, Mary and I were at one. It was an incredible, enchanting time, which we prolonged right up to the moment when the sun began to go down and the air became cooler.

For the return, we both had the same idea in mind. Make a detour by the almost identical shack that Cadell had rebuilt, a few steps from the one that had been destroyed by the fire.

There, in front of the logs that blazed in the fireplace, buried under a thick quilt, we gave our united bodies a fresh opportunity to vibrate in harmony. Never had we known such intense pleasure. Panting, soaked in sweat, we later savoured the serene happiness that follows carnal love. Nothing was more beautiful.

"We need to go back home," Mary said to me. "Mother will get worried."

"You're right, Mary. Let's not spoil this lovely day."

Lady Cheltenham was not worried, but was, all the same, happy to see us back before nightfall. As for Cadell, he wore a smile that I knew only too well.

EPILOGUE

The waves gently came and lapped the almost white sand. Some seaweed, scattered, here and there, lent a touch of colour to this idyllic setting.

Mary and I were sitting on a dune that overlooked the shoreline. Her head resting on my shoulder, she was contemplating, like me, the immensity of the sea and this reddish ball that merged with the waves.

We were on a beach in Ireland. After our wedding, celebrated in Gloucester in the intimacy of the family and workers from the manor, we decided to travel for a while. We had hired some horses when we arrived on the east coast and undertook a trip for several weeks through this beautiful land. We liked this country, indeed were enchanted by it. Here, it was all nature, rusticity and simplicity. The air was pure, the water was clear and the inhabitants had sincerity in their eyes and in their souls. They did not have any particular love for the English, but they must have liked our project, because they accepted us rather quickly. That was more than enough to get us to make a decision. We had thought a lot about it and we were going to take the plunge. And that was how we decided to settle in this country. Lady Cheltenham provided an important financial contribution in the purchase of a lovely expanse of meadows and woods that we had found near the village of Kilnamanagh, not far from the town of

Wexford. We had, in fact, given up our plans to go and live in France. Here, nature appealed to us and welcomed us with open arms; the place corresponded a lot more with our wish to have a peaceful life.

Mary, drew an ellipse on the sand and inside the figure, some rectangles and squares.

"What do you think?"

I looked carefully at her design.

"Where is south on your sketch?"

"Here. Why do you ask?"

"For the stalls. Not too warm, but all the same well oriented for the winter period. That's important. I'm a stableman; don't forget that… And this rectangle?"

"In the house?"

"Yes."

"The bedroom… for the baby."

And Mary burst out laughing with that crystalline laugh that delighted nature itself. Her happiness rose up to the heavens and began to run over the waves, making them dance with more vigour.

We were quite simply happy.

9 782914 644525